The Slasher

*#10 in the Edgar Award-winning
Dan Fortune mystery series*

Dennis Lynds

Originally published under the pseudonym Michael Collins

The Slasher e-book edition: 978-1-941517-18-5
The Slasher POD edition: 978-1-941517-19-2

For inquiries:
Gayle Lynds
P.O. Box 732
125 Forest Avenue
Portland, ME 04101-9998
www.DennisLynds.com

To Pat Gebhard

Acclaim for Dennis Lynds & His Novels

"*The Slasher* is smashing, [with a] plot that leaves the reader breathless." – *Publishers Weekly*

"A compelling novel of people with dark secrets." – *The Raleigh News and Observer*

"Briskly paced, tersely told." – *The Buffalo Evening News*

"[Lynds] juggles everything around like the expert he is, and the complications are nicely resolved." – *The New York Times*

"A fast-pace thriller … a good book to read at one sitting on a rainy evening." – *Minneapolis Tribune*

"[Lynds] writes with firmness and intelligence. His style is staccato, matched to the action and tone." – *Washington Post*

"Superb characters and excellent plotting." – *Booklist*

"[Lynds] is in splendid form." – *The Detroit News*

"[He] carries on the Hammett-Chandler-Macdonald tradition with skill and finesse." – *Washington Post Book World*

"… powerful writing." – *Library Journal*

"… engrossing and empathic." – *New York Daily News*

"A gripping story." – The Charlotte Observer

"Action and intrigue are nicely mixed." – *Publishers Weekly*

"A novelist of power and quality ... one of the major imaginative creators in the crime field." – *Ross Macdonald*

"Like Ross Macdonald, Michael Collins can write vivid prose and dialogue *and* plot a mystery." – *Ellery Queen Mystery Magazine*

"First-class ... suspenseful, character-rich, and absorbing." – *Kirkus Reviews*

"Some of the rawest, most unencumbered mystery writing extant in the genre." – *American Library Association*

"Tough, believable." – *San Francisco Examiner*

"[Lynds's books are] filled with as much closely observed incident and detail as John O'Hara short stories." – *Wall Street Journal*

"... hot mystery writer whose novels have reached mainstream status... ." – *San Diego Reporter*

"Collins is the Costa-Gavras of the PI world ... we might also call him the Captain Kirk of PI writers, boldly taking the genre where no colleague has gone before – and doing it so passionately that we can't help but sign on for the quest with him." – literary critic Francis M. Nevins, Jr.

"Lynds is a major contributor to the form, even a redefiner of it; whether or not he is ever given his just due, he should take satisfaction from the fact that he has written mystery novels of genuine distinction." – literary critic Richard Carpenter

Dan Fortune series, by Dennis Lynds, originally published under the pseudonym Michael Collins

Act of Fear, 1967
The Brass Rainbow, 1969
Night of the Toads, 1970
Walk a Black Wind, 1971
Shadow of a Tiger, 1972
The Silent Scream, 1973
Blue Death, 1975
The Blood-Red Dream, 1976
The Nightrunners, 1978
The Slasher, 1980
Freak, 1983
Minnesota Strip, 1987
Red Rosa, 1988
A Dangerous Job, 1989
Chasing Eights, 1990
The Irishman's Horse, 1991
Cassandra In Red, 1992

Paul Shaw series, by Dennis Lynds, originally published under the pseudonym Mark Sadler

The Falling Man, 1970
Here to Die, 1971
Mirror Image, 1972
Circle of Fire, 1973
Touch of Death, 1981
Deadly Innocents, 1986

Kane Jackson series, by Dennis Lynds, originally published under the pseudonym William Arden

A Dark Power, 1968
Deal in Violence, 1969
The Goliath Scheme, 1971

Die to a Distant Drum, 1972
Deadly Legacy, 1973

Buena Costa County series, by Dennis Lynds, originally published under the pseudonym John Crowe
Another Way to Die, 1972
A Touch of Darkness, 1972
Bloodwater, 1974
Crooked Shadows, 1975
When They Kill Your Wife, 1977
Close to Death, 1979

George Malcolm, private detective, by Dennis Lynds, originally published under the pseudonym Carl Dekker
Woman in Marble, 1973

Langford ("Ford") Morgan, ex-soldier, ex-CIA, ex-roustabout, by Dennis Lynds, originally published under the pseudonym Michael Collins
The Cadillac Cowboy, 1995

Other of his works include science fiction novels, literary novels, mystery short stories, literary short stories, short story anthologies, and poetry.

Table of Contents

Each year we make it easier to do more faster with less time to think about what we do or why we do it. Maybe we want it that way. Or someone does.

I thought about it as I watched the remote towns in the snow outside the train windows, and I thought about Marty and the telephone call from nearly three thousand miles and almost five years. I thought about how her voice across all those miles and years had sounded just as it had close to my ear in the small bedrooms of our good times. I thought about her words, "It's my husband's niece, Dan, someone killed her. I need some help."

I finished my fourth beer. I had forgotten how good it was to sit with a drink looking out at places I'd never seen, or not for a long time. The mammoth Mississippi frozen from bank to bank. Dodge City. The high plains of Colorado under a vast winter sky. A long way from Eighth Avenue.

There's a sense of distance on a train, of coming from somewhere and going to somewhere else. On a jet the only way you know you're somewhere else is by reading the timetable—it's 1:00 P.M. on a Thursday so it must be Los Angeles.

There's time to think on a train, and that's why they're vanishing. Action is the cry of the last half of the twentieth century. Keep it moving. Do, don't think. Thinking leads to questions. People might say to hell with those two weeks of plastic fun at the Kabul Hilton, and the whole country would collapse. We don't want questions, or someone doesn't, and on trains there is too much time so trains are out.

Even I was aboard only because of a wildcat airline strike, but before the sleeper turned west at North Philadelphia I remembered how much we'd lost when we traded the sleeper, diner, and club car for a fast subway ride in the sky. Now, late on the second afternoon out of Chicago, I sat in the crowded club car. In the morning we would be in Los Angeles, but today there was nothing anyone had to do and the long car was full of beer and laughter, Coke and conversation, politics and poker games. Most of them were young, or poor, or peripheral, or any combination of the three. The unaffluent having a lot of fun while I drank my fifth beer and thought about Marty and a murder.

The train swayed around the high curves of Raton Pass. Martine Adair, actress and woman. But not my woman. Not since she married her director because she wanted permanence, wanted the rewards of here and now, wanted her existence testified to by the recognition of others. Needs of our time. Needs a private detective with a one-room office/apartment couldn't fill.

But she was still the woman I saw in store windows, in the half-seen swing of a booted skirt. The woman I thought about late at night alone in a bed or a barroom the way I thought about my missing left arm.

And she had called me. To investigate the death of her husband's niece?

There were private detectives in California.

Did she really just want to see me? To talk to me after five years, maybe to? ...

I went for my sixth beer. The train moved on across New Mexico through a sweeping land of semi-desert and arid mountains white with winter snow.

We never give up. Deep down we know it's all some mistake. *They* will come to their senses, it's not really over, she (he) can't... . Love, or pride? Or just a kind of dream, a small illusion to make life a little better day to day, and was that the real reason I was on the train? I could have taken a jet from Chicago, or even a private charter from

New York. But the longer I took to get to L.A., the longer it would be before I had to meet her and know what she really wanted from me.

I drank my beer and looked out at the darkening country of the southern Ute. The train had passed through Las Vegas and on into the night west. I was stalling the time of meeting, and not just because of a romantic delusion. Five years can be a long time. I knew she had done two Broadway shows after she married Kurt Reston. I knew, she had left New York. But I didn't know when she had gone to the Coast—or when she had changed men again.

The letter with my retainer and the newspaper clipping about the dead girl had come on engraved stationery:

MR. & MRS. WILLIAM DEKKER

TORO CANYON   MALIBU

Where are your children?—Watch for the BIG one!

Who was William Dekker? Some movie mogul who even pushed his movies on his personal stationery? And what had happened to Kurt Reston? There *were* private detectives in California. Why did Marty really want me? Because I was safe? Or she hoped I was? How safe did she need? Suspicion goes with my work. A cop doesn't meet the most honest people, not even a private cop. Especially a private cop.

I got my seventh beer from the club car steward, and read the newspaper clipping again.

2

SLASHER'S TENTH VICTIM

Girl Needed Only A Mother To Love
But It Was Death That Embraced Her

LOS ANGELES. When Suzanne Emily Dekker was a baby, her mother deserted her.

A week before her tenth birthday, her father was shot to death in a shabby saloon.

When Suzanne was fourteen, she ran away to search for the mother she had never really known. A mother to love and to love her, and Suzy kept on searching for love. Some sort of love, and, in the end, any sort of love.

By the time she was in her mid-teens, Suzanne had turned to prostitution, and last week at the age of eighteen years, two months, and seventeen days her search for love ended when the so-called Canyon Slasher lured her to a remote cabin and murdered her—his tenth known victim.

Suzy was buried in a desert grave beside her father. She never had found her lost mother.

"But she was a happy girl," her aunt, Mrs. Jane Pearson, says. Then says, "No, that's what Suzy wanted to be, simple and happy, but she wasn't. I don't think there were many times in Suzy's life when she was happy."

Mrs. Pearson, a slim blonde woman in her early thirties, stares straight ahead as she sits on the couch in her neat tract home in Moorpark. The Christmas tree is still up a week into the New Year. On the mantel is a color photograph of her husband, a handsome man who works as a maintenance man on a large ranch-farm, and snap-shots of her two children and of Suzy Dekker's younger brother who lives with foster parents.

"After Stan was killed, Suzy lived with us for a few years," Mrs. Pearson explains. "But around thirteen she began to be very curious about her mother. At fourteen she ran away to New Mexico to try to find Peggy. That was her mother's name, Peggy Hill, and she came from New Mexico."

From then on Suzanne Dekker was on the run.

"Suzy was picked up for running and running and running and run-ning," Mrs. Pearson says, "and put in group home after group home. But that was never the answer for her. I don't know what the answer was for Suzy, if there was one except finding her mother, and by now that wouldn't have been an answer either. There are so many little Suzys running in our world."

Mrs. Pearson believes her niece probably became involved in prostitution at about the age of fifteen.

"I guess she got into that line of work as soon as she got to Los Angeles," says Mrs. Pearson. "For the first year or so she never said what she was doing to live, but I started to wonder. She was always like a little girl up here with me, but I knew she was unhappy down In L.A., and sometimes I'd ask if I could help her. She always said, 'No, Aunt Jane, you can't help me. It's too late. It's too late.'"

Suzanne was born In Flagstaff, Arizona, to Mr. and Mrs. Stan-ley Edgar Dekker. Her brother, Mrs. Pearson says, was a sometime garage mechanic, a high school dropout, who seldom stayed with any job very long. Suzanne's mother was a pretty junior college cheer-leader who married the handsome young mechanic when he took some courses at the college.

Suzanne was born, and Stan Dekker and the cheerleader left the college. Before Suzanne was two she had a little brother, and the family had moved to Barstow. About that time the mother deserted them.

When Dekker was thirty-one, Suzanne not quite ten, he got into a brawl in a Barstow tavern and was shot to death.

The boy was placed in a foster home, and Suzanne went to live with her aunt until she ran away to begin her search for her lost mother.

The search that ended last week in a Santa Monica mountain canyon.

Suzanne's roommate, Diane, describes that last day.

"Our outcall modeling service called about 8:00 P.M. Marilyn, the outcall operator, said that a man wanted Suzy to come to his Hollywood appartment."

As Diane recalls that night, she sits on a studio couch in the beach-community apartment while a baby sleeps fitfully in the single bedroom. She is a very attractive twenty-one-year-old with a stunning figure. Her eyes are hidden by tinted glasses as she explains the "modeling" service she and Suzy worked for.

"The service *does* get us modeling calls," she insists. "Okay, Suzy was into prostitution, but she modeled too! It's not fair for you newspapers and the police to label her only a prostitute because all the other girls he killed were! Just the day before she said she was through, she wasn't taking any more calls. She wanted to become a person society considers good, whatever that is."

But Suzanne Emily Dekker took one more call. Perhaps because the man asked for her specifically, perhaps for a last few dollars to tide her over.

Whatever her reason, Suzy left for her rendezvous just after nine that night. She failed to make the normal check-in call to the "service," and when Marilyn at the service tried to contact her the telephone number given by the man turned out to be a pay phone. Diane called the police. When they checked the address the man had given, it was an empty house. With no phone number or address, there was little the police could do that night, and by morning it no longer mattered what they did.

Suzy Dekker's nude body was found outside the cabin in the deserted canyon by some early hikers. She had been stabbed six times and her throat slashed—the tenth young woman to be found like that in outlying canyons in the last two years.

"I'm not convinced that it was the Canyon Slasher," Marty said, "if he even exists. There's something wrong with it, Dan."

She is a small woman, and the hair that hung over her left eye was still red. It had been other colors in our long years together. She is thirty-five now, no longer really young, but she still has the big eyes and the small face that could be the face of a boy.

"Did you talk to the police?" I said.

I had seen her the moment I came out of the long marble tunnel into L.A.'s Union Station—a vast temple to a vanished era when its soaring ceilings, marble columns, vaulted windows, and sleek marble floors rang to the arrivals and departures of the movie stars in the golden years of both movies and trains. Alone across the mammoth waiting room, far back from the crowd.

"Yes. They're polite, but they don't hear us. They see two emotional broads who won't face facts, Dan. Who can't believe a senseless, random murder."

She does everything quickly, eagerly. Her walk is a stride, almost a run when she's excited, and when she ran to me there in the echoing station, her arms tight around my neck, it meant a lot to me, but what did it mean to her?

"Two?" I said. "Her mother showed up?"

"Her roommate. She came to us two days after they found Suzanne and insisted something was wrong."

A rm in arm, she had hustled me out of the massive old station and across to the Plaza and Olvera Street—Old Mexico, preserved and recreated for the tourists, where the City Of the Pueblo of Our Lady the Queen Of the Angels had begun. Now we sat drinking coffee in a deserted cantina on Olvera while she told me that something was wrong about Suzanne Dekker's death. Still before 10:00 A.M., the restaurants were closed but the booths in the center were open, displaying their gaudy ponchos, over-priced serapes, and cheap leather goods.

"Senseless murders can be hard to believe," I said. The coffee in the cantina was harsh. "How are you, Marty?"

"Fine," she said, smiling that little-boy smile on the woman's body that had always been her gimmick.

She looked along the red-brick pedestrian street with its restaurants and food stands on both sides and the selling booths in the center. A bright early January morning in Los Angeles, with the pound and surge of traffic on Alameda and Sunset surrounding the empty silence of where we sat. Too early for people to come to Olvera Street. She sipped her coffee.

"I'm all right, Dan. They brought me out for a movie a few years ago. I wasn't quite what they'd expected, but I did four movies, medium parts, and I'm up for another now. I had a few TV shots, and there was a series that fell through. Par out here. I get back up on stage whenever they let me. The small theaters mostly, but one show at the Mark Taper. I model too."

Ask most of us how we are and we'll tell you about our love life, our fun life, our health, or our money. For Marty, her work had always been more important than anything else. Her acting work. The real work. She acts because she must, for its own sake, and that's the best reason there is. In the end, there isn't any other reason.

"No more G-strings and spangles?" I smiled.

"Not if I starve." She laughed. "I'm too old anyway."

"Not to me," I said. "What happened to Reston?"

She waved to the waiter for more coffee. I watched the formidable, muscular women behind the counter patting tortillas into shape. The waiter looked at me. I shook my head. He brought Marty's coffee. She drank.

"It just didn't work out, I suppose," she said. She smiled that boy's smile again. "Artistic differences, or sex differences, or maybe both. We never had either, did we?"

"Only philosophical differences," I said. "Dreams and life style. Or maybe just age." I decided to have some more coffee after all. The waiter brought it in disgust. I said, "And William Dekker?"

There is something that happens to women's eyes when they talk with an old lover about a new lover. A plea for understanding, a kind of wariness as if not sure what the old lover might do, a small thrill of fear bright in the eyes. She stirred her coffee, half smiled and half looked away along the arcade-like old Mexico street.

"He's a novelist, Dan. A powerful one, I think. I met him a year before Kurt and I broke up, got the divorce six months ago, and married Bill the same day." She toyed with the spoon in her coffee. "He's quite a man, you know? A cyclone courtship that didn't seem to leave me any choice."

"While you were still with Reston?" I said.

"Church morality, Dan? From you to me?"

I stirred my own coffee. "Character study. Some men are excited by the challenge, the sense of daring. Carrying her off on the saddle. A Roman rape. Bold."

"The detective," she said. "Bill's bold all right, and he makes a challenge of almost everything. Part of his background, I suppose, his whole life. You can feel the power, the sense of doing big things. It was all over with Kurt, but even if it hadn't been I think Bill would have gotten to me."

"Quite a boy," I said.

She laughed. "You mean the new one always is? That's not me, Dan. I never described Kurt that way. Or you. Because you're not like that. Your power is different."

"Yeh," I said. "Is he a good novelist?"

"I think so," she said. "More, I think he's an important novelist with a lot to say. He's seen so much, Dan."

Her eyes over the steam of her coffee cup were distant as she drank, as if trying to see all that her new husband had seen in his life. I waited, listening to her and watching her. Mostly watching her.

"His family came from Canada. They were *Metis*, half-breed Cree. His dad was a steelworker and lumberjack. He was killed when the boys were still very little and Jane was a baby. The mother had to work and struggle to bring them up, but she got them all the education she could. Stan was a year younger than Bill, a nice kid and a charmer, Bill says, but a dreamer looking for the rainbow and the gold. He could never stick long to any job or place; you've read that newspaper story. Jane, Bill says, is a plain, simple woman who never wanted more than a husband and a washing machine. Products of our society, Bill says."

"You've never met this Aunt Jane?" I said.

She shook her head. "Bill hasn't seen her in fifteen years. When Stan dropped out of school and Jane married, the family split apart. The mother remarried. Bill finished two years of community college and started wandering. In Africa he reported a famine and found he could write. By the time he got back to California he knew he *had* to write. He went to Berkeley for his degree in creative studies. Berkeley was in eruption then. Bill wrote a dense, white-hot novel about the evils of the society on campus and in the slums. By the time he finished it the publishers said people didn't want to be reminded about those problems anymore!

"So he quit, went into the mountains for five years, and wrote a sprawling epic novel about the same evils but making it sound like history. That was *Voices Of Violence*. It was a best-seller, a six-figure paperback, and was bought for a movie. Bill came to L.A. to do the screenplay. He bought a big old house in a Malibu canyon, did a small novel, we met and married six months ago."

The coffee was tasting more and more bitter. "What's that slogan on your letterhead? About the BIG one?"

"I don't know, something to do with the movie of *Voices Of Violence*, I suppose. Bill just had them printed, maybe because they're stalling on the movie."

I said, "Why send for me, Mart? L.A. has detectives."

She smiled. "I haven't forgotten how we always needed any dollar. I didn't think you'd become rich and secure. You'd never change that much in five hundred years much less five."

"To help me out? Some of your husband's movie money?"

She looked away toward the waiter as if she wanted to order more coffee but knew that she shouldn't.

"No, that's not the only reason." She fiddled with her spoon in the dregs of coffee still in her cup. "I know I can trust you. I know you'll be honest with me. I know you'll be on my side. I didn't want some stranger."

"No," I said.

She looked up at me. "Why did you come by train?"

"Airline strike in New York."

"I'd have paid for a charter."

"Five years is too long," I said. "Or too short."

"Perhaps both," she said.

I let it lie there between us. She knew I had stalled meeting her again; it made her smile, and if that meant that maybe the past wasn't dead I wasn't ready to push it any farther yet.

"Did you know the girl well?" I said.

Marty shook her head. "She came to the Malibu house a few times. When Bill came down to L.A. she read about him and looked him up. Searching for family, anything to help her remember her mother and father. She remembered Stan Dekker, but only his last years. She wanted to know the earlier years, hungry to hear about her grandparents, Canada. A history to put herself in."

"She spent a lot of time at your house?"

"Just a few visits, months apart and unannounced. She was a restless girl, her attention span was short. Immature and not very bright. She talked about modeling and her television jobs, but she was always hinting that she wasn't good enough for us as if she wanted us to suspect what she really did."

"She came to talk to your husband?"

"When he had time, but she seemed almost to want to talk to me more—Aunt Marty. What she really wanted, of course, was her

11

mother. The mother she described as a beautiful face with a sad smile that sounded like something she'd seen in a movie and probably was. It was her mother she was searching for, Dan, and that's part of what doesn't seem right."

"How?"

"We think she could have found her mother, or some real hope. The last time she came to Malibu, just over two weeks ago, she was tense yet exhilarated. She spoke of getting out of 'modeling,' of going back to school. She said, 'You've got to earn what you want, Aunt Marty, deserve what you get.'"

"You think she was giving up prostitution to be worthy of her mother?"

"Yes, and so does Diane Pasco, the roommate. She thinks Suzy had found her mother, and wouldn't have taken a call from a man looking for a prostitute."

"She thinks the call was something else?"

"And that Suzy *knew* the caller."

I watched the ladies pat their tortillas behind the counter. The waiter watched us. He had a fierce mustache, most Mexican men do. Like Armenians. I knew an Armenian intellectual who was totally Americanized and modern but who still had his mustache. He said he knew it was ridiculous, but he could give up smoking or drinking before he could shave off his mustache.

"If she'd found her mother," I said, "or even had strong hope, why not tell you or your husband? Why keep it a secret?"

"I don't know, Dan."

"Is that all the roommate has for her doubts?"

"There's more about how Suzy had been acting, what she'd been doing, but Diane can tell you that herself."

I waved to the waiter for the check.

"Their apartment's on the beach," Marty said. She held up some car keys. "I had a friend drive in our extra car for you."

The waiter came. When Marty paid, he looked at me and at my missing arm with a kind of surprised respect. We're irrational in all kinds of ways.

I said, "How did your husband get along with Suzy? He seems to have had no contact with his family, no interest in them."

The waiter brought her change. She put it into her purse, then took out a cigarette. She lit the cigarette.

"He liked her. He even tried to teach her about literature, but she'd had no education."

It was the first cigarette I'd seen her smoke.

"I've been trying to quit," she said. "Dan, I never even knew Bill had any family until Suzy appeared one day! He said that an artist couldn't be held down by conventional demands, feelings, or morals. He never even mentioned a brother."

"But he took an interest in Suzy? In the boy, too?"

She smoked. "No, not in the boy."

"Does he have any ideas about who killed her?"

"He *knows* who killed her—the Canyon Slasher," she said. "Bill doesn't agree with us, Dan. He says that Diane is evading the fact that their bad life killed Suzy. He's outraged at the society for neglecting such girls. He's made public statements that society and parents have failed. He agrees with the police."

"Does that bother you?"

"He isn't writing at home, and sometimes he's out all day, I don't know where."

"Have you asked him?"

"No."

"All right, I'll talk to him later."

Her cars were in the station lot across Alameda Street. A silver Mercedes sedan and a blue Subaru coupe.

"I'll try to get to Malibu before dark," I said.

She got into the Mercedes and drove off first. With one arm I need to know a car before I drive it, so I checked the Subaru over; but my mind wasn't really on it. I was thinking about Marty. I knew why she had sent for me. She wasn't sure of her new husband. Not at all sure.

4

In a certain sense the "beach" is Los Angeles, one of the unique styles that defines the freeway city. Elemental, where everyone is equal even in Malibu. A communal world where the sea and the endless hot sand belongs to everyone. A physical world without fences, where no one owns more than he stands up in.

You feel it when you turn off the freeways as they near the Pacific. It doesn't matter which beach, or that most of them aren't even officially Los Angeles but a melange of towns and cities with exotic names. Towns important, maybe, to businessmen and/or crooks who care about who runs the local show, but that mean little to the people who live in "Los Angeles" even if it is called Redondo Beach or Playa Del Rey.

Where Suzanne Dekker had lived was called Venice, and had canals to prove it. The address Marty had given me was a flimsy two-story cottage not far from a canal with outside stairs and an alley in back lined with narrow garages. Men in beards and beads, women in feathers and workshoes, wandered the street in the January sun. The defiant young, only these men and women were no longer young, as if Venice were the last refuge of lost rebellion or lost independence. A threatened refuge from the look of the expensive beach houses and condominiums on surrounding streets that towered over the cottages like invaders from nearby and affluent Marina Del Rey.

The names Pasco/Dekker were on the second floor apartment up the outside stairs from the alley. A tall, fair young man was polishing his car in the alley. A red Mustang that gleamed. One of the thousands of beach-and-highway youths who put more love and money into their cars than into their homes, their jobs, and even their wives.

"She ain't home," he said as I started up the stairs.

I leaned on the stair rail. "You know Miss Pasco?"

"Me? I mean, no." His large blue eyes were confused, eager but uneducated. The story of so many of the beach-and-highway kids. "I mean, I saw her leave, you know? I was working on.... You a cop?" He looked at my empty sleeve.

I came down. "Why?"

"That other kid, you know?" A certain confusion seemed to be his natural expression, trying to think but only looking blank. "I mean, I heard about the other girl. Suzanne Dekker."

"What did you hear?"

"You know, about the Slasher." I was really confusing him. Didn't I know? Was I a cop or not? "Real bad, you know? Some kind of psycho, right? Real sick to do that kind of thing. You find any clues yet? I mean, like, maybe you know who he is?"

"Not yet." I eased off on him. "Nice car. Sixty-eight Mustang, right? Hard to find."

He beamed at me. I knew about cars. He was a big, lean kid no more than twenty-three, with blond hair and a round, open face and those large blue eyes. He loved his car.

"She's a classic. Worth plenty. Rebuilt her all myself. Cost me plenty, too."

"You're a mechanic?"

He shook his head, serious. "No more. No money in it, and too slow. I mean, you got to move where the money is."

I came back at him, "What do you know about the Canyon Slasher?"

"Me? Gee, nothing. Only he got to be sick, right? Maybe can't make it with girls. You know what I mean? A creep. He never been nothing, never will be, so he got to go hurting girls. Weird. I seen guys like that back in high school. Creeps. Always going around alone. Not

15

like other guys. You don't know what they think about, what they want even. Never with the guys, or the girls."

"Where was high school?"

"Montana. Havre." He pronounced the town *have-er*. He was from Montana, and not too long ago.

"Nice country," I said.

"No action, I got out. Quit school and was in the Guard a while, worked in a garage, but a guy can't make nothing of himself up there. Not unless he owns a big spread, or oil land, or something."

"What do you do down here?"

He preened, grinned a little, as if he'd been waiting for me to ask so he could really impress me. Everyone's Hollywood in southern California, one way or another.

"I'm in the talent line. Agency work. Doing good enough to buy this," and he patted the Mustang, "but I'll do better."

"Model agency?"

"TV and movies, that's where the loot is."

The money was the game. Fast money for fast moving into the real action that was where and who movies, TV and the celebrity magazines said it was. (Not new or special. Since Babylon, popular minstrels have told the young what the good life is here and now.)

"When did Miss Pasco leave?" I asked. "Was she alone?"

"Maybe half hour ago. I didn't see no one else in the car. She got a 280ZX! Sure doing good at something."

I went on up the outside stairs as if I really were a policeman. In these beach areas the people live semi-communally, using each other's TVs, toilets, even showers. Doors are seldom locked. Diane Pasco's wasn't.

I went into a bright room furnished mostly with cheap rattan pieces. Table and chairs next to a stove and refrigerator. Bookcases and a TV in a "U" around two rattan armchairs. A long couch with its back to the rest of the room in front of a picture window with a wide view of the beach and the Pacific.

In the single bedroom there were twin beds, two bed tables, some chairs, and a crib against the right wall. An empty crib. I returned to the main room—and stopped.

A pair of polished men's western boots stuck up on the couch where the high back had hidden them. Boots with feet.

5

A hand appeared above the back of the couch at the other end from the boots. A hand holding a leather case with a badge. I could see the silver word: *Sheriff.*

"Sheriff's office," a smooth voice said lazily. "You a friend?"

"Yes," I said. "Isn't this L.A.P.D. territory?"

The hand disappeared but the voice continued unseen except for the cowboy boots. "A case this big crosses boundaries, we all work together. A friend of which girl?"

"Both," I said, stalling. It was too early for me to have to justify being here to the police.

"A client?" The voice came alive, and as he talked he stood up. "Can you tell me about it? How you met them, where, what you paid them, what they talked about when you were together?"

I saw a tall, dapper-looking man in a soft three-piece gray flannel suit, striped blue shirt, and dark blue tie to go with the western boots. He had thick black hair, a deep California tan, and stopped talking when he saw me. He stared at my missing arm. Longer than I liked.

"That'll take some time," I said, still stalling.

He turned to the picture window, stood looking down at the street. "What does she do with the baby?"

"Baby?"

This time he didn't seem to hear me. He walked to the bedroom doorway. His eyes were very dark, almost black, and he was younger than I'd thought. No more than forty, if that. His hands moved in the air as he talked. Quick hands, even graceful.

"She leaves it with neighbors," he said, staring as hard at the empty crib as he had at my empty sleeve. "It's a circle. The kid will grow up the same way the mother grew up. And Suzy Dekker. Children raising children. Abandoned children bringing up neglected children. Where is the experience, where are the adults? Where's the shelter, the help, the love? Where's the wisdom of the family, the grandparents?"

His voice had become rich, strong. A beautiful voice used to speaking for an audience. And the words, too, were like something for an audience. With that voice and those clothes, he had to be some top man, a captain or even an under-sheriff, and very young for both.

"Most kids manage to grow up all right," I said.

"Do they?" He looked at me intently with those dark eyes that seemed to gain power from focusing on my face.

"Diane Pasco seems to be making it," I said.

A furrow deepened between his eyes. As if in pain.

"But how?" he said. "With what future? Existing isn't making it. Yet what chance have we given her? Any of them? The running children, the thousands of abandoned out there?"

He continued to stare at me as if he wanted an answer, but I had the impression that if I did answer that pain line would come between his eyes again. So I made no answer, and after a time he sighed, "Well, I have things to do."

"Do you know where Diane Pasco went?" I asked.

"Maybe her TV studio," he said as he went out.

I crossed to the picture window. Marty's Subaru was the only car on the street. I watched him pass without taking my license number or even looking at the Subaru. He hadn't asked for my name nor my identification. He hadn't leaned on me even lightly—a man who had walked into the empty apartment of a murder victim.

He wasn't a captain or an under-sheriff. He was no man from the sheriff's department at all. I couldn't explain the badge, except that I hadn't really had a good look at it, but he was no cop.

Not a cop, and I had the sudden certainty that whoever he was he knew me. Or knew about me. The way he had stared at my empty sleeve a shade too long and stopped asking questions. My missing arm meant something to him.

I thought about those dark eyes and that rich voice while I searched the whole apartment for anything that could remotely indicate a motive for the murder of Suzy Dekker by someone other than the Canyon Slasher. There wasn't a lot to search, neither girl seemed to have owned much beyond her clothes. All I found was a sheaf of letterheads for Unicorn Productions, with an address on North Vine Street in Hollywood.

In the alley the blond youth and his red Mustang were gone. But as I climbed into the Subaru I had a glimpse of what could have been the Mustang at the next corner. By the time I got there and made the turn it was gone, if it had ever been there, and I drove on to Venice Boulevard.

6

It was on La Cienega Boulevard that I had the sensation of being followed. The blond car-polisher? Or could I have been wrong about the dark-eyed "sheriff's" man? Tailing me? Was that why he knew me, why I had not seen his car on the Venice street?

The lanes of cars moving in a pack between traffic lights constantly changed position, cutting in and out. Normal city traffic anywhere. I didn't see a red Mustang, or anything that looked like a sheriff's car. The next cross street was Pico. I made the turn on the arrow, speeded up along Pico, and then went slow along the boulevard. I saw no cars that appeared to be on my tail, so turned into the Avenue of the Stars, drove on through the tall buildings and theaters of Century City, took the ramp onto Olympic Boulevard, and headed back to La Cienega.

Halfway to La Cienega a blue Chrysler appeared three cars behind me. I watched it until I turned left on La Cienega in my original direction toward Hollywood. The Chrysler also turned, and then there was a gray Buick. I had the definite impression I had seen them both somewhere behind me earlier.

I lost them before I reached Hollywood, but the impression remained.

7

The Capitol Tower stood in the distance beyond the waiting people like a giant stack of phonograph records, and there are times I think there is little left in this world but promotion. I drove on past the building of Unicorn Productions and parked in the lot behind. I walked through a narrow alley to the street where the people waited in two separate groups.

One group, orderly and in line under the theater marquee, were an unmistakable combination of tourists and professional daytime TV goers. The pros headed the line: two old women, with their knitting, seated on folding stools; an older couple, probably retirees, on canvas chairs and eating lunch; a middle-aged blonde in a long dress and a floppy hat with studio ticket stubs pinned all over the hat. People whose lives were waiting in line for some daytime TV show. The tourists gawked at both the habituals and the passers-by, clutched canvas airline bags, and had the eager eyes of those who had planned this for months and a thousand miles.

The second group waited in a clump outside the double glass doors of the offices of Unicorn Productions. From time to time they each stared nervously through the doors to where a haughty young man behind a desk ignored them. They ran the gamut from businessmen in three-piece suits and women in chic dresses and boots, to students in sports jackets and T-shirts and bearded semi-drifters. They were tense and talkative, total strangers making jokes to each other in sudden group camaraderie, like seekers after some job or nervous army recruits.

I went inside to the desk of the portals guardian.

"I'd like to see Diane Pasco."

"Just wait with the others, you'll get your turn." He didn't even look up.

"Turn?" I said.

"You're not here for the contestant interviews?" He looked up now. "Anything else for Pasco, come back next week."

Outside I looked at the group waiting to be interviewed. There were at least forty. Diane Pasco was going to have a busy afternoon and maybe evening, and I was going to have a long wait. Unless… . A fat youth in a dirty T-shirt and leather jacket looked at his watch and paced restlessly at the rear toward the far corner. I walked to him.

"Going to take all day," I said.

"Shit," he agreed.

"You won't make it anyway. Ten bucks for your papers."

"You bought a deal."

For the ten he handed me a form letter that gave the rules and telephone numbers to arrange an interview. The show was called "RISK!," and the youth had written time, place, and location on the letter. It had all been done by phone, so I'd be okay. All eyes turned to assess what competition I'd be as I joined the hopefuls. Some of them smiled at my missing arm, some frowned, and a sixteen-year-old page swaggered out, herded us into a line, and marched us to an unmarked side door.

"How'd you lose the arm?" a man asked beside me.

"Crocodile," I said. "In Vietnam."

"Christ," the man groaned. "They'll hate the arm, but they'll love the story. You got an edge."

On the second floor we trooped along a hall and into a small room full of chairs with attached desk-arms. A young girl stood smiling at a table in the front of the room. She was tall, with long black hair and the stunning figure the *Times* reporter had admired. I admired it too. The dark glasses were missing, and her smile was totally television. Not exactly fake, but a role she played, part of the "makeup" of a welcoming interviewer.

"My, so many brainy people!" The makeup smile. "If I didn't work here, they wouldn't even let me in the room!" She waited for, and got, her laugh. "Okay, then. I'm Diane, I'll sort of guide you, do the preliminary interviews, and give the written tests. Are there any questions before we start?"

"Yeh, I've seen you somewhere," a brash young man said. "Tell us where."

"No, you haven't seen me." Her voice had an edge, and then the smile returned. "Now, first, has anyone been on a game or quiz show before? The network only allows two shows per person, with a year between the two. No one? Good. Okay, now all of you fill out the questionnaire on your chairs, and I'll explain what we're going to do for the rest of the day."

She had a pleasant voice, light yet firm. The girl next door putting us at our ease, but brisk and businesslike. There would be the written test, and while it was graded she would talk to each of us briefly. Those who passed the test would stay, do a practice session of the show for a producer, and be interviewed once more. No one was guaranteed a spot on the show by passing the test, which meant that, in the end, the producers would mold the show any way they wanted.

As Diane Pasco distributed the tests she saw my arm. There was a reaction, but not recognition. Surprise, even alarm—the deformed and crippled don't appear on daytime TV shows.

I took the test—as much ego as the next. It wasn't easy. "RISK!" seemed to be an authentic quiz show, not a gong-run-and-scream show. It probably wouldn't last too long.

Diane Pasco collected the tests, they were taken from the room, and she began her interviews. She read our names off the questionnaires, and we stood and told her what we were, why we were there, and how interesting we were.

"Daniel Fortune?" She still had no recognition.

I stood. "Dan Fortune. From New York. I'm a private investigator here on a case, but I had some free time."

The recognition came this time. A stiffening, a flicker of those dark eyes. She covered beautifully. Bantering with me.

"Is your arm a handicap in your profession, Dan?"

"Not often. Sometimes it even helps."

"The enemy underestimates you?"

"I disarm them."

While the room groaned, Diane Pasco smiled. A real smile, deeper and older. It didn't blend with her hostess role, and vanished as quickly as it had come. She finished the interviews, and they brought in the results of the tests. She read the names of the winners. I'd made it. The result of all my haphazard education, the in and out of colleges, the reading on all the slow ships I'd sailed on in the old days. What an old professor I'd had in San Francisco once called learning a lot without increasing my market value an iota. Or maybe Diane Pasco just wanted me to stay.

The incredulous losers took a long time leaving. They couldn't have failed such a simple test of their knowledge. Something was terribly wrong. Ask them the questions again right now. Ask them anything. Illusions never really die.

The rest was a lot of waiting and playing the show—competing to answer questions better, faster and more often until one contestant survived and could risk all his won money on a last big question. (What will you do, Dan, play it safe, or—RISK? The audience screaming: "RISK! PLAY IT SAFE! RISK!—I'LL RISK, WALTER!" Gasps, cheers, applause.) In groups of four, until it was dark outside and I was as tired as I was hungry.

"All right, boys and girls, that's it. If I had my way you'd all get on 'RISK!', but we have a lot of considerations, so we'll have to let you know. You were all wonderful, I want to personally thank you for coming. Now, I don't know about anyone else, but I want a drink and some dinner!"

Laughing like old friends, we trooped out of the room. Diane Pasco shook my hand at the door. I went down the stairs to the street with the others. Southern California is essentially a desert and the night was chilling rapidly. Evening traffic was heavy on Vine and the boulevards. I looked at the small note Diane Pasco had slipped into my hand. *Parking lot in back, ten minutes.*

I left the rest of the aspiring contestants, and walked back through the narrow alley to the dark parking lot. There were few cars left.

A group behind the building that had to belong to the studio staff, and a yellow Datsun across the lot near my Subaru. The overhead light was on in the Datsun like a distant one-room cabin dwarfed in the vast parking lot.

The driver's door of the Datsun was open, which was why the light was on. An arm stuck out of the door, which was why the door was open. The arm looked broken. I opened the door.

The dead man had been shot in the head. At least twice by the holes in his face. A young face, probably just twenty. Some small gun. Bigger than a .22-caliber. Maybe a 7.65-mm. He had been sitting in the front passenger seat. The bullets had entered the right temple knocking him over to where he lay on the driver's side under the steering wheel. His legs were still in the passenger's well, and his left arm was flung out of the driver's door and broken when someone slammed the door on it.

"Is he dead?"

Diane Pasco stood behind me. I nodded.

"Know him?"

She stepped closer. The dead youth had been nothing special to look at. Dark brown hair, a squarish face with a small, crooked nose that could have been broken once. Just under six feet tall, wearing a dark blue double-breasted blazer with brass buttons and pale brown bell-bottom slacks. His shoes were cordovan boots, he wore a digital Timex watch and no other jewelry.

"No," Diane Pasco said.

"Maybe the car?"

"No." Her voice was deeper, harder out of her role as hostess. It had begun to shake. She leaned on the Datsun.

"Wait for me somewhere," I said.

She nodded. "The Brown Derby. It's across Vine."

"Get a brandy."

I didn't like it that the Datsun was so near to my Subaru. It could be coincidence, but I didn't believe that. Murder breeds murder. I began to search the dead man and the car.

8

"Alan Welker," I said. I took a long drink of my beer. I needed it. "Registration in the glove compartment, and he had some letters and a name tag in his jacket. His wallet was gone. It could be robbery."

The Brown Derby lounge was still half empty before 6:00 P.M. Only the bar along the left of the narrow room was full. An enormous bowl full of matchbooks stood at the front of the bar as you came in. I lit Diane Pasco's cigarette with one of them. And my own. She was on her second cognac.

"No," she said, "I don't think so. I know him after all, Mr. Fortune. His name anyway."

She had her tinted glasses on now. Part of her other life. Close across a booth table she was even better looking. Her almost perfect face more mature, more individual, with a small scar on the chin and thoughtful eyes. And, at this moment, unaware of herself. Hunched under her long black hair inside a rich dark brown suede jacket as if she were cold.

"Who was he, Diane?" I said.

"Suzy's contact at a big model agency. She talked about him a lot the last month or so, but I never met him."

"Could he have been coming to see you? Maybe to tell you something?"

"I don't know." She shook her head, drank her cognac, opened her suede jacket now as if she were too hot. A light brown turtleneck, beige slim skirt, and cordovan boots showed her figure nicely. "But he's part of the whole thing, Mr. Fortune, and it proves Suzy wasn't murdered by some anonymous psycho! He was one of the big changes about her, you know? She'd only known him a few months, but all of a sudden he was very important to her. She was all excited ..."

Her voice had risen enough to make some men at the bar turn, and her manner was becoming more and more agitated. I put my hand on her arm.

"Take it easy."

She watched me from behind those dark glasses. Her arm was very alive under my hand. She had already gotten to me. The way she called me "Mr. Fortune" now, not "Dan" as she had back in the studio. The "Dan" was part of the commercial role, the game. In private she did not use first names so easily. She was thirty years younger, and I knew what she did for an extra dollar, but I liked her.

"We'll get the answers, okay?" I said.

She nodded. I took my hand away. I didn't really want to but she *was* too young, and I *did* have a job.

"Start at the beginning," I said. "Tell me everything that made you decide she wasn't killed by the Canyon Slasher."

Maybe it was giving her something definite to do, or maybe it had been my hand on her arm, but she calmed. She warmed her cognac between her hands, and sat silent for a time as if putting her thoughts in order.

"Suzy wasn't too bright, Mr. Fortune. She had no career dreams, no sense of a special future, so she dreamed about the past. The family she never had. Does that make sense to you?"

I nodded. Suzanne Dekker had needed something to belong to, a "home," the same as the rest of us. A place, a career, a person. That's what a dream is, somewhere or something to belong to. A sense of continuity, of really being someone somewhere.

"It was all that was really important to her," Diane said. "I don't mean day-to-day every day. She liked clothes, money, men, movies, dancing, swimming, long weekends somewhere special, and all that. But the need she had in front of her like a goal, the something that made her feel different from all the other girls she knew, was her family. She built crazy fantasies about the mother she'd never really known. She used to cry over her father, asking why he had had to get killed like that, why it had happened that way to her."

"You think her father's death could be somehow involved in her murder? Maybe more to the killing eight years ago than the newspapers said?"

"I don't know, Mr. Fortune." She watched a handsome young man enter the lounge and stop in the entrance where everyone could see him. "I only know that the newspapers were right, she was an unhappy girl. You never knew what crazy scheme or hope she might get into her head."

Most of the pain of life comes from the difference between what we want and what we get, and it's especially sharp in the teens when the hopes are usually so wonderful and the reality so often nothing. A few, through hard work and good fortune, make the hopes into reality. A few fail in the dream, are unable to accept reality, and are destroyed. Most, rich or poor, sooner or later bring the dream down to reality and settle for what is. Had Suzy Dekker been one of those who refused to settle, and who pushed too hard?

Diane drank her cognac. "I know that she was always looking for her mother. She went into modeling just because her mother had modeled and she hoped that somewhere, someday, she'd run into her! She always carried an old photo that was the only one she'd ever had of her mother."

"You think she found her mother?"

"I'm sure she had some kind of lead to her mother." She looked at me. "And Alan Welker was part of it."

I needed another bottle of beer, and her glass was empty. I called the waiter. We sat in silence until the drinks came. Diane warmed her cognac.

"She'd been excited the last week or so," she said. "Eager and nervous at the same time. Hints that something was going to happen, but she couldn't tell me because that was bad luck."

"She didn't actually mention her mother?"

"No, but nothing else could have excited Suzy so much."

I saw why she and Marty had met trouble convincing the police. She didn't have facts, she had judgments.

"What about Alan Welker?"

"Suzy'd been with Regent Model Management almost a year—a good size eight All-American girl. She'd mentioned Welker a few times, complaining that he was after her too much. Then about a month ago she started going out with him! She saw him a lot toward the end, and he called her almost every day, but she never brought him to the apartment."

"Is this other agency like that 'outcall' one?"

There was a small smile behind the dark glasses. "No, Regent offers modeling jobs, that's all."

"Sorry. It could have been important."

"Don't apologize, Mr. Fortune." Her mouth turned serious, but the wrinkles at the corners of her eyes showed that behind the glasses she was still smiling. "I don't."

"But Suzy did? For what she was doing?"

"Sometimes." She drank her brandy. "I told you Suzy wasn't too bright. She worried about doing 'bad' things, about not being 'worthy' of her mother, but she never did much except talk about it. Regent Model called her a lot, but she turned down most jobs. It was hard work for low pay compared to turning a trick or two. Men even take you out, it's more fun."

"But recently you felt she'd changed, really planned to give up the trade?"

She nodded. "She was seeing a lot of that Alan Welker, and just the weekend before she was killed she went out of town on a modeling job."

"You think Welker and that job had some connection to her mother?"

"I'm sure of it!" She was fierce. Her friend was dead and no one really cared why. "She came back only the day before she died. She was keyed up, almost bursting, but when I asked about the weekend she said it had been nothing special. Normally she chattered up a storm, but this time she told me nothing about where she'd been or what she'd done. She was out most of all that day, talked more about quitting and maybe leaving Los Angeles, got that phone call, and I never saw her again."

She looked up, still fierce behind those dark glasses. "I know she'd never have taken a call from a john, and I'm sure she knew the caller."

"A girl might take one last trick, the way the *Times* suggested, and the caller could have been some regular customer."

"Suzy never had regular customers. She said only professional whores did that and she was a model. A matter of degree. Any woman would understand."

Degree and self-image. Call it self-delusion if you want, but I understood it too. I also sensed that Diane Pasco would not need such delusion, would face reality head on, and wouldn't say what she didn't believe.

"Could it have been something else that had her excited?" I said. "Some other dream? Some other change in her life?"

"Such as what, Mr. Fortune?"

"What other dreams did she have?"

"The usual: marriage, a man in a white Mercedes, getting rich, having her own kids, a big house, the country club. The standard dreams of dumb young girls."

She drained her cognac as if the standard dreams of dumb young girls gave her a bad taste to wash away.

"TV, movies, acting?" I said. "Some other career?"

"This is Los Angeles," she said. "Sure she had acting ideas, but not for long. I got her a job on 'RISK!' with me. She couldn't even act enough to do the interview bit you saw. No talent, no education for any career, and not many brains."

In her voice I heard a deep feeling that Suzy Dekker had been a victim of more than the Canyon Slasher or any other killer. A victim of being given dreams that could only benefit others, not her.

"It's one of your dreams?" I said. "Acting."

"Mine?" I could feel her pull back behind the dark glasses. "I'd like to act. I'd like to do a lot of things. Right now I've got myself and a son to support."

"Sorry again," I said.

She looked down at her empty glass, then up at me. The dark glasses reflected the now crowded lounge with its posing actors and beautiful women drawn from all across the nation.

"You do believe me. About Suzy?" she said.

"I don't believe or disbelieve. I find out."

"The Canyon Slasher didn't kill Alan Welker out there."

"You don't know that," I said. "Welker could have seen him, a witness. He could have stumbled over some clue."

"No," she said.

"You have anything more to tell me?" I said. She shook her head. I waved for the waiter. "Then you better go home. Be careful. Someone did kill Welker, and we don't know why."

We passed the plush dining room of the Brown Derby as we went out. Neither of us had had dinner. In the night chill and traffic of Vine Street between Sunset and Hollywood boulevards I suggested we go to some less expensive restaurant. She declined. She was already late for her babysitter.

Her car was still in the lot behind Unicorn Productions. I had driven mine to the Brown Derby to get it away from the body, but I wanted to check to see if the killing had been reported yet. It had been. The police were all around the yellow Datsun. I hid in the alley from Vine while Diane Pasco went to her car. A patrolman stopped her and a detective talked to her.

I watched her explain who she was, show her identification, and answer a few questions from the detective. They let her go, and she got into her 280ZX, but by then I wasn't watching her or her car.

I watched the other man hiding in the shadows.

He had been standing among the detectives around the yellow Datsun. When the patrolman called one of the detectives to talk to Diane Pasco, I saw him slip quickly into the darker shadows of the buildings. A tall man in a dark suit who stood now close against a wall in the deep shadows.

Diane Pasco drove away in her expensive 280ZX. The detective who had questioned her returned to the group around the yellow Datsun. The patrolman returned to his patrol car at the entrance to the lot. The man in the shadows lit a cigarette and moved out of the shadows. He continued to watch the police work.

The medical examiner's van left with the body. A tow truck came to remove the Datsun. The various teams of detectives finished their work and left. The patrol car followed and the lot returned to the night—silent and empty.

The tall man in the dark suit walked north toward Hollywood Boulevard, turned east on Selma to Vine, and went across Vine to the parking lot of the Brown Derby. When I eased into the lot he was standing near my borrowed Subaru. He wasn't doing anything, just looking at the car and at the rear of the restaurant.

It was the dapper man in the gray flannel suit and western boots who had said he was from the sheriff's office.

He turned from my Subaru to a flashy Lotus sport convertible with a dark green fiberglass body and a roll bar, took a pack of cigarettes from the glove compartment, and went on into the Brown Derby lounge through the side door. He had a Scotch.

I sat down at the bar beside him.

"Looking for me? About Alan Welker's murder, maybe?"

His face was impassive under the thick black hair, but I saw the surprise in his dark eyes. There and gone.

"If you're tailing me," he said, "I wouldn't go on."

"No," I said, "you must be tailing me. Unless you came to watch Diane Pasco. Want to talk about it all?"

He drank his Scotch, fixed those intense eyes on me.

"I could have run you in at the beach. I still can, but I won't. Just walk away right now."

I smiled in his face. "You can't run me in, you're no cop. But you know who I am, you knew the first time you saw my arm. Or didn't see my arm. You knew the Subaru so well you had no need to check it, and you were hiding from Diane Pasco."

"Get lost!" His voice had lost some of its richness, and his manner its confidence.

"Why don't we just go on home to Malibu, Mr. Dekker," I said. "Okay? We can talk with Marty too."

10

The Lotus sometimes moved ahead out of sight on the Santa Monica Freeway, but William Dekker pulled it back each time until he saw me behind him again. It was hard for him, he needed to put the gas to the floor and fly—violent and bold. I held him down by refusing to break my steady sixty, and when we blended into the Coast Highway in Santa Monica the traffic held him more.

Through Santa Monica and Pacific Palisades, the beach and ocean dark to the left, the Lotus weaved and darted in the heavy traffic like a nervous, restless animal. I followed it on past Topanga Canyon into Malibu until the Lotus turned right into Malibu Canyon. Dekker took the curves with squealing tires as we drove deeper into the coastal mountains, and soon turned again into a narrow side canyon.

The narrow side road climbed rapidly and became gravel, twisting higher and higher and finally emerging over a sheer drop with a vast view of what seemed to be the whole world of night. The dark sea, Malibu like a strip of miniature lights between, Los Angeles a sweeping sea of light to the south and west, and the dark mountains to the north rank on rank.

Almost directly above was a lighted Spanish-style house perched like a Moorish hacienda. The gravel road curled and came to a dead end behind the big stucco house. William Dekker had found an entire canyon to call his own.

Marty stood framed in a small doorway at the rear of the house as the two cars pulled into a courtyard of olive trees. Her red hair looked like copper against a slim black jump suit, and her large eyes were on her husband, puzzled and uneasy.

"We bumped into each other," Bill Dekker said as he walked past her into the house.

I explained about the meeting at Diane Pasco's beach apartment as Marty took me into a large old-California-style living room with a low beamed ceiling and a terra-cotta tile floor. It was full of antique Spanish colonial furniture, its white walls hung with serapes, rugs, and ancient Spanish weapons. A very modern picture window had replaced the small windows in the front wall to show off the sweeping view.

Bill Dekker made Marty and himself a Scotch at a corner bar. I had a beer. A Mexicali. It was good beer.

"All right," Dekker said, "what has the New York detective found out so far?"

Marty said, "He hasn't had much time, Bill."

"Time?" Dekker said. "All the time in the world isn't going to change how Suzy died or why."

His rich voice was back, and his hand rested lightly on the back of a heavy, throne-like old California chair. The *hidalgo* in his elegant suit, dark hair, and shining western boots.

"I've found," I said, "that the girl's uncle is snooping around. That doesn't sound like someone convinced that she was killed by a chance psycho. Incidentally, what was the badge?"

"Honorary sheriff." Dekker began to walk, his glass held in both hands, intense and intent. "Chance? It's not chance that sends these girls to their deaths. It's not chance that makes them vulnerable like sheep to a stalking tiger."

"What does?" I said.

He sat down in the high-backed chair. He drank. "When it happened, when I heard that Suzy was lying naked and dead in some canyon, I knew no psychotic phantom had killed her. I had!"

"Bill!" Marty cried.

"We," Dekker said, "all of us! Us and the world we live in. By neglect. By indifference."

It was another part of the same speech he had given me in Diane Pasco's beach apartment. Marty shifted restlessly on the couch, sipped at her Scotch.

"You feel guilty about Suzy's death?" I said.

"Yes, I feel guilty. We all should."

"A general guilt? We all failed her?"

Tall in the throne-like chair, he still held his glass in both hands, his head bent to look at the glass as if it were a crystal ball. "Another guilt too. A guilt I felt the instant they told me she was dead. Like a hammer blow, you know? A revelation. I'd just found my brother's daughter and now I'd lost her again. Why? How?"

He looked around at us but I knew he didn't want an answer now anymore than he had at the beach apartment in Venice.

"My brother's child." He intoned the words like a priest. "An uneducated nothing. A zero. A prostitute. Her mother abandoned her, her father failed her, and what did I do? When my brother died, where was I? What have I done that was more important than a child? What are we all doing that's so important?"

"You were finding out what you could do," Marty said. "You couldn't sacrifice yourself for your brother's failure."

Dekker drank. "Perhaps."

"So you feel guilty," I said. "What are you doing about it? Why the snooping around playing sheriff?"

His drink was empty. So was my beer. He got me a beer, made himself a Scotch. Marty shook her head. Dekker began to pace.

"I thought about Suzy for days, and then I realized that Marty and the Pasco girl could be right about one thing—Suzy *had* known the killer. She knew that madman! The Canyon Slasher was someone she had met before!"

"Someone like Alan Welker?" I said.

He knew at once what I was hinting—that he had been there when Alan Welker was shot, and that he had a motive. He stopped and studied me over his whisky. His dark eyes were cool.

"You were there too, Fortune, so was Diane Pasco. I never met Alan Welker, didn't know him."

Marty said, "Alan Welker?"

Now I told her about the dead man in the yellow Datsun in the Unicorn Productions parking lot and what Diane Pasco had told me about him. Marty listened. She seemed surprised.

"Suzy *did* mention a name like that. He annoyed her. She told me she didn't much like him."

"She changed her mind," I said, turned back to Dekker. "When did you get to that parking lot? What did you see?"

"I saw nothing. I knew nothing until I saw you find the body in the car."

"When did you get to Unicorn Productions?"

"About five-thirty."

"Why?"

"Because I knew you'd go to talk to Diane Pasco. I watched from across Vine, saw you come out, followed, and saw you find the body. I tailed you to the Brown Derby in my car, then went inside and watched you and Diane from the bar. You never even saw me." He grinned, pleased with himself.

"Clever," I said. "Why did you return to the parking lot?"

"I couldn't get close enough to hear what you and Diane Pasco were saying, so I went to see what I could find on the dead man, but the police were already there. I have a press card, asked them what had happened. They said it looked like robbery, but I saw the auto registration and remembered Suzy mentioning a name like Welker."

"Did the name mean anything to the police?" I asked.

"It didn't seem to," Bill Dekker said.

"And you still think the Slasher killed your niece?"

"Even more! That Welker boy must have known him too, or have seen him with Suzy. He *is* someone Suzy knew, and there must be some clues to him in her life." His dark eyes held a fury. "I'm going to find this madman. I'm going to talk to him. In his life, somewhere, is why this happened, why Suzy had to die."

"Bill!" Marty said. "You can't chase a murderer!"

"It's not your job," I said. "Let the police handle it."

"The police have ten victims and they'll have more; the city is full of lost girls waiting to be victims. The police won't look in the life of one girl for some tiny clue."

"That's why I hired Dan," Marty said. "It's his work."

"I'm not man enough?" Dekker said.

"Man enough," Marty said, "but not skilled enough."

I said, "You could get into a hell of a lot of trouble, not to mention get hurt. Let me do what I'm paid for, okay?"

The habit of holding his glass in both hands gave Dekker an appearance of wisdom. He had a young face for his forty-odd years, and I guessed that he had adopted the habit early to seem older. Now it served to make him seem to think carefully before he spoke. Maybe he did.

"Perhaps you're both right," he said. "The worst thing a writer can do is think he's one of his own heroes, eh? The actor who forgets he's not as tough as the character he plays." He smiled and finished his Scotch. "I'm tired. Marty?"

"Dan and I'll talk a while," she said.

Dekker held out his hand. "Dan, I'm glad you came out."

We shook hands. He had a slim hand, soft but not flabby. He hadn't worked much with his hands. His smile was neither flabby nor soft. A friendly, open smile. I had the feeling that he worked a lot with the smile.

11

The big house was silent.

Isolated high above Malibu, it had a stiff, orderly silence as if it had rarely known noise at all. Marty brought me a new beer. She had a fresh Scotch. We sat dwarfed by the giant living room and the vast night outside. Marty watched the distant lights of Malibu and the coast highway far below.

"You didn't tell me about Alan Welker," she said. "You told me you met Bill in Venice, but not about Welker."

I listened to the silence of the remote house. When he left the room, Dekker could have vanished from the earth. I drank.

"I don't know what's going on here, Marty. I don't know what happened and what didn't. I don't know who did what or who wants what. I don't know which side anyone is on. I don't even know what the sides are. All I know is that two people connected to your husband and you are dead."

Her voice was tight. "You don't seem to know much."

"No, I don't." I drank again. "I don't know what Bill's relations were with Suzy. I don't even know what your relations to her were."

"Mine I told you. A few visits, some talk. She needed to talk to an older woman. Almost any older woman."

"And Bill?"

She took my empty bottle and went into the distant kitchen. She returned with another bottle of the Mexicali, made herself another Scotch at the corner bar, and sat down again.

"I don't know what their relationship was," she said.

"A niece he'd never known or even met," I said. "He might not have felt much like an uncle."

She listened to the silence and the night. "He liked her, Dan, I saw that. I don't know how he liked her." She moved in her chair. "He's an iconoclast, a maverick. He thinks his own way, and does what he wants."

I felt that we sat at the bottom of a great pit with the eyes of the world watching us. Small and insignificant, exposed under a giant microscope to unknown eyes.

"How are the two of you getting along?" I said.

She went on listening where there was no sound. "I don't know. Sexually we're all right, and it's only been six months. But I don't really know how we're getting along. There's something in the air. I don't know what, or if it's him or me."

"Before or after Suzy was killed? This something in the air?"

"Both," she said. "There hasn't been that much change."

The doubt I'd heard in her voice on Olvera Street was still there. Nothing definite, only a sense of uncertainty.

"Does he always talk that way?" I asked. "Speeches, theories?"

"Not with me. With other people he tends to."

"How did he get along with Suzy's parents in the past?"

"I don't think he ever even met the mother, and as far as I know he never saw his brother Stan again after they both left home up north. Bill isn't much for family relations."

"Until Suzy came around."

"Yes," she said. "Until Suzy came around."

I decided to let it end there for now. She'd had a long day.

"It's probably all nothing," I said. "I'll go into high gear tomorrow." I smiled at her in the silence of the big old hacienda, and enjoyed the last of my bottle of Mexicali.

"Where will you sleep tonight?" she said.

"I'll find a motel."

"You can sleep here."

"I don't think so."

"Why not, Dan?"

I finished the beer, stood up. "I'll start with Alan Welker. The address on his registration was in Redwood City, but he worked down here and must have had an apartment or a room."

"Can I work with you?"

"No."

"Then sleep here. Talk to me."

I turned to the door.

"Dan? It's a very big house."

"Not that big."

The outside door closed almost silently behind me. In the Subaru I could still see her sitting there in her slim black jump suit with her feet tucked up under her and her large eyes watching me from under the thick red hair.

I drove down carefully. My eyes were on the twisting gravel road, but my mind was on the house behind me and the man and woman in it. Would she go to bed with him now? I thought about something else.

On the Coast Highway I turned south and was in Pacific Palisades before I found a motel with a vacancy.

12

They say a soldier comes to feel when the enemy is near. In my work you come to feel danger. You know when someone is outside your door. The way a secret agent in his hidden room knows just when the violent knock is about to come.

Sometimes there is no knock.

"Okay, up!"

Two men in dark suits with the motel door open behind them. A thin man and a short man. Both with guns. The thin man patted my clothes, tossed them to me.

"Get dressed."

Two more of them moved around the motel room opening everything. Another stood outside the open door.

"What—!" I sat up.

"Don't talk," the thin one said. "Read him his rights."

The short man read me my rights. I got dressed. They had my bag packed. Some of them were still looking down drains, taking fingerprints, snapping photos. The short man had handcuffs. He turned me around and swore. He'd noticed my missing arm.

"Cuff him to yourself," the thin one said.

They hustled me out and into a black car so fast I barely saw any daylight. We drove out of the motel with another car in front and one behind and went left toward the sun. It wasn't yet 7:00 A.M., the highway less than half full and the broad beach to the right empty. My companions sat with drawn guns as if they feared an attack or a rescue any minute, and I knew what was happening. At the police station I was hustled in as fast as I'd been hustled out, walked down corridors and into a windowless room. My suitcase and loose change were on a long table. Three older men came in and sat behind the table.

"He been read to?" the youngest of them said.

"Yeh, Lieutenant," my shorter one said.

"He got a gun in the case," my thin man said.

The lieutenant looked at me as if he suddenly liked me. The oldest of the trio at the table went through my wallet. He held it out to the next oldest. They would be at least captains. The second oldest handed the wallet to the lieutenant, whose smile faded. They had found my investigator's license.

"You're Daniel Fortune? From New York?"

"Yes, Lieutenant."

"When did you come to Los Angeles?"

"Yesterday morning, for Mrs. William Dekker," I said. "I'm not the Canyon Slasher, Lieutenant. Sorry."

"Shit," the oldest of the trio said.

He stood and walked out. The second oldest followed him. The lieutenant said, "Why the hell didn't you tell my men?"

"Lieutenant," I said, "the day hasn't come when I try to talk to a roomful of cops who think I might be a psycho mass murderer."

The lieutenant just sat for a time. Then he waved his men out, stood up, and motioned for me to follow him. I picked up my suitcase and sundries from the table, and we went to his office. I lit a cigarette. My hand shook only a little.

"You were spotted at the girl's Venice apartment," the lieutenant said. "We've got it staked. You were a stranger. Sacramento returned the license of the Subaru as belonging to William Dekker of Malibu. We thought we'd made a big break."

"Sorry again," I said. The cigarette tasted very good. Handcuffs aren't something you get used to. I was glad I wasn't the Canyon Slasher.

"Her aunt hired you? Dekker's wife?"

"Yes."

"Why you? All the way from New York."

"We're old friends."

The lieutenant poked his desk with a wicked switchblade that looked like the memento of some case but now served as a letter opener. He was a short, heavy man with black hair and a sharp hooked nose in a round face.

"You can't carry a gun in Los Angeles."

"I know that," I said. "It stays in the case."

"You're not licensed to work here."

"The girl's family has a right to find out how and why she died. You can check me out in New York."

"We know how and why the girl died."

"Then I can help get the family off your back."

He swung his battered desk chair. It needed oil, rasped harshly in the small office.

"I don't like it, Fortune. This is too much case for a P.I., especially an out-of-towner. You better go home. Tell the Dekker woman the Slasher is out of your line."

"If Suzanne Dekker was killed by the Slasher."

"She was," he said.

"You don't know that, Lieutenant. You won't until you catch him and sort out the real victims from the copy-cats, coincidences and imitations. Somewhere out in this city you could have a murderer hiding his killing behind the Slasher's method."

He was too experienced a policeman to deny my suggestion, but he didn't want it.

"You have anything to base that on besides theories?"

"Not yet."

"And you won't."

"Maybe not," I said, "but I'd like to see the details on Suzanne Dekker's murder."

He didn't want that either, only he was a good cop. If I wasn't going to go away, I might be some help. He took a thick file from a drawer, leafed through, and found a single sheet.

He read, "Nine-ten A.M. Female Caucasian in her late teens found in upper Collins Canyon by two male hikers. Victim was positioned on her back, without clothing, twelve feet from an abandoned cabin. Cabin was locked, had not been entered. No—"

"The *Times* implied she was killed in the cabin," I said.

"The papers usually get it all ass-backwards. We even like it that way, don't say anything, because it could confuse the killer. She wasn't even killed in that canyon, none of her clothes were there. Most of his victims were killed somewhere else and dumped in the canyons." He went on reading. "Stabbed six times, throat cut, and shot once in the head. No evidence—"

"Shot?" I said. "Were any of the other girls shot?"

"No."

"What killed her? The knife or the gun?"

"M.E. can't say for sure. Either or both. She was shot and stabbed about the same time."

"What caliber gun?"

"Seven-point-six-five millimeter."

I thought about that. For a long minute or so.

"You don't think it important she was the only one shot?"

"No," he said. "Two others were strangled before he cut them up; one had been clubbed before the carving. Once he forgot to cut the throat. Each killing has minor variations, but put them into the computer and all ten come out loud and clear—slashed, naked, in canyons, young, hookers, and a lot more."

"Go on," I said.

He read, "No evidence of any other person was found within half a mile of the body. Cabin is half a mile from a road. No tire marks near the body. No signs of dragging. Victim was apparently carried, but no usable footprints have been found."

"He carried her half a mile? A dead body?"

"He could be a big one, but we figure two men."

"Two?"

The lieutenant nodded. "It's pretty certain there were two men in one of the other killings."

"The Slasher is two men?"

"No, but we think he has a friend who helps him out."

"That's quite a friend," I said.

"Loyal," the lieutenant said. "We get every kind."

"What else is there on Suzanne Dekker?"

"That's it." He filed the sheet, returned the file to the drawer. "We haven't found her clothes, the weapons, the car, or where she was killed. Maybe we do, maybe not. In six cases we did locate the murder site, in three we still have zero."

"And each time there've been differences?"

He nodded. "He's inventive, or unpredictable."

"What's different with Suzanne Dekker besides the gun?"

He thought. "Nothing. A perfect Slasher job."

"In the other cases there was more than one difference?"

"Usually, yeh."

"Maybe Suzanne Dekker's case is too perfect."

He studied me. "What's that, New York police work? If it all fits it can't be true?"

"I think I'd like it better if everything except the gun didn't match. Makes me wonder if someone didn't try too hard."

"You know what I think?" He went on studying me. "I think you're a crook, Fortune, a hustler. I think you're out to make a good buck out of the Dekkers. Shock and fear, right? The Slasher is like blind chance, and people don't like blind chance. It scares them. Anyone could be killed any time. Maybe them. That's what you play on to make your cheap money."

I stood up. "Then I won't bother you, right? Just take my money and do nothing. Can I leave?"

"Stay out of our way, call in anything you think you find out— anything. Keep away from trouble, and don't get out of line with the citizens."

"You'll get your Slasher, Lieutenant."

"Beat it."

In the corridor no one took any notice of me. By now the two older cops were back at Parker Center, the day was in full swing. The name on the office door said I'd been talking to Lt. Stepanic, and the thin detective from the motel sat at a desk across the corridor. He told me my Subaru was in their lot. He gave me the keys, said they'd paid the motel bill with my money, and returned to his paper work.

The January morning sun was high as I walked out. The day was growing hot. I tossed my bag into the Subaru, found Sunset Boulevard, and drove toward Hollywood.

I hadn't told them anything I'd done. If Suzy Dekker had not been a Slasher victim, she'd be just another street girl killing to them, and they got fifty like her a month. So far I had little to change that; the less they thought I knew the more they'd stay out of my way, and maybe I could get something that would change their thinking.

I found a telephone booth and looked up the address of Regent Model Management. An address in Hollywood.

It looked like they hadn't connected Alan Welker to Suzy Dekker or to me, and didn't know about Regent Model Management. This meant that they hadn't seen me with Diane Pasco last night, that in the parking lot Diane had told them nothing about Welker, and that they didn't know that Welker worked locally. That, or they were playing me like a fish.

And Alan Welker had been killed by the same size gun that had shot Suzy Dekker.

13

It was a three-story building on the edge of the Sunset Strip, with a go-go saloon and a narrow pornographic bookstore on the first floor. Regent Model Management had the third floor. The elevator was self-service from a narrow lobby of beige imitation marble. It opened directly onto Regent's reception area of couches and glass tables on three inches of gray carpet presided over by a tall blonde who looked like she herself had only stopped modeling yesterday.

"Yes?" Her voice had been to school, and had a question mark at the end now as she looked at my empty sleeve.

"Mr. Alan Welker, please."

"I'm sorry, Mr. Welker isn't in today. Perhaps someone else can help, if you could tell me just what—?"

"It's private," I said. I made my voice serious, even ominous. "About one of your models—Suzanne Dekker."

I watched and it hit her, but she never lost her smile. She moved a shade too precisely to pick up her telephone, press a button, and speak stiffly.

"Mr. Barton? A gentleman here asking about Mr. Welker and Suzanne Dekker. Yes. A private matter." She listened and hung up. "Mr. Barton will come out."

Mr. Barton wasted no time. He came out of the side wall where a knobless door was barely visible. A short, thin, ramrod straight older man with a quick walk. His silver gray hair shined with bluish undertones, and his rich gray suit ended in soft dress boots with two inch heels and lifts inside. He looked me over, then motioned for me to follow him.

The door in the wall closed behind us, and we walked along a narrow, soundless corridor hung with paintings—all abstract and original. A rear passage for executives only, with three doors opening off it. Barton's was the last door. The boss. I was more important to them than I had expected.

The quick little man went in first and sat behind a desk that looked like an aircraft carrier sailing on a sea of chocolate brown carpet. He pointed me to an Eames chair—a real one in cocoa-colored glove leather so soft it felt as if I could eat it. Mr. Barton watched me silently from behind his desk.

"You're a policeman?"

"A private detective working for Mrs. Martine Dekker."

"Mother?"

"Aunt," I said. "My name's Dan Fortune."

"Yes," Barton nodded. The high back of his desk chair reached six inches above his head. "Actually, Miss Dekker did very little work for Regent. On the few assignments she did take from us she performed her modeling work well, gave no difficulties, and attended strictly to business. We knew nothing, and can tell you nothing, of what she may have done outside this office or in her private life."

It was a prepared statement, carefully constructed word by word and memorized. He must have had it ready for over a week. Since the morning Suzy Dekker had been found naked in the canyon. But I didn't think he'd had a chance to give it before.

"Is that what you told the police?"

"As I said, she hardly worked here at all. The police had no reason to—"

"The police never talked to you or anyone here?"

"No," Barton said.

"You didn't go to the police? No one here? Not even Alan Welker?"

"As I said, we knew nothing of what Miss Dekker did—"

I nodded. "All right, Mr. Barton, I've got your official position. It's fine with me. You don't want to be involved in what really doesn't involve you, and neither do I. All I want is some help, off the record, okay? With any luck Regent's name will never come into it."

He thought about it for a time. Not too long. He was a man who could make decisions.

"Yes, that's all I want. The girl really did very little work for us, I see no reason why we must bleed."

"You think you'd bleed?"

"White," Barton said. "You've seen the newspaper stories. What do you think people would say about another 'model agency' where Suzanne Dekker worked? Too many already assume we sell the models not the modeling. We'd lose our clients and our models."

"And you don't sell the models?"

He sat there small in the high-backed chair and closed his eyes. "There's a lot of money in it? We must be crazy?"

"There's money in it," I said.

He sat silent. "All right, I'll try to explain." He opened his eyes. "My father built this business. A service for a group of talented and needed women who could profit from professional help in managing their careers. A good, honest business. Now it's mine. It does well, I like my work, I make enough money. I don't need cheap money from a different kind of service. If I did take such money I would lose what my father built and what I enjoy doing. You understand?"

He sounded like the type of man you don't find often in Hollywood. Or anywhere else.

"But you know what the girls do on the side."

"Some of them," he said. "Yes, I know. Los Angeles gives a girl every opportunity for an easy dollar. A boy too, for that matter. I can't change it, but I have no intention of adding to it."

It was something I could agree with. I hoped it was all true. Mine is a cynical business.

"You sent her on a big job out of town about two weeks ago. Where? What was the job?"

He was surprised. "You must be mistaken, Mr. Fortune. I sent her on no large assignment. She wasn't on the out-of-town roster. I don't think she ever wanted to be, and I only send my most reliable models on such assignments."

"I'm sure she went on one two weeks ago."

He pushed a button. His intercom beeped. "Yes, sir?"

"Bring me Suzanne Dekker's file. The inactive section."

"You don't waste time," I said.

"I have an efficient office manager. She's dead, so she's inactive. A little callous, but necessary in agency work."

His secretary brought in a thin file. Barton flipped through it.

"Well I'm damned. You're right. Who the devil—?" He shook his head, studied the file. "She went up to Santa Barbara two weeks ago to work in the annual Christmas season fashion showings of Elite Imports at El Mirador Hotel and Beach Club. They put on a show on each of four weekends to buyers from the best chains and specialty shops. We've had the model contract for many years and it's one of our very best. I always approve the list of models, and would never have sent the Dekker girl. Someone must have changed the list. I'll find out who—" He reached for the intercom again.

"Never mind," I said. "I think I can tell you who put her on the list. Alan Welker."

"Welker? Why would—?" He sat back. "You think he was involved with that girl? Damn it, I'll fire him!"

"I don't think you'll have to," I said. I didn't tell him why. "How long has he been off the job?"

This time he picked up his telephone receiver. "Personnel. Yes. How long has Mr. Welker been ill? A week? Thank you." He hung up, frowned at me. "He's been out a full week or more. In fact ..." He blinked, thinking. "I don't think he's been in the office since the girl was killed."

"Do you have his home address?"

"We should have." He went through the intercom/secretary routine, and handed me Alan Welker's address. "He's been with us just over a year. Not too much education, but he's eager, ambitious, and hardworking, and he gets along well with the girls. There's a knack to this work, a matter of personality in some ways. Alan has it, I think, but if he sent that girl up to Santa Barbara for his own advantage I'll fire him cold."

"She may have talked him into it," I said. "Well, thank you, Mr. Barton. I appreciate the help." I got up to leave.

Barton stopped me with a gesture. "You mean you think the girl could have had some reason for wanting to go to that show in Santa Barbara? That they both could have had a specific reason? Then …" The small, ramrod-straight man stopped. Then he shook his head with its silver-gray hair. "No, don't tell me anything more. I really don't want to know."

14

The police hadn't given me time for breakfast or fed me, so I stopped for a hamburger and a beer on Wilshire in Santa Monica around the corner from the address of Alan Welker. I left the Subaru in the fast-food diner's lot, and walked.

In the sunny early afternoon the side street with its old palm trees and stucco buildings was quiet. Alan Welker's building was one of those massive apartment houses built in the twenties to look like Moorish palaces—or some second-rate local architect's gaudy idea of a Moorish palace. Yellow brick and stucco, decorated with bulging windows and towers, set with tiles in what was supposed to be arabic mosaic. It was built around a lush open center courtyard and occupied half the block.

The long, red-and-yellow tiled lobby echoed to my footsteps. At the far end giant French doors opened into the trees and shrubs of the center court, and cool corridors led right and left in a rectangle around the open courtyard. Alan Welker's apartment, number twelve, was to the right on the first floor and halfway along the silent tiled corridor. I made sure I was alone in the cool, dim hallway, then used my ring of keys.

There was one large, high-ceilinged living room, a small bedroom, smaller kitchen and bathroom. The living room was sparsely furnished with a few ill-assorted pieces that looked like they had been barely saved from the city dump. The bedroom was no better—a functional double bed, unmade, a lamp-bed table, a battered bureau, and a single wooden chair. The floors were wood badly in need of polishing. Alan Welker had not been a man who spent his money on where he lived.

He hadn't spent his money on clothes either. One blue suit, a dress shirt, and a pair of dark brown oxfords were all that was in the bedroom closet. There were no suitcases, and no desk in either room. No tables with drawers, a single drawer in the bed stand that was empty, and the bedroom bureau.

The program was in the top bureau drawer. For a fashion show at El Mirador Hotel and Beach Club of the South American clothes of Elite Import, Inc. On New Year's weekend. A series of names under Elite Imports had been circled in ink.

I heard the key in the lock, came out of the bedroom as the stocky man closed the outer door. He stood blinking at me.

"The super," he said. "He gimme the key. My boy's stuff."

He was a wide man in his late forties wearing work pants, a wool plaid shirt, sneakers, and a gray hat he took off to reveal a bald bullet head. His hands were large and had the permanent dirt under the nails of a man who worked with the hands. His small, quick eyes looked everywhere except at me.

"I'm sorry," I said. "Can I ask some questions about him?"

"Who're you?"

"Dan Fortune," I said. "Private investigator working for Suzanne Dekker's family."

"Who the hell's Suzanne Dekker?"

I told him. "The police didn't tell you about Suzanne?"

He continued to look around the sparse living room. As if he still expected his son to appear any second. Or hoped.

"Hell, Dan, I don't know nothin' about no Suzanne Dekker. The cops didn't say nothin' to me."

"Alan never mentioned her to you?"

"We didn't keep in touch so good." Welker's heavy face was confused. Perhaps trying to understand. "You know how it is with kids away from home. You want to keep in touch, only you don't, you know?"

"You have no idea why Alan was shot?"

"We got no ideas, nothin'. Got in with bad people, I guess. We never got to know his friends." He rubbed a dirty finger in his eye and the back of his hand against his sniffling nose, still didn't look at me. "They know who killed this Dekker girl?"

"The police say the Canyon Slasher."

"That psycho? Christ, maybe he got Alan too?"

"Why would he kill Alan, Mr. Welker?"

"Clyde," the stocky father said. "Hell, I don't know. Maybe Alan was with her, yeh? Maybe he *saw* this crazy Slasher."

"Why didn't he tell the police? Where was he between when Suzy was killed and he was killed?"

Welker scowled. "Yeh. Good questions." He seemed to have a sudden thought. One he liked. "Hey, maybe you oughta work for me too! I can pay pretty good. I'm a pressman. Do real nice, you know? Maybe get my own print shop soon."

"I've got a client, Mr. Welker. I'm not allowed—"

Later I knew that I'd been listening to the sounds for some time. Out in the corridor. Sounds and lack of sounds. First the soft, echoing footsteps of two people. One to the right and one to the left. Stepping slowly toward the apartment beyond the closed door. Then nothing.

No sounds. No footsteps. Only silence. And it was the silence I heard. I stepped to the door, opened it.

They were there to the right and left along the dim, tiled corridor. Leaning silently against the shadowed walls. Two men in dark suits.

I closed the door.

"Cops?" Clyde Welker said.

"I don't think so," I said. "The windows."

Welker didn't wait. He dropped out the window into the central courtyard. I dropped. We ran through the small trees and green shrubs along the bench-lined stone walks.

Heads and faces at the windows behind us. Silent faces. Inexorable. With guns.

We ran in through the rear French doors, and around into the long opposite corridor toward the front lobby. Apartment doors lined the cool, silent corridor. I rang a bell. An old lady opened the door. She screamed. We ran through her living room, jumped out her windows into a narrow alley. A blind alley.

The only exit was into the street at the front of the building.

Steps between iron railings led down to a basement entrance. The door was locked. My third key opened it. Inside we listened in darkness. We listened a long time.

The knob turned in the door.

We watched the knob turn.

The footsteps went up into the alley and away.

"They missed us!" Clyde Welker whispered.

"They'll be back. All we have is some time."

I found the light switch. The basement was divided into a maze of passages lined with slatted storage rooms. One room for each apartment. With heavy padlocked doors.

"Stay at the door," I said to Welker. "When you hear them again, signal with the light switch and lie low."

The rows of cubicles led in all directions. I found no windows and no other exit. The slatted cubicles were full of furniture. Broken and loose boards hung from some.

Daylight glared behind me. Someone ran up the cellar stairs and out into the alley. I waited.

Footsteps in the dark cellar. The same soft steps.

Clyde Welker had not signaled. Welker had run up out of the cellar. They had not gone after him. They didn't want Clyde Welker. They wanted me.

15

They knew how to quarter an area, how to keep all; escape covered. Silent in the dark cellar.

They would push me steadily back until I was penned into a smaller and smaller corner. I tried to remember where I had seen a cubicle with a loose board.

They were unhurried. Slow footsteps in the darkness on a concrete floor.

I found the loose slat. The nails were still in it. I squeezed through the opening. I fitted the board into its nail holes, pulled as hard as I could with my lone arm. The board tightened almost flat against the upright beams. Inside the cubicle I sat behind two old trunks and breathed slowly.

They came.

First a shadow through the slats. The lock rattled metallic. The door shook. The shadow moved on.

Behind my head the second bumped unseen against the cubicle wall. The loose board held. The steps passed on, faded away.

I waited.

Without sound or warning, quick shadows returned. They shook the lock and bumped the walls. Again.

Then silence.

I sat in the silent cellar for five hours.

After a time I smoked the way a soldier smokes in a fox hole, cigarette cupped in my solitary hand. After a longer time began to think about them, about Clyde Welker, about all of it. Who and what were they? Some kind of gunmen. Professional. Welker had left me to face them alone. To hurt me or to save himself? He had run without hesitation up in the apartment, as if they could be after him. But they hadn't been. Only me.

Five hours, then I walked through the dark basement and up into the alley. A late afternoon sun angled low down the alley. There were no shadows waiting for me. Victory is often only a matter of who can wait the longest.

I walked slowly back to the fast-food restaurant parking lot where I had left the Subaru. It was just luck, chance, I'd parked it there instead of in front of Alan Welker's building. Victory can be that too. They had missed the car. But they wouldn't miss much. Whoever they were, they were pros. Some kind of pros.

16

On the way to Santa Barbara I called Marty from Malibu.

"Suzy was in Santa Barbara the weekend before she died. Does Elite Imports, Incorporated, mean anything to you?"

"No, Dan," Marty said.

In the phone booth of a sleek saloon where the custom-made beachcombers were massing for the night, I had the program from Alan Welker's bureau. "How about Henry Wayne, Helga Kasmer, Judson Graham, or Eva Wayne?"

"No," she said. "Dan, I never heard of any of those names! Are you sure they meant something to Suzy?"

"No, but they seem to have been important to Alan Welker," I said. "Is Bill at home?"

There was a silence. "He went out early. After the police called to ask if we'd hired you. I told them we had. Okay?"

"They already knew. Bill hasn't returned all day?"

"No," she said. "Why didn't you stay last night?"

"Maybe because I wanted to," I said. "Mart, let me do my job. What you hired me to do."

I hung up. Damn women. Damn men. Damn the need. It was hard enough in my work without my mind somewhere else. Did she know that?

17

The red glow of freeway taillights narrow between sea and mountains. Distant floating lights of oil platforms. A series of wooded promontories washed by a ghostly surf. Santa Barbara.

Off the freeway, on a dark curving drive of large houses that loomed above towering hedges of trumpet vine and oleander under palms and eucalyptus, El Mirador Hotel and Beach Club was a sprawling frame structure on ten acres between the drive and the sea. A vast lawn flowed gently among the buildings to the sea. It would take a small army to maintain, and that was the mark of true privilege in a time when there were no more peasants or immigrants.

The desk clerk looked at my old sportcoat, wrinkled gray slacks, and lone arm and was still polite. That costs money.

"The shows are held in the beach club, sir. For one more weekend. Someone from Elite Imports should be there."

The lawn had the soft spring of velvet, and a cold fog was drifting in through the palm trees. The beach club was a modern glass-and-concrete complex of central buildings around an olympic-sized pool. The two-story-high lobby had a wall of glass facing the sea. It was guarded by a doorman in uniform.

"The fashion show? They expectin' you?"

"I'm a private detective from New York. It's a murder case and I need some fast answers.

"Murder? Well—?" He was interested in murder, but you never knew when someone was trying to steal a free swim.

"It's a matter of time."

The urgency got to him. He was a policeman himself.

"Upstairs. The ballroom."

The second floor landing overhung the lobby and faced the dark ocean through the glass wall. In the empty ballroom a man and a woman leaned on the stage studying papers. The man looked up. Probably in his early thirties, he had a stiff, crooked smile, with blue eyes and dark blond hair. A young face, but there was something wrong with his eyes.

"Elite Imports?" I said. "A few questions."

"What? Yes, all right. My sister can help you." He went back to his papers, his thin fingers tapping.

The woman came to me. "Helga Kasmer. I handle public relations. You're a reporter?"

She was a big woman maybe ten years older than the man. Taller than he was, and much heavier. Overweight, with ragged true blonde hair she wore shoulder length and slow moving blue eyes. In a shapeless dark wool dress, she had a certain resemblance to the slender man, but not much.

"A private investigator," I said. "Dan Fortune. Looking for information about a model in your New Year's weekend show. Suzanne Dekker."

The man looked up again. He looked at me. He moved slowly as if having difficulty focusing his mind. "Who?"

"Suzanne Dekker," I said.

He returned to his work. "I don't remember that name."

"I think so, Henry," Helga Kasmer said. "That all-American girl, size eight? The one who was late for rehearsals? Modeled the Quechua skirts and most of the serapes?"

I heard a faint accent in her voice now. Not much, a trace. The man, Henry, didn't have it. He looked up again, distracted.

"The one who flirted with some of the buyers?"

I said, "You're Henry Wayne?"

"In charge of sales," Helga Kasmer said. "The buyers are his territory, so he'd notice that."

"Did she flirt with any particular buyer? More than flirt?"

"I don't know, Mr. Fortune," the stout woman said. "We have an agency, they send a rep to supervise the models."

"Was that Alan Welker?"

"No, a woman." She thought. "Some name like Barton."

Henry Wayne didn't look up. "Regina Barton."

"Some relation to Regent Model Management's president?"

"Probably," Helga Kasmer said. "We're only vice presidents, Mr. Fortune. Our mother still handles the top-level contacts."

"Would mother be Eva Wayne?"

"That's mother," she said. "Principal owner, chairman, president, what have you. It's her company. She has the taste, the connections, and the know-how."

"Where can I talk to her?"

Henry Wayne made an angry noise, pushed his papers aside. He was unhappy with the interruption, my questions, or both.

"Mother is out of town," he said. "Helga, can we get some work done?"

"Don't push me!" she snapped. She stared at him. "When did mother leave town?"

"This morning."

"She never told me!"

"She told *me!*"

She was older, but he was a man. The family battle that has been going on for centuries and only now is the woman sometimes winning. But this time Helga Kasmer did not go on with the debate. She only went on staring at her brother.

"Is there anyone I can talk to about Suzanne Dekker?" I asked. "What she did up here? Where she lived. Who she met, talked to, went out with. Anything special or unusual that might have happened?"

Henry Wayne slammed his pen down on the stage, snapped, "Whenever you're ready again, Helga!" and stalked out of the ballroom.

Helga Kasmer frowned at me. "Is there something special about this girl, Mr. Fortune?"

"She's dead," I said. "She was killed the day after she left Santa Barbara."

"Killed?" she said.

"The police say by the Canyon Slasher."

"How horrible!"

"Some people think the police are wrong, that she was killed by someone else using the Slasher to try to hide his motive."

Behind the slow eyes and the drab appearance there was a sharp mind. "And she was up here just before she died. I see. You think someone here could be involved?"

"Have you had any trouble lately in your business? Violence? With competitors or clients? Those buyers, maybe?"

She half laughed. "We're not high fashion, Mr. Fortune. No one comes to steal our designs. We simply import all kinds of native fashions from South and Central America. Mother does have her special suppliers she keeps secret, but anyone who really wants to import can find suppliers."

"What about buyers? Trying to undercut, deal direct?"

"No," she smiled. "It wouldn't be worth it, and it is tricky to do business down there if you don't know your way."

"Elite is a relatively small business?"

"Medium-sized, but a gold mine. Mother is a shrewd trader. I'm afraid the villagers don't get rich, but everyone else does: middlemen, wholesalers, retailers, and investors."

"So you're having no business troubles?"

"Nothing out of the ordinary."

"Who can I talk to about Suzanne Dekker?"

"Perhaps Jud Graham. He—"

"Judson Graham?" The fourth circled name on Alan Welker's program. Only, according to Henry Wayne and Helga Kasmer, Alan Welker had not been in Santa Barbara that weekend. Then where had he gotten the program?

"Yes," Helga Kasmer nodded. "Mother's partner, the silent kind. He's a member of this beach club, so he gets us the club for the shows at just about cost. To do it he has to help with the shows, so he and his wife Janice sort of mother the girls. You know, arrange where they stay, the various logistics of rehearsals, time off, parties, all that."

"Where does he live?"

"Eleven-twenty-four Tucker Canyon Road." She laughed. "Wait until you see it."

"Are any of the same models here now?"

"Yes, some. They're staying all around town, but you might find a lot of them over at the bar of El Mirador."

"Join me?" I said.

"I never *join* anyone, Mr. Fortune."

She walked away. Her drab and sloppy clothes, ugly grooming, and excess weight weren't accidental. She worked on being unattractive, the rejection of any man's desire or even interest.

18

I gave the guard a smile and a nod of thanks as I went out. He looked like he would have preferred a tenner, or at least some good scandal, but I didn't think he'd earned those.

The fog had slid softly through all the trees and across the dark lawn to the hotel buildings and beyond. Soft, damp and silent under the palms and eucalyptus, the shrubs and bushes like ghosts as they lightened and darkened with the moving fog. A muffled world with motors sounding far off and long fingers of shrouded light probing toward the hotel as a car turned in.

And muffled footsteps walking rapidly behind me. I stepped behind a thick royal palm. Henry Wayne came hurrying through the fog from the direction of the beach club. He was not going toward the lobby of the El Mirador. Oblivious, he went straight ahead without looking right or left. I followed through the fog. He went on around the main building to a side entrance. A tall man in a dark suit and hat came out to meet Wayne.

They stood in the fog and dim light of the side entrance and talked briefly. Then they went inside. I didn't move. Another shadow appeared out of the fog to my right and closer to the side entrance of the hotel. Someone who had approached the hotel from the same direction but a different angle. Who followed the two men inside and passed under the dim entrance light. Helga Kasmer.

I couldn't follow too closely, and by the time I went in after them they had all vanished.

The same polite desk clerk smiled at me as I entered the lobby. Large and rustic, with high redwood ceiling beams in the cathedral style almost native to early California, the lobby led on the left into the sitting-room lounge and the bar lounge. A large bar lounge out of time and place. The long, high bar on the right, the old-fashioned glassed-in cabinets, the overhead wooden fans, the dance floor, and the rattan furniture were like something east of Suez in the days of the empire.

An almost empty bar on a winter Wednesday, except for a group of young women at two tables who talked, laughed, drank, and danced with each other to the heavy beat of a yawning three-man band. Like the last survivors of a summer resort at the end of the season. I approached them.

"Are any of you ladies from Regent Model Management?"

"A man!"

"Are we from Regent Model Management, kids?"

"Grab him!"

"Not far enough from it!"

They were in a manic mood after a long day's work a long way from Los Angeles and the weekend still three days away.

"I'd like to talk to any of you about Suzanne Dekker."

There was silence, only the dancing and the band.

"She's dead," one of them said.

"He knows that, stupid," another said. "Cop?"

"Private," I said. "For her uncle. Can you tell me anything about her while she was alive and up here New Year's?"

"What's to tell?" a third said. "It goes with the territory. You're a woman, creeps and psychos kill you."

One of them was a few years older than the rest. A gaunt brunette with alert eyes. "Dance with us, and you can ask your questions."

"All of you?" I said.

"Hey, wow! I never danced with a one-armed guy!"

"Or did anything else," a young one giggled.

The older one with the alert eyes and easy smile danced first. She was tall and thin, stood eye to eye with me, and danced close.

"You knew Suzy Dekker?" I asked.

"Not well. She didn't take many jobs at Regent."

"What about the weekend up here? See her much?"

"Not much. She never seemed to be around, when I think about it. Try Kate Lennon, she roomed with Dekker that weekend. She's not here tonight."

"You say she seemed to vanish often that weekend?"

"Showed up for the work, but late a lot," she said. "You dance pretty well."

"For a one-armed man."

"I didn't say that."

The next two who cut in hadn't known Suzy Dekker or been in Santa Barbara that weekend. They laughed more than they danced because they were cutting in on a man! We could have been back in the fifties. Everything goes in circles.

The fourth was a petite blonde. She had known Suzy a little, but she hadn't been in Santa Barbara with her.

"She wasn't supposed to be on the list to come up here," the girl said, "but the Hollywood cowboy got her on."

"Alan Welker? Why would he do that?"

"Chasing her, what else? Favors for favors, right? I guess it worked too. She never gave him the time of day until maybe the last month. He must of done something right."

"Did she have a reason for wanting to be in this fashion show? Maybe to come up to Santa Barbara?"

"The pay's good. It's fun, and they pay everything."

"But I heard she didn't spend much time with the group. Went off on her own."

"I don't know, I wasn't here. Maybe Welker was around."

The next and the next had been up in Santa Barbara that weekend but hadn't known Suzy Dekker, and after that I began to lose track of which one I was dancing with and who I was talking to. Except for the tall, older one with the almost green eyes, they all blended into one.

"Who's Regina Barton?"

"Boss's daughter. Modeled herself, but she's around forty now so she just works in the office and chaperones."

Redhead.

"Alan Welker wasn't up here with you?"

"Not that I know. I mean, I never saw him."

Blonde.

"You think Welker could have been up here?"

"I wouldn't be surprised. He got her on the roster for some reason, right?"

Blue eyes.

"Kate Lennon ought to know best. They roomed."

Henry Wayne appeared in the lounge and they grabbed him too. He resisted, angry, but they dragged him onto the floor. He danced like a stiff prep school boy, an overage Ivy Leaguer with a bland, youthful, handsome face that didn't fit with his rigid smile. Helga Kasmer came in to sit alone at the bar. She watched her brother. The models found another candidate. A tall man, older than Henry Wayne but far from old. Lean, brown hair worn short, gray suit, a thin smile, and eyes that told nothing about him. He could have been the man Henry Wayne had met out in the fog, if he'd changed his clothes and gotten rid of the hat.

Black hair.

"Did she go anywhere special? Meet anyone?"

"Maybe. We get lots of free time in the day and after the show, you know? I mean, I don't remember seeing her around much with the rest of the girls."

Another brunette.

"She never went on the tours and picnics Mr. Graham fixes up, or even the parties. Maybe a couple of the parties. And she went out to meet old lady Wayne with all of us."

The tall stranger smiled as he danced. He gave no sign of knowing Henry Wayne. Wayne didn't smile, but he danced. Helga Kasmer still drank alone at the bar. I finally got back to my tall older model with the easy smile and the almost-green eyes.

"I think," I said, "I'm about worn out."

"Nonsense."

"Down to the bone."

"I wonder how long you'd have danced if you hadn't had so many questions to ask?"

"Not long," I said. "No one has any idea if Suzy Dekker had a special reason for wanting to come up to the show here?"

"The only thing I ever heard her really talk about was her mother. She had an old picture she showed everyone."

"You didn't see Alan Welker that weekend?"

"No, but that doesn't mean he didn't come up."

"No," I said. Her almost-green eyes were directly in front of mine. "My name's Dan Fortune."

"Kay Michaels."

"Can we go somewhere else?"

"Not tonight."

"Some other time then," I said.

She smiled.

I left them still dancing with the tall man. Henry Wayne had escaped, gone. Helga Kasmer no longer watched anything but her glass. And me. She watched me as I walked out into the lobby and on into the fog. The grounds were wet and wreathed in fog under the palms, the parking lot all but empty. My car was out of sight somewhere on the far side of the lot.

Muffled footsteps walked again behind me.

I found a shrouded oleander bush to hide behind. All the bushes looked like shapes from some horror story covered in a white fungus. The footsteps continued somewhere in the fog. Slowly this time. It is hard to tell just where fog muffled sounds come from. No one came out of the fog. There were no more footsteps.

At the Subaru I looked back. Somone leaned against a palm tree at the far edge of the parking lot. A hatless shadow that smoked in the fog and looked toward me. Some hotel guest out for a last cigarette? I didn't believe that, but I made no move to go closer. I knew that as soon as I moved toward the silent shadow in the night it would vanish into the drifting fog.

I got into the Subaru and went back along the curving drive into the coast village of Montecito. On a Wednesday night in January even the De Anza Inn Motel had a vacancy.

19

Cool sunlight and the endless song of a mockingbird woke me to a vision of the shadow leaning casually against the palm tree last night in the fog. Watching me, I was sure, only why? I hadn't learned much that seemed dangerous to anyone. Was I getting closer, or seeing shadows that weren't there?

Showered and dressed, I went to find some breakfast. At the desk the clerk said the Biltmore Hotel served the best breakfast in Santa Barbara, but there was a chili, egg and hamburger cafe right next door. I took the shorter and cheaper route, had a mushroom omelet, muffin, and coffee at Peabody's next door. The omelet was good, the coffee hot, the winter sun growing warmer, the Pacific blue in the distance to the massive Channel Islands, the mockingbirds loud and cheerful, and as I sat over my second cup of coffee I decided maybe I'd never go back to the East.

Retire and sit in the sun. Call it quits. Watch the sea and wait. Easy living can be insidious. Luckily I still had a job to finish. Work is the only answer.

20

"Wait until you see it!" Helga Kasmer had said. Parked on the shoulder of the steep road I looked up at Judson Graham's 1124 Tucker Canyon Road house high on its mountain slope.

An enormous series of gray squares, circles, and angles in cast concrete and glass with dark wood accents, it covered the entire top of a ridge that jutted out from the mountain. It was like some fortress dominating its canyon with the mountain sweeping on above. A massive modern bunker ready for an attack.

I drove up the twisting driveway and the mammoth house changed into an almost delicate series of interlinked glass boxes that blended easily into the sweep of the mountainside in the morning sunlight. High, spacious, airy like some fine Japanese house.

As I passed closer around it, like some architectural chameleon it changed again into an abstraction of concrete blocks, cylinders, and wedges like a Magritte painting or some giant cubist sculpture.

And behind the house, in the blacktop parking area on the level with its roof, it changed once more into what looked like part of some freeway interchange with the Pacific, the city, and the coast far below.

An exciting house, probably unique and controversial, and certainly worth a fortune. So Judson Graham had money, maybe taste, and probably daring. Any of which could make him a target for someone.

A maid answered the bell. The door led into the kitchen. A modern open kitchen in plain view of the rest of the house. Another Chicano lady smiled at me as she deftly dismembered a chicken. A kitchen like those in many middle-class tract houses, only larger and with more facilities. Much larger. A kitchen of the modern rich who are just like everyone else only with more money. Much more.

"Mr. Fortune?" He strode into the kitchen with his hand out. "How can I help you?"

He was a big man in all ways—height, width, hand, and manner. Over six feet, barrel-chested and heavy-necked, he had to weigh at least 220; he wore brown corduroy jeans, a deep brown flannel shirt, a handwoven Irish fisherman's sweater, and low black boots. His large face had a deep tan under dark blond hair, and small blue eyes sunk in wind and sun creases. An outdoor man. He carried his head tilted slightly backwards, his chin slightly raised, so that he looked at you from a height and distance as if observing and judging.

I told him how he could help me.

"Private investigator?" His expansive manner cooled a bit. "Come into the living room."

We went into a living room that would have passed for a theater lobby back in Chelsea. The walls were all concrete, hung with giant paintings and what looked like South American Indian capes and ponchos. Except the wall facing the ocean far below which was all glass, house high, and had a terrace outside. The furniture was glass, steel, soft leather, and free form, some pieces so unusual I didn't even know what they were.

"I really don't remember the girl very well," Graham said.

He was still polite, but restless now as if he didn't have time for me. The kind of man who had no friends in low places.

"Dekker, eh? Perhaps my wife could help you." He needed someone else to handle me, someone not so involved with people and matters of greater public substance.

While I waited again I had a good look at the mammoth living room. It seemed to be about two-thirds of the house, with the bedrooms and everything else in a wing on one side. But it was the giant paintings I looked at most. All were dated this year, and all had something loud, grotesque, macabre, or sensational. Super realism with giant male organs, bloody car crashes. Neoprimitives with horror and violence.

Semi-abstracts of pain and screams. Violent, even psychotic, colors. Macabre landscapes of grotesque plants and demons eating people.

"You know painting, Fortune?"

Judson Graham had returned with a slender, black-haired woman in her late thirties or early forties. His own age. She smiled to me but said nothing, waiting for him to tell her what she was supposed to do.

"I've read some," I admitted. I don't admit that in Chelsea. It would make the regulars awfully suspicious about me.

Graham gestured proudly at the walls. "Every one of them shocked people. Critics said none could be hung in a living room. You'd lose your friends, if they didn't shoot you. Well, I hung them. Our friends probably would like to shoot me, but that's what it's all about, right? You've got to own your own space."

I was getting a picture of Judson Graham.

"Sort of like the house itself," I said.

"You saw that, did you?"

"Jud?" his wife said. "I was in the middle of planning—"

"In a minute, Jan, in a minute!" His hearty manner was back as if he'd forgotten I wasn't important. "This architect in L.A. wanted to see what could be done residentially with cast concrete in a radical design on a large scale. I liked the idea and the design. It would cost a million, but I knew it would be a good investment. It had to become a contemporary classic if only from its size and construction. One of a kind, and I was sure to resell it at two or three times the cost."

He rubbed his big hands together. "But what really got to me was the idea of building it right here in Montecito in the middle of Spanish haciendas and Victorian mansions! You should have heard my banker when I told him where I planned to put it. The old residents screamed like banshees. We had some battle while it was going up, and a lot of the red-tile-roof gang still hate me, but that's where the vibrations are, right? That's where it is for me, where I can get in touch with myself, own my own power, know what I can do."

It was the murky vocabulary used by the pop psychologists so busy these days saving the souls of the rich and the bored and the uncommitted. People of all ages with too much time in a world too comfortable and nothing in particular to do except make money. Graham made a lot of money, or had a lot of money.

"What do you do at Elite Imports, Mr. Graham?"

"Very little," he laughed. "It's a very good investment, though. Investments, some real estate, is what I mostly do. I trained as a marine biologist, still do some expeditions."

"Jud is a good scientist," his wife said. "He's done a lot of books and expeditions. Even a college textbook."

"There's money in textbooks," Graham said.

What it meant was that he had inherited his money, a great deal of money to live in a house worth some three million, and so there was nothing he had to do to make a living or carve out a place. Nothing required of him that he could prove his worth by doing. So he went in for pop psychology and sought out the controversial. He bought and hung the bizarre paintings, built and lived in the radical house. A "daring" life. To feel manly, virile. To prove himself.

"So Elite Imports is only an investment?"

"Mostly, but a first-rate one. Good profit every year."

He would need that too, the making of money on anything he did to prove he was as good as his father or grandfather.

"You do nothing in the company itself?"

"Jan and I go to board meetings. Sometimes we help out, such as with the fashion shows, but essentially we're the silent partners."

"Full partners?"

Graham laughed again. "Not quite. We now have about thirty percent. Helga has ten and Henry five and the rest is Eva. No one is a full partner with Eva Wayne. She's an independent woman. It's her business, her ideas, her contacts. She's something of a genius the way she knows how to get the best clothes from the remotest villages, and the way she knows how to merchandise them to turn a good profit. The stuff is in big demand, and she's really the whole company."

"You have a lot invested in Elite?"

"A fair amount. But it's really Jan's operation. She found Eva, saw the potential, and I let her run our interest mostly." Graham looked at his watch and then up and over my shoulder as if looking for something better he should be doing. "Jan, this is Dan Fortune, a private investigator looking for information about one of those models we're mothering. What was the name, Fortune?"

"Suzanne Dekker," I said.

"I remember her," his wife said. "A size-eight blonde, very wholesome type. Not really good for South American style. It was her first time up here, and probably her last."

"Late for rehearsals or something?" Graham recalled.

"Yes," Janice Graham nodded, "and she disappeared on her own all the time too. Not the caliber girl we usually get from Regent. In any case, she hasn't come back again."

I told them why Suzy Dekker hadn't come back. Graham fidgeted in the vast living room with its metal and rich leather shining in the sunny morning until I got to the Canyon Slasher. Then he seemed to stop thinking about whatever he wished he was doing instead of talking to me. His small blue eyes watched me. Janice Graham listened without any change of expression. She had a long face, cool and composed, with regular features as elegant as the showcase living room but a lot more reserved.

"Good God," Judson Graham said. "You're not serious? One of our models? The Canyon Slasher!"

His voice was shocked, but eager too. Something important, unusual, had happened close to him, and he was a man who had to be in the swim, involved in big events. Unless it was maybe a way of covering up. Not really shocked or even surprised?

His wife may have been shocked, if she didn't show it on her calm face, but she wasn't surprised.

"I remember reading about that tragic girl," Janice Graham said. "But I never connected it to one of our models. What a terrible thing!"

"The poor kid," Graham said. He shook his head, sadly yet almost savoring the tragedy of it. "I wish I could really remember her."

"Because they're so impersonal, these Slasher murders," Janice Graham said. She seemed to shiver. "You feel so helpless, vulnerable. It's all so senseless and indifferent."

"He doesn't even know his victims, does he?" Graham said, shook his head. "It's hard to accept that kind of random killing, and ..." The big man's face went momentarily blank as he searched his mind for some elusive recollection. "Prostitutes!" He turned to his wife. "The newspapers said all the girls he killed were prostitutes!"

"At least amateurs," I said. "According to the police."

Graham still faced his wife. "What in hell was Regent Management doing sending us a girl like that? We can't have Elite Imports involved with prostitutes."

"Elite wouldn't be blamed, Jud," Janice Graham said.

"If she solicited the buyers? Maybe that's where she disappeared to all the time! Why she was late for rehearsals!"

"We'd have heard," Janice Graham said.

Graham stood frowning in the enormous living room. Finally he nodded.

"I suppose you're right, but we're going to have to talk to Regent about her. You know what a lot of people think about the fashion business already. All they'd have to find out is that Elite uses prostitutes as models and we'd be in real hot water if we weren't out of business."

"I don't know," Janice Graham said. "Times are different now. Women are different. A woman can do just about whatever she wants to do, and most people realize it's her own business and no one else's."

He shook his head, thinking about it. "Morality is the business of everyone, Jan, the whole country, and I'm not sure we should be that liberated. At least Elite *wasn't* dragged into it."

"No," Janice Graham said, but I saw that her cool eyes were watching me and seemed to say that Elite Imports hadn't been dragged into it *yet*. Graham didn't notice.

"What makes a girl do such things?" he asked.

"You'd have to be a woman to understand at all," Janice Graham said.

I said, "Lack of identity. Lack of somewhere to really belong, a place for her. Neglect. Indifference. The sense that no one anywhere cares about her. Or maybe that no one anywhere cares about anyone. An indifferent world. A sense of being alone and not wanting to be alone."

"I wonder why we aren't all prostitutes," Janice Graham said. "If any of that is true."

"Maybe we are," I said.

"No," Judson Graham said. "That's all excuses, Fortune. Anyone can get in touch with himself, or herself. All you have to do is face yourself honestly, listen to your feelings not your brain, learn your own space and live within it. It's too easy to blame society, the world. No one is to blame for you, and you're to blame for no one else. Find yourself."

He had the jargon down pretty well. I didn't know exactly what it all meant, but I had an idea of what it added up to.

"You have no children?" I asked.

"No," Janice Graham said. "Do you, Mr. Fortune?"

"I never got married."

"I had no idea that was still required," she said.

"Children," Judson Graham said, "are a terrible time drain. They limit your space more than anything else. The world has too many people now. I'm glad we never had any children. It wouldn't be good for us or them, eh, Jan?"

"It's hard to fulfill children and yourself," Janice Graham said. "When you're poor you must neglect yourself, when you're rich you tend to neglect them."

There was a sudden distance to her low voice as if turned inward. People accidentally reveal more than they mean to by their opinions, but it was hard to tell if she meant more than she was saying. Her long face had that calm manner of what used to be called the "well-born." Not necessarily meaning rich, but that whatever money there was had been there long before she was born. Self-contained, very erect and even haughty, her slim neck corded and beginning to wrinkle at her age, but not hidden or evaded. A woman who faced herself.

"The poor neglect too," I said. "Did the Dekker girl ever talk to either of you about her family? Say anything about her mother to anyone?"

Graham looked at his watch. "As I said, Fortune, I don't really remember the girl all that well."

"Why would she talk about her family to strangers?" Janice Graham said.

"Because her mother was the most important thing in her life, and I don't think she came up here just for your fashion show." I told them the history of Suzy Dekker and her mother and father. "I think she had some lead to her mother, and that could be why she kept disappearing."

"Her mother?" Graham looked up from his watch. "What would that have to do with the Canyon Slasher?"

"It has nothing to do with the Canyon Slasher," Janice Graham said. She sat down in a high-backed leather chair and crossed her good legs. She lit a cigarette now, shook out the match carefully and deliberately. "I wondered why a private detective would be concerned with a mass murderer. You don't think this Dekker girl was killed by the Slasher, do you?"

"My client has doubts," I said.

"And you?" she said.

"I'm beginning to have doubts too."

"You mean," Judson Graham said, "you've been lying to us? She never was one of the Slasher's victims? Why would you—?"

"The police are still sure the Slasher killed her," I said.

"Then," Graham scowled under his heavy brows, "you're just speculating? You're up here on some kind of guess?"

"Because," Janice Graham said, smoked and blew the smoke in a hard stream, "he thinks someone up here killed her. Perhaps one of us."

"I think," I said, "that she could have been killed because of something that happened up here. That doesn't mean I think someone up here killed her."

"But nothing happened up here!" Judson Graham snapped.

"No trouble at the fashion show?"

"Trouble?" Graham was incredulous. "Of course not."

"Or at Elite Imports? Problems with competitors, or the buyers, or maybe the South American suppliers?"

Janice Graham shook her head. "Not that we've heard, Mr. Fortune, and I'm sure we would have heard."

Graham was back looking at his watch. "If you have questions about Elite you should talk to Eva."

"Mrs. Wayne is out of town."

"Eva?" Graham seemed startled. "Eva never goes out of town during the fashion shows, or damn near any other time for that. Who would run the business or the shows?"

"Henry Wayne and his sister seem to be running the show."

Janice Graham said, "Perhaps she's mellowing, Jud, giving Henry and Helga a chance. She has to give up some time."

Jud Graham laughed aloud. "She'll never give up, and she'd never let Henry run the business even if she did. Helga maybe, but not Henry."

"Why not?" I asked.

Graham snorted, "He's no executive and never will be. Too easy-going, soft. If Henry ever ran the company I'd start to worry about my investment. He's too nice. Strong mother and weak father. George Wayne was just like Henry."

"The only kind of man a woman like Eva could marry," Janice Graham said.

It didn't sound much like the Henry Wayne I'd met, almost like two different people.

"Wayne is a medium-sized man, average build, blue eyes, dark blond hair, early thirties?"

Graham nodded. "Thirty-two or so."

"But the sister is different? She could run the company?"

"Half sister," Janice Graham said. "An earlier marriage."

"She's no great leader," Judson Graham said, "but a lot tougher and more efficient than Henry."

"How old is she?"

"Early forties," Janice Graham said.

"Or late thirties," Judson Graham said.

"She's lived here all her life? Never married?"

"As far as we know she's been here all her life," Judson Graham said. "I've never heard of any husband."

Janice Graham was careful. "I think I may have heard that Helga once ran off for a time when she was a lot younger. Gone for a few years, I think. In those days it seems that Helga and Eva got along even less than they do now."

"They don't get along now?"

"Maybe they're too much alike," Judson Graham said. He did his watch looking. "I'm afraid I must get back to—"

"That weekend," I said before I lost him, "could the girl have been seeing a man from Regent Management named Alan Welker? Did she ever mention that name? Did you maybe see Welker?" I described the dead youth in the Hollywood parking lot.

The Grahams shook their heads to each other and to me.

"And you can't say anything about where she was or what she did when she was off on her own?"

"I'm sorry," Janice Graham said.

Jud Graham edged closer to the door out of the living room.

"Kate Lennon," I said. "She had a room with Suzanne Dekker that weekend. Where can I find her?"

"At the San Marino, I think," Jan Graham said. "I'll check."

Graham and I smiled at each other in the mammoth living room. In his heavy Irish sweater, his chin raised and head tilted back, he looked like a pompous bear. A bear who very much wanted to be somewhere else. Anywhere else where there might be important action. At least, he wanted to get away from me.

"San Marino Hotel, room forty-four," Janice Graham reported. "She shared the same room with the Dekker girl."

She gave me the address on a slip of paper. Up close the wrinkles and cords in her neck came not from age but from slimming and the sun of Southern California. In her late thirties. At the most.

"How long have you two lived in Santa Barbara?" I asked. "How long have you been married?"

I looked toward Graham. Or toward where he had been. He was gone, had finally slipped away.

"Judson is a native of Santa Barbara," Janice Graham said. "We've been married ten years."

"Where are you a native?"

"New York. The city," she said. "Are you sure the girl wasn't killed by that madman? Sure the police are wrong?"

"No," I said. "I'm not sure. But I will be."

21

Room forty-four at the San Marino Hotel was half of a white-and-green duplex cottage hidden in broad-leafed tropical vegetation at the end of a winding asphalt path.

The short drive from the Graham house high on its dry mountain slope to the San Marino on the green semitropical Pacific shore was like moving between different worlds. From the hot, brown, dusty austerity of nature, to the cool, shaded, privileged creation of man. From California as it had been for millions of years, to California as man had made it in less than a century. And the San Marino Hotel occupied the next man-created wooded point to the east of El Mirador Hotel and Beach Club.

A more informal complex of detached two-story units around pools, tennis courts, and the open beach, plus secluded single and double cottages, everything at the San Marino was painted white with green roofs, doors, and shutters. The clerk in the office gave me the big smile you only get from clerks in the off season or during a gasoline crisis. He directed me to room forty four.

The curving paths under the palms, banana trees, and eucalypti were thickly bordered by plants I couldn't name. Leprous, a sense of lizards. I stood in front of cottage forty-four and listened to the sound of freeway traffic close yet unseen, almost like a memory as I stood in a remote jungle.

The voice that answered my rings was as remote as the freeway or the jungle. "What? Yes? Who is it?"

"Miss Lennon?"

"What?" The voice muffled, distant.

I went around the cottage and through the vegetation to the bedroom window. "Miss Lennon?"

"Am I late?" Bedclothes rustled and small feet hit the floor. "What time is it, for God's sake?"

"Ten-fifteen," I said.

"Ten—!" Disbelief. "Then what the hell... . Who are you?"

I spoke up to the small window that was above my head. "My name's Dan Fortune, Miss Lennon. I wanted—"

"Oh, the guy Kay said wanted to talk to me?"

"That's right. Did Miss Michaels tell you what—"

"Yeh, poor Suzy. Hey, give me fifteen minutes. Go get some coffee, and bring me back a cup in fifteen. Okay?"

"Okay."

Coffee would be good.

I never heard or saw what hit me.

22

I breathed slowly.

I had turned away from the cottage window, thinking about a cup of coffee, and … what? A step, a sound, something that moved through the air … pain and exploding light… on my face in leaves … dirt… darkness …

I opened my eyes.

Darkness.

The pain was small. Almost no pain.

Why darkness? Why … something hard against my nose.

Only a sore throb to the back of my head.

Flat and hard and rough against my nose. Against my hand. I touched. Wood.

A light-headed dizziness sweeping over.

Wooden boards on top of me.

Nausea.

The odor of dirt.

I lay without moving. I always check my arm. I did not check my lone arm. I looked up at the darkness, touched the wooden boards above me, unaware of the pain, the nausea, or my only arm.

I lay on my back in darkness with a wooden board against my nose and an odor of dirt. Soft, wet dirt.

I began to pound at the boards above me. I kicked at the unmoving boards. I screamed, "Help! Help! Help! Down here!" My only hope… . How long did I have? … "Help! Help!"

Light?

Thrashing, I saw a distant line of pale light. And in the instant of seeing that far-off line of unexpected light a whole new focus slipped over my eyes. A different focus like waking from a dream. The line of light wasn't distant, less than five feet away. There were boards over me, but none right or left or underneath. I lay not on wood but on dirt. Damp dirt. And leaves. And there was air. And I began to laugh. And my arm was unhurt. And there was only a little blood oozing from the bump on my head. And I wasn't buried. And ...

I lay under some house. In a crawlway. A low crawlway with wet dirt and dead leaves and plants outside where the light was. I turned over and crawled out and stood again under the bedroom window of room forty-four in the San Marino Hotel. My watch showed that less than twenty minutes had passed, but there was no sound from inside the cottage. I went around to the front.

The cottage door was open.

Inside there were three rooms and a bathroom, all small. A nightgown lay on one unmade twin bed. A toothbrush was wet in the tiny bathroom. The living room was empty. In the bathroom I washed my face, put wet towels on the oozing bump on my head. Who knew I wanted to talk to Kate Lennon? The Grahams, and the girls last night at El Mirador. Kay Michaels.

I searched the cottage. There was little to search, a transient room, and I found less. A large group photo with a Christmas tree in it: two girls I didn't know, Helga Kasmer, two men I didn't know, Judson Graham, a smiling Henry Wayne, and an unsmiling Suzy Dekker. I took the photo with me.

The desk clerk smiled, asked if I'd found Miss Lennon.

"Just missed her," I said. "Bad luck."

"A shame," the clerk agreed. "Care to leave a note?"

"She must have just gone out with someone."

"Really? I didn't see her," the clerk said.

I showed him the group picture. "Which one is she?"

He pointed to one of the two unknown girls—small, Irish, dark-haired, with a mischievous smile and wicked eyes.

"How about this girl?" I pointed to Suzy Dekker. "Ever see her with anyone? Going in or out?"

"She's not here this weekend."

"But she was New Year's. Went out a lot. Know anywhere she went, or who she went with?"

The clerk shook his head.

"How'd she travel? Her own car?"

"Taxi, other cars, walking."

"So you do remember her."

"Who'd forget one like that?"

"She met men?"

"I don't know who she met."

"But she took taxis, you know that."

"Sometimes, mostly at night."

"Which taxi company?"

"We've only got one: Montecito Taxi. In the coast village."

"Thanks," I said. "I appreciate the help."

"*De nada*" the clerk smiled. "Sure that's all you need?"

"That's it," I said, "unless you want to tell me who paid you to tip him or her when someone came asking for Kate Lennon. Especially if a one-armed man asked."

His smile had gone long ago. He straightened a few forms, squared the registration tablet on the desk, flicked a speck of dust from his cuffs.

"No one paid me. Only the hotel pays me. If there's anything else—?"

"Of course someone paid you," I said. "It's okay, I'd just like to pay too. How much to tell me who it was?"

His smooth manners went. "Good-bye, mister."

"Hey, sure," I said. "I understand. You have to live here, right? Some local big shot. Okay, I get it."

"Beat it!"

I smiled as I walked away.

23

Four men played poker on the sidewalk in front of Montecito Taxi Company. They barely looked up at me. One, the dealer, jerked his head toward the right side of the battered garage up against the freeway when I asked where the office was. The only one in the littered office was a slender black-haired young woman with a wonderful figure and a better smile. She sat at a small desk with the dispatch book open in front of her.

"Hi, can I help you about something?"

"I hope so," I smiled in return. A real smile, not the same one I'd left with the clerk at the San Marino. "I'm trying to trace a young woman who stayed at the San Marino Hotel on New Year's weekend. I know she took a taxi a few times, but I'm not sure when or where except that it was at night."

"Ouch, you don't know much," the girl laughed. She turned pages of the dispatch book. "Lucky this is a small town, and we don't get a lot of calls to the hotels. The people come to the hotels just about always drive. Okay, New Year's weekend." She read through only a few pages. "We had seven calls to the San Marino that weekend, and four of 'em was to a big bash on the Sunday, New Year's Eve—too drunk to drive, so they had to be locals not hotel guests. The other three were all at night, two on the Friday, one on the Saturday."

"Where did they go?"

"Well," she read the book. "Two were to the same place—one on Friday and one on Saturday: number 435 East Alcazar Street in town. The other was Friday to Pietro's Shop."

"What do you mean 'in town'?"

"Santa Barbara. The city itself."

"How about Pietro's Shop? What kind of shop and where?"

She laughed aloud. "It's up in Capitan Canyon, and it's a tavern. Very old, very popular. Everyone goes up to it."

"How do I get there?"

She told me.

Capitan Canyon Road crossed a deep, wide gully on a high steel bridge. Just before the bridge a road led off to the right. A sign on this road read "Pietro's Shop."

Down under the high bridge in the shadows of the deep gully, on a twisting blacktop road that had to have been the original route up the canyon into the mountains, Pietro's Shop was a meandering con-glomeration of low frame and log buildings among dark pines. Inside was a long tavern room around a magnificent old high mahogany bar, a smaller side room with a fireplace and a shorter bar, and a dining room of blue and white checked tablecloths. The large main room was closed. A matter of heat. The smaller bar was for winter with a great bed of glowing coals in the fireplace and crocks of cheese on the bar beside bowls of crackers.

A modest crowd had gathered for the noon hour. I joined them, ordered a beer, helped myself to the excellent cheese and crackers, and snowed the bartender my photo of Suzy Dekker.

"Nope," the bartender said, "and I'd remember that one if she been here as recent as New Year's. Friday the twenty-ninth? Lively that night, but she wasn't around, unless maybe she was in the cabins."

"Cabins? You have overnight cabins?"

"Sure. Go ask the manager. That's him at the end of the bar."

The manager shook his head at my photo. "Never saw her. We only had three couples that Friday, all older than that kid."

I had another beer. The other patrons at the bar were five couples and three solitary men. The tavern had sounded to me very much somewhere Suzy Dekker would have gone. I had more free cheese. It was as good a lunch as any.

That the bartender and the manager didn't recall her did not, of course, mean that she hadn't been here, but it did mean that if she had been I wasn't going to pick up her trail without coming back at night to show the photo to everyone I could. Maybe coming back for a lot of nights. I still had the address on the east side of Santa Barbara to try before that damned slow work, but I felt weary just thinking about it. I had one more beer.

Outside I walked around to the back and looked at the cabins. There were six, all small and built of logs. They seemed to have no heat except open fireplaces. Cozy. Just the place for a girl to meet someone special. A hideout. But, somehow, from the look of the dead youth back in the Hollywood parking lot, not Alan Welker's style. An older man. If Suzy Dekker had been here at all.

In the Subaru I came up out of the dark glen and drove across the high steel bridge toward the mountains ... the mountains? No, that wasn't right. Was it? No, I was going *into* Santa Barbara, *away* from the mountains. *Down* the canyon, not *up* the canyon. Not *to* the mountains. *Away*. All wrong.

I laughed aloud.

The car waited at the side of the road. I sat in the car that waited at the side of the road. Stopped car pointed toward the mountains. Turned the goddamned wrong way! Stupido!

Half turned across the road.

Half up the dirt bank ... oops. Easy does it, Dan. Easy boy. Slooooowwwwww ...

The long bridge undulated in a thin haze.

I drove carefully through the fog on the swaying bridge as ... the monster leaped at me with four glowing eyes! A looming monster that was ... a blue Chrysler careening too far over ... going to hit ... side-swipe ... push me over the edge of ...

(Blue Chrysler? Where? ...)

I stamped on the accelerator. The Subaru jumped ahead with spinning wheels and skidding tires and the blue car was past. Slam against my rear. The Subaru slewed across the bridge swinging its tail from rail to rail as I got control and was off the bridge and driving on toward …

The Subaru sat at the side of the road. I sat in the Subaru at the side of the road. We sat. Pointed toward … fog. Shivering … fog … rolling … I … *drugged?* The beer … *drugged* … men in the tavern … tall and thin and passing …

I sat in the Subaru at the side of the road. I bit my hand to clear the fog from inside my eyes, *awake*, and … the blue Chrysler in my rearview mirror. Coming up fast behind. I started the Subaru. *Stay awake.* In reverse I lurched backwards through the clouds of dust on the dry shoulder of the canyon road and the blue car veered and screeched and was gone on through the dust and … fog … drifting … *stay awake.*

Gone … but would return … aware I was drugged … yes … knew … return to push me over … swaying canyon and road and trees and ravine and steep slope over the edge and down into fog … thick fog … *stay awake!*

I turned the wheels of the Subaru toward the steep gully. Out, I reached in. Arrow on "drive." Moving. Vanished.

I walked over the edge of the ravine. Down the steep slope. Running. Stumbling. Falling. Face, dirt, brush, stones … rolling … rolling … down … dark …

25

Distant sounds rising and falling like cars passing from time to time on a highway somewhere.

I moved my fingers. I moved my lone hand, and my arm. I moved my shoulder. Nothing hurt, everything moved, and I lay and listened to the distant sounds like cars passing.

They *were* cars passing. On a road. Above me.

And where the hell was I this time?

I opened my eyes. I was groggy. I ached all over. My mouth was full of fungus. I was getting damned mad.

I sat up and whacked my head against rock right on the tender bump of the morning. Jesus!

There was ragged light ahead. I crawled and came out among large boulders behind brush and fallen trees. I had been inside a narrow cul-de-sac among and under the rocks. A mini-cave. And now I stood at the bottom of a deep, broad ravine in a fading twilight.

And it all came back at once. Blue Chrysler. Drugged. In the beer at the bar in Pietro's Shop. Chased. Two tries to run me into the ravines. To escape ran the Subaru off the road in one direction, and myself into the gully in another. Somehow, I'd crawled into the niche before passing out cold.

I looked cautiously all around the fading light of the ravine, gully, gulch, glen, whatever they called it around here besides just the bottom of Capitan Canyon. Nothing seemed to move, I heard no sounds beyond the passing of the occasional car up on the canyon road.

The Subaru was some hundred or so yards away nose down against the thick trunk of an old oak two-thirds of the way down the slope. It hadn't burned, but was clearly damaged. I hoped Marty had proper insurance for letting a guest drive it. The police didn't appear to have spotted it yet, and whoever had been in the blue Chrysler had either taken it for granted that I was in the wreck—dead or injured and unconcerned which—or had found I wasn't, searched the area, but failed to spot me in my crevice as I slept off the drug.

I climbed back up the steep slope. My head was clear, but my whole body ached and shook from the effects of the drug and the stumble-and-roll down the slope. On the road the passengers of a car stared out at me in horror as it passed. No one was going to pick me up in the fading dusk, I was in no mood or condition to walk to the coast and my motel, so I went down into the gully to Pietro's Shop and called a taxi.

I had been hit on the head, shoved under a house, scared to death, drugged, chased by a murderous car, and rolled down a rocky slope of thick and savage brush. A long day, and when the taxi delivered me to the De Anza I fell into bed.

To sleep and to dream.

But before the sleep I fought with two stubborn thoughts. Someone in Pietro's Shop had drugged me: I tried to remember faces along the bar, but it was all a blank with only the vague impression of a tall, lean shape passing once behind me. Someone had been trying to stop me from the very start: to hide the killer or something else, the attacks were getting stronger so I was getting closer. To something. It was as far as I got before sleep.

Then the dream.

She came through the window. Tall and slender, an older woman with quick eyes and a slow smile. Almost skinny, with almost-green eyes. She floated through the dim light of distant red neon somewhere outside, bent over me. She kissed me.

"Hello, Dan Fortune," she said.

The apparition looked exactly like the tall model who had led the dancing in El Mirador's lounge. Kay Michaels. Floating in through the motel window, saying, "Hello, Dan Fortune."

"What time is it?" I said.

"Another time."

She did not seem to be wearing much.

"You've been hurt."

"All over," I said. "Battered and bruised."

She wore nothing. Skinny on the bed. Not too skinny. Long dark hair and soft skin.

"You said some other time." High breasts and long legs. "It's some other time."

"Now?"

"Why not now?"

"I'd never make it."

"You'll make it."

A dream world. A very nice dream floating beside me, under me. High legs. In dreams everything is possible.

26

The January morning sun was cool. Outside the open motel window the mockingbirds made their racket. My mouth tasted like a stable, and my body ached at every joint. Yet I lay in the motel bed with my eyes closed, smiling in an overall sense of euphoria. I was relaxed. I could smell the perfume.

I lay for a time with my eyes still closed listening to the mockingbirds and an angry scrub jay, enjoying the cool morning air and the pale warmth of the early sun.

Eventually I opened my eyes and looked at the indentation in the other pillow. Close, the other pillow smelled more intensely of whatever perfume it was. I picked three long black hairs from the pillow. Kay Michaels. Not a dream.

I closed my eyes again. "Some other time," I'd said, and she had decided when and where and what. An exciting woman. For me? For her own needs, desires? Or for something else, someone else? Another way to try to stop me?

They say an actor can never really enjoy the theater or the movies, too concerned with the skills, the mechanics. A painter can't ever see a painting for itself after the first few years, a writer can never read for simple pleasure, for enjoyment. Maybe after a time a detective can't really enjoy people, too concerned with what makes them tick, their motives and hidden corners. Maybe a detective sees too many people at the wrong times, lives with suspicion.

I felt too pleasant after my night "dream" to care about the aches in every bone, but I took a hot shower to try to ease them. For a middle-aged roustabout hot showers are almost as good a friend as a ready pot of morning coffee. Warm the body, cool the solitude, and clear the mind. I had been drugged and attacked *after* reaching Pietro's Shop, so whatever I wasn't supposed to find out wasn't at Pietro's Shop, but I was coming closer. Maybe very close.

The police would find the Subaru, if they hadn't already, and would call Marty or William Dekker. They would be alarmed, at least Marty would. So I called the Malibu house. There was no answer. Down in the motel office I asked the clerk to rent me a car with power steering and no stick shift, left my license and credit card, and went next door to Peabody's for another breakfast omelet and plenty of coffee.

I called Malibu again. There was still no answer.

The motel clerk sent me into town the scenic back way as the quickest route to the upper east side. It had once been the elite part of town where the substantial locals lived after the Mexican *rancheros* had had their day and before the really rich began to build their estates in Montecito. Since then it had been down and was now on its way up again. But number 435 Alcazar Street looked like it had never been down.

A big Victorian frame house with turrets and bay windows, it was on a solid acre of well-kept trees, bushes and lawn and painted an independent shade of blue-gray with white trim. That was a lot of land for a city house, and the trees and lawn had been there a long time. The houses around it, big and small, old and new, had a lot less land, and the blue-gray house looked like the only survivor of another time. A high hedge encircled the rear behind the house, but in front only trees and a low white picket fence separated it from the street.

The name on the gate post was Wayne.

At the front door there was no answer to my ringing.

Across the street an older man out pruning his roses stared at me. I went across the quiet street. The older man didn't seem too friendly. I gave him a sincere smile.

"Good morning. I was looking for Mrs. Eva Wayne."

"That's her house."

"I didn't get any answer."

"I guess she's not home."

"You mean she lives alone in that big house?"

The man straightened up and arched his back after the bending. "Your husband dies and your kids grow up, you tend to end up alone no matter what size house you have."

"I guess so," I agreed. I was trying to figure what he was being belligerent about. "Has there been any trouble over there lately?"

He laid down his tools. "We don't pry around here, mister. She's a nice, quiet woman and a good neighbor."

"Something unusual happened recently, maybe?"

"What are you? From some damned magazine?"

"Private detective. On a case and looking for this girl." I showed him the photo of Suzy Dekker. "Did she come to Mrs. Wayne's house?"

He looked at the photo. "A lot of those fashion models come to see her during her fashion shows; this girl could have been one of them, but I couldn't swear to it." He handed back the photo, and seemed suddenly friendlier. "Eva goes to her office about nine-thirty, but when she works nights for the fashion show she goes in later. She should still be at home."

"Unless she's out of town," I said.

"Never noticed her leave," the man said, "and I'm sure her car is in the garage."

He pointed toward a garage visible on an alley behind the big blue-gray house. I could see that its doors were closed.

"She's probably out back in her garden," the man said. "She has one of the best gardens in town."

I hoped Eva Wayne was in her garden.

27

There was still no answer to my rings. Only the bell echoing far off somewhere inside the big house.

A narrow brick path led around the house to where another gate between the high hedge and the house opened into the rear yard. It wasn't locked. As I lifted the latch I heard an ominous growl.

"Quiet," a voice said in the yard. "Yes, who's there?"

It was a woman's voice.

"Mrs. Eva Wayne?" I called out.

There was a pause.

"You can come in. The dog won't bother you."

I unlatched the gate and walked on around the big house into a large and incredibly crowded garden behind it. Shrubs, bushes and flowers grew in profusion everywhere. Every inch had been planted in precise rows and beds with almost no space between them. Rigorously tended, I couldn't see a weed. The dog lay in the shade of the high hedge between a neat hibiscus and a geometric bed of slender Iceland poppies. It watched me quietly. A pit bull as immobile as a palace guard.

"A well-trained dog," I said.

The woman sat on a low canvas folding stool methodically removing dead blooms from a large bed of calendula.

"Bred and trained," she said. "An animal is only as good as its breeding and training. Even a garden needs good seed and the proper care."

Her voice was firm and clear. Not loud but not especially low. Strong yet slow. A deliberate voice, almost weary.

"It's a good garden for January," I said.

She stood up and brushed her hands together to remove the soil. They were large hands that moved as deliberately as her voice. Tall and ramrod thin, she wore a long flowered smock. Her short hair was all gray, her deeply tanned skin was full of wrinkles, and she had to be in her middle seventies, but she seemed to be in good shape, well-kept and healthy. A square and angular face with a sharp nose and thin lips. She would have been almost mannish except for her large brown eyes, long legs below the smock, and high breasts even at her age.

"We can grow some flowers all year," she said. "If you plan correctly you are never without either color in the garden or cut flowers in the house. A great advantage of our area. What can I do for you, Mr.—?"

"Dan Fortune," I said. "I was afraid you were out of town."

"Then I'm glad I'm not."

"Your son said you were."

"Ah," she said. "I changed my plans and forgot to tell Henry. Just who are you, Mr. Fortune?"

"A private detective."

She smiled. "Have I done something?"

"I hope not."

"Ah?" She went on smiling, half amused and half questioning, as if saying that if I really thought she might have done something I was taking a risk coming to her to talk about it. It's something I've thought about a lot myself, every cop does, real or private, but there's not much we can do about it except to change work, and that's not easy to do for any man.

I showed my photo of Suzanne Dekker. "Did she come out here the Friday and Saturday of New Year's weekend?"

"Yes she did," Eva Wayne said. "One of our fashion show models. Suzanne Dekker, I think."

"You've got a good memory."

"Yes."

"What did she want here?" I said.

Eva Wayne took a cigarette from the pocket of her smock. She lit it. "Why do you want to know, Mr. Fortune?"

I told her. About all of it from the Canyon Slasher to my talk with the Grahams. She smoked. The cigarette was one of those extra long ones in a brown paper wrapper. She never took it from the far corner of her mouth.

"You aren't satisfied with the police investigation?"

"My client isn't."

Smoke drifted up into her right eye half closing it. She watched me with her other eye. I felt like a butterfly on a pin. One of her subordinates.

"If you agreed with the police you would have persuaded your client by now."

"Let's say my mind is still open."

"To the possibility that someone at Elite Imports might have killed the girl?"

"Her trail led here, Mrs. Wayne."

"So did the trail of many girls, why would she be killed because of Elite Imports?"

"If I knew that, I'd know the answer."

"There is no answer, not at Elite. We have had no problems, no troubles, and no unusual events. The Dekker girl had no real connection to Elite at all."

"Then why did she come to see you," I said. "Twice."

"Because she was looking for her mother."

She said it in that deliberate, oddly weary voice, and seemed to have no idea of its impact. For me, a breakthrough. It was the first time since I'd started on the trail of Suzy Dekker's death that someone had confirmed what Marty and Diane Pasco were sure of—that Suzanne Dekker had been actively looking for her mother. It was no longer just a theory.

"Why come to you?" I said.

"She had an old photograph of her mother. For some reason she seemed to think I would recognize it as someone I knew now. I didn't. She was disappointed and left."

"What made her think you might know her mother now?"

"I have no idea. She'd only been here once before. To the small reception I give for all the models."

"But she came back again?"

"For the same reason. Was I *sure* I didn't recognize the photo. It was sixteen years old, the person might have changed a lot. Please look hard. Very insistent the second time."

"As if she'd been talking to other people and getting nowhere?"

"Yes, something like that," Eva Wayne said.

"And you never did recognize the woman in her photo?"

Even her half-closed eye was surprised that I asked the question. Obviously, if she had known the woman in the photo she wasn't going to tell me. The cigarette smoke rose from her nose, and her face was a little contemptuous, and yet maybe a little admiring too, as if she knew that it was just such a question that made people reveal themselves.

"When your daughter left home as a young woman," I said, "did she maybe get married?"

"Helga?" Eva Wayne pinched out her cigarette, stripped the paper, scattered the remnants of tobacco, and put the paper and filter into her pocket. "Who told you that Helga left home?"

"I heard it," I said. "When were you in the army?"

"The army?" She stared, and then her eyes brightened. She was a quick thinker. "The cigarette? Not the army. When I was young my first husband and I lived in a mountain fire area. He taught me to always pinch and strip a cigarette." Talking about it made her find her packet of cigarettes in her pocket and light one. "People must jabber and gossip. Like old women. Speculate and gossip, and most of it is useless. Sheep. Too stupid to do more than jabber like monkeys without purpose and without vision." She shrugged and smoked the long brown cigarette. With the smoke closing her eye she looked like some fierce, wounded eagle. "Yes, Helga left home. It was unimportant."

"How long ago was that?"

She blew smoke. "Nineteen years or so. She was gone over two years. She did not get married. She did not have a child."

"What did she do?" I asked. "Where did she go?"

"I've never known, and I've never asked. I have better to do than gossip about a forgotten past."

"Then how can you be certain she didn't get married?"

"Because no man ever appeared to ask for money," Eva Wayne said. "No man and no child."

"Maybe they couldn't find her," I said. "Until now."

"My daughter was not the woman in that photograph," she said. "She is not the kind of person who could abandon a child. It would not be in her."

She had said Helga Kasmer *could* not abandon a child, not *would* not abandon a child. There is a big difference—"would not" is a moral judgment, "could not" is only psychological. Helga Kasmer could not act so harshly, but, by implication, Eva Wayne could and would. A tough woman, but too old to be Suzanne Dekker's mother, and without any evidence I had no way to challenge her story of Helga Kasmer.

"She never married at all?" I said.

"No."

"But she doesn't live here with you."

"I live alone, Mr. Fortune."

"Not even with your son?"

"Henry *is* married," she said. "He has a wife, three children and his own house."

"Where would that be?"

"Coyote Road in Montecito. Number 250."

I wrote it down in my notebook. Eva Wayne watched me with her half-closed eye, her head slightly tilted away from the acrid smoke of her cigarette. There was a faint curl to her lips, a distant expression close to contempt. A kind of sense of general contempt as if for the whole world, and there was something intimidating about her silent scrutiny. I guessed that she was a good executive.

"How well do you know the Grahams?" I asked.

"They invest in my company."

"Did Suzy Dekker talk to them about her mother? Did she say anything to you about Graham or his wife?"

"She said nothing about either of them. I don't know if she spoke to them about anything."

"They're only silent partners?"

I saw that small curl of contempt again. "I needed cash for a large expansion some years ago. Jan Graham made an offer. It was good for me, they've made a good return on it, and I see that Judson Graham stays far away from the operational side."

"You don't like him?"

She brushed that away with a curt gesture that said she did not deal in like and dislike, at least not with Judson Graham. "He's a rich man's son with little ability and a lot of ambition to be important. That does not make for a good businessman, or very much of anything else."

"What about Janice Graham?"

"A pleasant enough woman with a difficult life."

"You mean married to Graham?"

"A spoiled man rigid in his views and narrow in his ways. He must be pampered. I would not find that possible, but other women have other needs it seems."

From time to time her speech seemed to become formal, even stilted, as if not quite natural. Yet she had no trace of the faint accent I'd heard in her daughter's voice. I had been listening, but she had no accent at all.

"What did Mrs. Graham do before she married him?" I asked.

"I have no idea."

"You know where she grew up?"

"I have heard New York, but I really don't know."

It was what Janice Graham had said, but Janice Graham could also have been who Eva Wayne heard it from. Along with Helga Kasmer's two missing years, it might be something to check out.

"With your first husband," I said, "did you live abroad?"

While she pinched and stripped her cigarette again, she seemed to look me over with a certain interest for the first time.

"Yes, for our first ten years," she said. "What made you think of that?"

"Helga has a trace of an accent, but you don't."

"Ah?" She nodded. "Yes, Kasmer was a Norwegian. Helga didn't come to the States until she was ten. That was very observant. Really quite good."

The approval in her voice was real, the voice suddenly a little less weary as if one of the few things that still interested her was someone who could do his job with some degree of skill. She continued to look at me like an army sergeant who has just found hope in a new recruit as she rummaged in her smock for still another cigarette.

"Does the name Welker mean anything to you?" she said.

"Maybe," I said. "Why?"

She lit the long brown cigarette, waved the match out in the sunny morning air. "The second time the girl came to see me that weekend, as I said, she was so insistent, grasping at straws, that I could see she was beginning to doubt that her mother was in Santa Barbara. That was when she talked about an Alan Welker, seemed angry. I had the impression that he was part of her coming here, that he was romantically inclined but that she was not, and that she was annoyed with him. I also had the impression that Welker could have been up here in Santa Barbara."

"Only an impression?"

"That was all."

"And you can tell me nothing about her mother?"

She shook her head.

"You'll be in your office?" I asked.

"After eleven," she said.

The dog watched me all the way to the corner of the big old house. Eva Wayne returned to removing the dead calendula blooms. I glanced at my watch. It was twenty minutes to eleven. With her cleanup, and the drive to her office, she would probably have five more minutes to work at the most. I would have skipped those five minutes, so would most people. But apparently Eva Wayne would work to the minute.

28

Coyote Road was a sharply climbing back road between the green coastal estates of lower Montecito and the rocky brown slopes of Mountain Drive. Number 250 turned out to be a low, rambling ranch among dusty live oaks and brown wild oats down a long dirt road. On the lip of a deep barranca there was a one-story main house, rows of dilapidated horse stalls beyond a working corral, and some ramshackle barns and outbuildings.

I parked under a pair of old sycamores in front of the house that showed that the barranca was for part of the year a real creek. The low stucco house had a roof of curved red tiles and was covered with trumpet vine and purple bougainvillea. With the stables and barns it was old and rundown, bare brick showing through the stucco and the roof tiles blackened and broken in many places. Yet there was no feeling of decay.

As I stepped out of the rented Chewy I felt a sense of revival. It had been in a lot worse shape and was now getting better. The signs of repair and renovation were everywhere, even to ladders against the buildings as if people had just stopped working a moment ago. A sense of coming back from neglect, but not rushing about it. A new door here, some patched roof there, repaired stucco somewhere else. In new, loving, but easy-going hands. A pleasant house, benign.

Until as I walked closer to the house the feeling changed. A motionless silence seemed to hang over the whole ranch. A kind of vacuum that was not benign. Across the deserted corral horses moved restlessly in their stalls. Cows wandered around the barns, and some burros complained in pens. At this hour they should all have been out in the fields. Two dogs lay near the corral with their heads down on their paws as if waiting for someone to return, and as I neared one of the ladders set up to make repairs the tools on the ground were flecked with rust.

A child of no more than five came running out of the house stark naked. A red-haired woman in sandals, a purple Mexican blouse, and a loose red and purple skirt came after in close pursuit. Scolding and laughing at the same time, the woman pounced on the little girl just at the edge of the barranca. The child squealed and kicked and the woman threw her high over her head in the sun in mock anger that fooled neither of them. In the midst of their laughter the little girl saw me.

"Mommy!"

The woman turned. She held the child under her arm like a loaf of bread.

"Hello." She smiled. "I didn't see you there."

"Mrs. Wayne?"

"Yes." The little girl was now hiding behind her and she rubbed the child's hair as she watched me. "Can I help you?"

"Is Mr. Wayne at home?"

"No, he's at work."

I would have been surprised if Henry Wayne hadn't been at work. It wasn't Wayne I had come to talk to. Suzy Dekker *had* been in Santa Barbara to find her mother. Now the question was had she found her mother? Henry Wayne's wife was neither tall nor large, but there was a sturdiness and an easy calm that told me she wasn't a young mother. She was almost like a girl playing with the child, but she wasn't a girl. Despite her look of sturdiness her long face was thin and beginning to wrinkle in the sun and wind, and her blue eyes had seen more than a few hard years. She looked older than Henry Wayne, in her mid or even late thirties.

"I'm afraid you just missed him," she said.

"After ten?" I said. "On a Friday? Because he worked late on the fashion show again?"

"Late work and the trips to L.A.," she said, not happily, and looked around the silent ranch in the warm January sun. "He's really supposed to be on vacation, he doesn't usually do much at the shows. He even started all kinds of work on the house and stables, but I guess that'll have to just wait. The company is his work, right? If they want him to work nights and go down to L.A., I guess he has to go." She laughed now. "I mean, we've been fixing up the ranch so long a couple more years doesn't much matter."

She seemed a gentle and pleasant woman, with an easy voice and the speech of a younger person. A college girl's manner of speaking, perhaps a cheerleader? It was only eighteen or so years ago that Peggy Hill Dekker had been a cheerleader. A woman with a young family, a woman who stayed home on a somewhat isolated ranch, might keep a young speech pattern.

"How many children do you have, Mrs. Wayne?" I asked, smiling at the small naked girl still hiding behind her.

"Only three." She smiled back.

"Is that the oldest or the youngest?"

"Goodness, you must need glasses. Sandra is youngest and, I hope, the last."

"All of them Henry Wayne's kids?"

"What?" She blinked at me. "I don't understand—?" She reddened. "Who are you? What do you want?"

"Were you married before, Mrs. Wayne? Maybe in Arizona? Do you come from New Mexico?"

She was angry. "I'm a native Californian, I don't know what you're talking about, and why did you want to see Henry?"

I snowed my photo of Suzy Dekker. "You know this girl?"

"No."

"You're sure? New Year's weekend, at least?"

"I never saw that girl anytime."

"Not even at the Elite fashion shows?"

"I don't go to the shows or mix in Elite."

"Your husband and your mother-in-law both talked to her New Year's weekend."

"Well I didn't! Henry keeps his work and his home life as separate as he can. It's not easy to work for your mother." She stopped. "You know Eva Wayne?"

"I do now."

"Now?"

"I talked to her before I came here."

I could almost see her close up, an almost physical withdrawal that seemed to make her smaller and older. The child sensed it too, clutching her mother's skirts and looking up.

"Who are you?" she said.

"My name's Dan Fortune. I'm a private detective."

"Who is that girl?"

I told her. She said nothing for a time, stood there with no expression on her long, weathered, ranch-woman face. Her hands reached down to hold the naked little girl. She held the child tight against her skirts. It was cool in the shade of the sycamores, while out in the heat of the winter California sun the animals moved restlessly in their stalls.

"Poor child," she said. "You think I'm her lost mother?"

"How old are you?"

"Thirty-seven."

"You could be."

"Of course," she said. "Did I kill her too?"

I heard the car coming fast along the dirt road.

"Did you?" I said.

The cloud of dust hung above the road and moved toward the ranch.

"My own daughter?" she said. "I'd need a very good reason, wouldn't I?"

"I've learned that you never can tell what could seem like an important enough reason for murder."

The car was a dirty yellow station wagon from before the last energy crisis. It stopped with a lurch under the sycamores. Henry Wayne ran toward us, small and slender in a dark blue suit. He was angry, the same crooked mouth but without the smile, his blue eyes glaring toward me under the dark blond hair that fell over his eyes as he ran.

"Stop bothering my wife, Fortune! Damn you!"

"All right." I watched him. The rage was deep in his eyes. An inch taller than his wife, slimmer, his whole wiry body was shaking. "I came to talk to you anyway, I'm glad you got here."

"Me?" He seemed startled, his anger slipping from focus.

"You told me your mother was out of town. She wasn't. Why didn't you want me to talk to her? Because you didn't want me to find out that Suzanne Dekker visited her twice that weekend, and you had to know the Dekker girl better than you let on the other night at the beach club?"

His wife was looking from one to the other of us, her lean face confused. Wayne didn't look at her, only at me.

"My mother was supposed to go out of town, she changed her mind and forgot to tell me. I wasn't trying to keep you away from her, and I knew nothing about the Dekker girl. My mother doesn't tell me very much." There was a deep bitterness in his voice. An angry bitterness, violent. Almost excessive.

"She told you I was here," I said. "It's the only way you could have known. She must have called you right after I left her house. And your story about her going out of town is her story. She primed you so your stories would agree. You know what I think? I think you're all covering up something."

"I don't care what you think!" Wayne raged, his anger back in focus and on me. "Who are you to come here digging dirt, accusing people! That girl wasn't even killed up here! Get off my land! Don't bother my wife again!"

"No," I shook my head. "Something's wrong at Elite Imports. Something that made you break your vacation, work on the shows, and go down to L.A.—if that was for the company."

Wayne turned on his wife. "Damn it, Marian, is there anything you forgot to tell him about me?"

"Henry!" The little girl began to cry. Marian Wayne soothed the child softly while she faced Wayne. "I didn't know what he was doing, Henry, or what he wanted. He's clever."

"I'm sorry," Wayne said, nodded. "Of course you didn't know what he was doing. We have nothing to hide anyway."

He put his hand on her shoulder. They smiled to each other. With his other hand Wayne smoothed the little girl's hair until she stopped crying. His voice was suddenly pleasant, even gentle. The voice of a man who lived up a dirt road on a battered ranch he was rebuilding himself but not hurrying. A man with a wife and family and not worried about the passing years.

"Why don't you take Sandy in and put some clothes on her," he smiled. "Get me a beer. Fortune too."

"Yes, dear." She looked toward me. "And he didn't come to talk to you no matter what he says now. He's being clever again, making it sound that way, but he really came to talk to me about that girl. He thinks I could be her missing mother."

She took the little girl into the house, but not before Wayne had bent and whispered in the child's ear and made her laugh. Then he patted her bottom and they went on inside the low ranch house. Wayne turned back to me. His anger seemed to have gone. His blue eyes calm, even thoughtful now.

"She was looking for her mother?" he said.

I told him the story. "You didn't know that?"

"How could I? I barely remember the girl. So that's why she was late all the time, off on her own."

"She told your mother what she was doing."

"I don't see that much of my mother out of the office, or even in it, and what would it all have to do with Marian anyway?"

"I think Suzanne Dekker found her mother."

The burros were braying in their pens. Henry Wayne looked toward them. "And that had some connection to her death?"

"Something caused it," I said.

"Not Marian." He laughed, almost relaxed. "I'm her only mistake."

"How long have you known her?" I asked.

"We've been married twelve years."

"That's not exactly what I asked."

"I knew her a year or so before we married."

"Suzanne Dekker was eighteen."

He shook his head. "You'd have to see Marian with our kids to realize it was impossible. Abandon a child? No."

"You never know what pressure can make a person do."

The braying of the burros, the restlessness of the horses in their stalls, seemed to be bothering him. He stared toward the outbuildings, and then beyond them to the dry mountains clear in the January afternoon. He shifted his weight back and forth from one foot to the other as restless as the animals, began to walk in small circles under the sycamores.

"If that girl found her mother, it wasn't Marian."

I said nothing. He went on walking around in his small circles under the trees. Marian Wayne came out carrying two cans of beer. I thanked her. Wayne seemed to have forgotten he had wanted a beer.

"If that girl found her mother," he said, "how would that have killed her?"

"I don't know yet," I said. "Maybe her mother's disappearance sixteen years ago had more to it than we know."

"I see." Wayne nodded.

Marian Wayne stood very close to him, her body touching his, and her hand moving slowly on his arm.

"There was a man you met," I said, and described the tall man in the dark suit Wayne had met in the fog at El Mirador. "Who is he?"

"You've been following me!"

"Not yet," I said. "I happened to see you that night."

Marian Wayne said, "I know him, don't I, Henry? I've seen him with you?"

"A business associate," Wayne said.

"Does he have a name?" I said.

"Joseph Murray."

"What does he do?"

"A salesman for International Instrument Corporation."

"What business do you do with him?"

"Mine."

Each answer was shorter and sharper, the anger back in his voice. He moved his arm away from his wife's hand as if the anger isolated him.

I said, "Your mother called you at work. You're too busy to finish your vacation, but you can rush out here to stop me asking questions. Why, if nothing is wrong at Elite?"

"Because I don't want any cheap opportunist private snooper bothering my wife and family!"

"Henry!" Marian Wayne said again. "That poor child is dead. Mr. Fortune is only trying to find out the truth."

Whatever it was angering Henry Wayne, isolating him in his restlessness, it wasn't his wife. He put his hand on her shoulder, gently. "You're right, I'm sorry."

With his small hand still on her sturdy shoulder, he turned to me. "There's nothing happening at Elite, Fortune, but you have my permission to investigate and talk to everyone there if you want to."

"Thanks," I said, turned to leave.

Wayne thought. "I suppose that if it wasn't the Canyon Slasher, something to do with her mother did get her killed."

"Probably," I said.

At the San Marino Hotel I was back in the green coastal lushness of Montecito. There was still no answer at cottage forty-four, and no sign of the Lennon girl, so I drove on into Santa Barbara and stopped for some pizza at a parlor on Milpas Street. For the West Coast it was decent pizza.

The main office and showroom of Elite Imports, Inc., was a two-story red brick addition to the front of a warehouse on the lower east side of the city. The offices were on the second floor. I asked the receptionist for Helga Kasmer. She announced me, and sent me through a door into a vast area of low half-glass partitions and endless rows of heads bent over desks.

A center aisle between long main partitions divided the enormous room into two sections and led on back to where there were offices with walls and doors. The left section of partitioned cubicles was: SALES… CUSTOMER RELATIONS … STOCK CONTROL … PURCHASING. The right section announced: ADVERTISING … PUBLIC RELATIONS … PERSONNEL … BOOKKEEPING.

Helga Kasmer had her office at the far end of the right area of cubicles, larger than the rest but no more private.

"Who," I said, "has the offices with the doors back there?"

"Only mother. The rest are conference rooms."

The large woman sat at a messy desk behind the low half-glass partition. As I came in she leaned back, lit a cigarette.

"You're in charge of everything on this side," I said, "and Henry handles everything on the other side?"

"It keeps down overhead to have just two vice-presidents. Miss Inside and Mr. Outside."

"Which also keeps it in the family."

"Which also holds down the overhead," she said. "On the future hopes, you can pay relatives low salaries."

"Not to mention overworking them," I said. "It looks like the two of you have the whole business about covered. What does Eva do with her time, watch you two?"

"You forget the most important part of a business."

I thought. What had been missing from the eight categories assigned to the two sections of cubicles?

"Production?"

Helga Kasmer nodded. "At Elite that means finding the fashions, the clothes, down in South America. The contacts, the trips, the buying. Only Eva does all that, and she does it alone. That keeps down the overhead too."

There was an edge to her voice, a hint of bitterness. Was this the trouble at Elite Imports? That Eva Wayne kept too tight and narrow a hold on the power, on the business? The "boss" of everything including her children's livelihoods and maybe even their lives? Judson Graham had said nearly as much, and Helga Kasmer didn't sound any more relaxed than her brother. In some battle with "mother," bitter about it? But how would that have ended up killing Suzanne Dekker?

"Your mother's not so young. She should be long past retirement," I said.

"Sometimes I think Eva's younger than any of us," Helga Kasmer said, "and she'll never retire."

"Maybe someone here would like to make her."

She had put out her cigarette. Now she lit another.

"We think about it, I suppose."

"Maybe," I said, "someone wants to do more than think. Or maybe someone already tried."

She seemed to think about that carefully as she smoked and looked out over her low partition.

"Not that I know of, Mr. Fortune."

"Are the Grahams your mother's only partners?"

"Yes."

"No other executives besides Wayne and yourself?"

"No."

"What about Joseph Murray?"

She stopped swinging, looked back at me. "Who?"

I described the tall, silent man in the dark suit. "The one we both saw Henry meet at El Mirador Wednesday night in the fog."

"I don't know who he is. Some friend of Henry's."

"Why were you watching Henry?"

"I wasn't," she said. She stubbed her cigarette in a large ashtray. "I had something I'd forgotten to tell him, so I went after him. I saw him meet that man, didn't care to interrupt, and talked to him later."

Possible? I didn't think so. I remembered how she had come through the fog that night.

"What's happening at Elite, Miss Kasmer? A power fight? Against your mother? Some other kind of business battle?"

"Nothing is happening at Elite," she said.

"Henry broke off his vacation."

"We had some unexpected delay on the fashions from Brazil, Eva needed quick help to get ready."

"And the trips to Los Angeles?"

"Trips?"

"Henry's trips," I said. "Or didn't you know about them?"

"I knew," she said evenly, "but we all took trips to L.A. the last weeks, we usually do. Even Eva and Jud Graham. I didn't know whose trips you meant. Henry had to go down to round up some special lights and stage decorations Eva wanted for the shows this year, and probably some other errands. Eva has a way of sending people on sudden errands."

It was as possible as her explanation for following Henry Wayne in the fog, only if she was hiding anything this time she wouldn't be doing it alone. There had to be collusion, at least with Henry Wayne, and if I checked into the details I would probably find them vague and impossible to pin down. Call it a dead end for now.

"You lived on your own for a few years," I said. "About twenty or so years ago?"

"Yes."

"Where?" I said. "Where did you go, what did you do?"

She slowly stubbed out her cigarette. She didn't light another, but closed her eyes and sat in silence for a time as if recalling those long ago years. Out in the vast room of tiny cubicles typewriters clattered and voices hummed like the drone of some giant machine. Helga Kasmer rocked in her chair, her eyes still closed, her voice slow and distant.

"I ran, that was all. Nowhere special. I wasn't running to anything, I was running from something—an alien home, a stepfather, a brother, Eva, everything. I took jobs in Los Angeles, a lot of jobs. I lived on the beaches: Redondo, Hermosa, Venice. In furnished rooms, at the beach bars. The whole act of the late fifties, early sixties."

"Men?"

Her eyes were still closed. "No one in particular."

"That's unusual," I said. "In our world, then and now, a girl usually runs with men. Only boys run alone."

"I'm special."

"And still alone."

"Yes."

"How are you special, Miss Kasmer?"

She opened her eyes now. "That's not your business."

"It is," I said, "if you ran not to L.A. but to New Mexico. If you then wandered on to Flagstaff, Arizona, and got married. If you had children, moved to Barstow, California, before you came back home."

"Children?" She seemed to think about children, silent and almost detached, and yet I saw a flash of something like regret in her eyes. As if she would have liked children, a child, but something had stopped her. Or as if she had lost a child? "What is your big interest in children?"

I told her Suzy Dekker's whole story. "Eva didn't tell you that Suzy Dekker was looking for her mother up here?"

"No." Helga Kasmer now lit another cigarette.

"The Dekker girl never showed you the photo she had of her mother?"

"Perhaps. I can't recall," she said. "You think I was that girl's mother?"

"You could be."

"But I wasn't. I never married. Not in New Mexico, not in Arizona, and not here."

That odd feeling I'd had the first time I met her returned suddenly—that she rejected men, their desire or even their interest in her in any way. Men, or was it marriage? Marriage and children? Eva Wayne had said that her daughter could never abandon a child. Somehow, Helga Kasmer herself seemed to be saying in her every action that she could never have a child, or would never have one.

"Did your real father have anything to do with your run twenty years ago?"

"My father died before I was six, Mr. Fortune. I never really knew him."

"That was in Norway?"

"Yes," she said. "In Norway."

"How old were you when Eva remarried?"

"I was ten."

"And that was here in Santa Barbara?"

"Yes."

"Why don't you live with your mother?"

"I prefer not to, Mr. Fortune, if it's any of your business." she said. Then she smiled. "You know grown women can't live in the same house."

"But you can work for her?"

"We all have to earn a living doing something."

"And better a vice-president than a stock clerk."

"Always."

I got up. "One of your models, Kate Lennon, is she around somewhere?"

"I don't know the models by name," she said. "Most of them are probably resting for tonight, but you might try the lounge at El Mirador again."

30

In the middle of a Friday afternoon the lounge of El Mirador was all but deserted. Two older men drank alone at each end of the bar, and Kay Michaels sat alone between them. The bartender was reading a newspaper. I sat on the stool beside the tall, gaunt, green-eyed model.

"I had a dream last night," I said.

"Was it a pleasant dream?" she said.

"Very pleasant," I said. "You could say spectacular, but unbelievable. Impossible even. I'm an old man."

"Funny," she said, "I didn't notice."

"Then you must have been dreaming."

"If that's the way you want it," she said. She smiled at me. "I don't mind a dream."

"Dreams don't last," I said.

"What does?"

By now the bartender had finally noticed me and put down his newspaper. I indicated that a beer would be nice, he brought one, and went back to his newspaper. The two men alone at the bar paid no attention to us. I realized something about Kay Michaels, she was a woman who would make up her own mind about what she wanted and what she would do, make her own decision. After that it would be time for me to make a decision.

"Where are the rest of you girls?" I asked.

She smiled again. "I thought you were too old for even one model?"

"This is work."

"Sorry. Which one do you want?"

"Kate Lennon."

"She usually has a swim and a rest before a show."

"She's not at her cottage," I said, and told her about the attack on me at the San Marino yesterday morning.

"Someone hit you?" She drank her Scotch. "You think someone here doesn't want you to talk to her?"

"It looks that way."

She thought about it for a time before she took another drink. Her green eyes were fixed toward me, unblinking.

"And that means you don't really believe the Canyon Slasher killed Suzy Dekker down in L.A. You think someone up here killed her, or knows who did."

"Yes," I said.

"Do you know why, Dan?"

"I don't even know where or when or how," I said, "not to mention who."

"I'll find Kate Lennon for you."

I sat in the lounge finishing my beer, watching the sunny winter afternoon outside and the sea beyond the lawn and the beach. I didn't appreciate the view or the beautiful climate. I was thinking about the case, about Marty and Suzanne Dekker and the whole thing, and my mind was a blank. Something had killed Suzy Dekker. What? All I had was a young semi-prostitute late for show rehearsals because she had supposedly been off by herself searching for her mother, and who had died in Los Angeles a day after returning from Santa Barbara. The boy who had sent her up here was dead in Los Angeles too. Someone didn't want me around, and there did seem to be something wrong at Elite Imports, but what, and how could it have killed Suzy Dekker and Alan Welker?

I ordered another beer and turned my back to the sun and view to see if that would help me think. It didn't, but I did see Judson Graham crossing the El Mirador lobby. I waved him into the lounge. He looked at his watch, then came in and sat at the bar beside me.

"Well," he said, "how goes your business?"

"Slowly," I said.

The bartender saw him a lot faster than he had seen me, quickly folded his newspaper and hustled over. Graham ordered beer, and nodded as if answering a question.

"Yes," he said, sipped the beer as the bartender brought it instantly. "I've been thinking about it. There just isn't any way she could have been murdered by anyone up here. At least, not by anyone connected to Elite or the shows. We hardly knew her, and she'd never been up here before. It looks to me like the Los Angeles police must be right about that Slasher madman."

"It's possible," I agreed.

"But I understand why you have to investigate," Graham added. "It would be hard for the family to accept. A faceless killing. Pure chance, pure accident. We can't accept that."

"Most deaths are faceless," I said.

He didn't hear me, or didn't want to. He had his own ideas on his mind.

"The idea that just anyone can walk down the street and kill you is too hard, too unfair."

"She could have found her mother," I said.

He heard me this time. "Found? No, she couldn't have. If she had, why hasn't the mother come forward? I mean, after she was murdered, wouldn't her mother have come to the family, the police?"

"Not if the mother killed her," I said.

He drained his beer glass. "I suppose such people do exist. Can I buy you a beer?"

"Sure," I said. When the beers came, I said, "Did you tell anyone I was going to talk to the Lennon girl yesterday morning? After I left you and your wife?"

"What?" He scowled at me as if he didn't like the question, as if he'd been accused. "Oh, yes, Kate Lennon. I'm sorry, you did ask us about that Dekker girl's roommate, didn't you. No, I spoke to no one about her. Only you."

"How about your wife?"

"I don't know," Graham said. "Why, did anything happen when you talked to her?"

"I didn't talk to her," I said, and told him of the attack on me at the San Marino Hotel. "Either that clerk tipped someone that I was there, or someone was told I was going to be there and was waiting."

"Well I told no one, and I doubt that Janice did," Graham said. "Who else knew? Did you ask anyone else about her?"

It was my turn to not like the question. Who else had known I was looking for Kate Lennon? The models, but not all. Maybe one or two whose names I didn't know, and Kay Michaels. She had been the first to tell me about Kate Lennon rooming with Suzy that weekend. Kay Michaels, who had been a very pleasant dream in a motel room. An unexpected dream, almost unbelievable to a one-armed roustabout going nowhere in particular in this world. I've said it often, I have a rotten profession.

"You met your wife in New York?" I said to Graham.

"Jan?" He finished his second beer. "No, in San Francisco. She was working up there in a museum. She comes from New York, though."

"Was she ever married before?"

"Hell no! I'm first and last, eh?" He grinned. "Number one all the way."

That would be important to him too. His wife. Maybe not a complete virgin, not in the last half of the twentieth century, but nobody really important before him.

"You know a man named Joseph Murray?" I said, described the tall man Henry Wayne had met at El Mirador. "He's a business contact of Henry Wayne's."

"Never heard of him," Graham said, and waved to the bartender. "I've got to go."

"You've been down to Los Angeles recently? On trips?"

"I'm always on trips somewhere." He paid the bartender, nodded to me, and walked out of the lounge.

The question was, should I have one more beer, or should I wait for Kay Michaels in the lobby? I don't like to wait alone in hotel lobbies;

on the other hand too much beer on the job has never been good for anyone. Fortunately, my news-hungry bartender was still ignoring me, giving me plenty of time to make up my mind. Maybe he didn't like one-armed men in his bar. It wouldn't be the first time I'd run into that. Or the last.

I might have been still there making up my mind with no help from the barkeep, if Janice Graham hadn't come into the bar after maybe ten minutes and spotted me. She joined me. The bartender was there in a flash, all smiles. It pays to be known.

"White wine, Bill," she said, and to me, "Have you seen my husband, Mr. Fortune?"

"Another beer, Bill," I said quickly and loudly, and to Janice Graham, "He left about ten minutes ago."

"Damn!" Her voice was still low, and she still sat very erect, and her long face was as reserved as ever, but she chewed a fingernail. "He was supposed to be in the lobby, but I looked in earlier and he wasn't there. Then I was held up."

"My fault," I said. "I lured him into the lounge here to ask questions. Something urgent?"

"With Judson everything is urgent," she said. Then she laughed. She had a nice, youthful laugh. "I'm sorry. No, nothing very vital. It's just that Jud is totally accustomed to his life being what he says it is. He decides how he should live, and then sees to it that he lives precisely that way. It's a nice trick if you can get away with it."

She was wearing a dark green brimmed hat, and took it off when her wine came with my beer. I got a shock. Her black hair was now strawberry blonde. She wore wigs. She was wearing a green tailored suit now, and the blonde hair went with it well. The new wig suited the outfit, and it suited her too, made her look even younger. It was only the long face and corded neck that added age to her. She wasn't naturally so slim. I wondered if the heavy dieting was part of Graham wanting his life to be what he decided it should be. The decision that he, Judson Graham, had to have a slim wife.

"It's nice to be rich too," I said. "What color is your real hair?"

"Gray, mostly," she said. She drank her wine. "What did you question Jud about?"

"Kate Lennon mostly."

"The girl who roomed with Susan Dekker? What about her?"

"I wanted to know who you and he might have told I was going to talk to her that morning."

"I told no one. Why would I? I barely recall you asking about her."

That was a lie. She had known at once who Kate Lennon was and what I was talking about. She recalled my asking about the roommate very well. For whatever importance it had, she was lying through her teeth. I eased away from it.

"That's what your husband said," I agreed.

She nodded as if saying "of course Graham had said the same because there was nothing else to say." She sipped at her wine but seemed to barely taste it as she realized there had to be something more behind my asking who they had told about me and Kate Lennon.

"Did something go wrong when you talked to Miss Lennon?"

"I didn't talk to Miss Lennon," I said, and gave her the story of the attack on me yesterday morning.

"Do you have any idea who it was or why?"

"None."

She took a better drink of the wine. "Is that all you asked Judson?"

"No."

"What else?"

"I'd asked him where he'd met you, and if you'd been married before."

"San Francisco," she said, and laughed. "I was working in the marine section of the natural history museum and one day in he walked." She looked at me over her glass. "I'd been waiting for him a long time, Mr. Fortune, you understand? To get married."

"That seems important to him."

"What does?"

"That you hadn't been married before."

"It is to a lot of men," she said. "Was that all?"

"Of what?"

"Your questions to Judson?"

Murder cases tend to turn a lot of people into snoopers. There's a morbid excitement, and it seems to make most people more curious than usual. But I was getting the feeling that Janice Graham was pumping me. When I thought about it, Graham hadn't appeared to be waiting for anyone when we talked. Had she been looking for Graham or for me?

"I asked him if he knew a man named Joseph Murray."

"Did he?"

"No," I said. "Do you?"

"No."

"And I asked about his recent trips to Los Angeles. Do you know where he went down there?"

"Not off hand," she said, finished her wine.

"How about your trips? Where did you go?"

"I haven't been on any trips. To Los Angeles or anywhere else."

Another lie? Or was it Helga Kasmer who had been lying this time? Maybe about both of the Grahams? Graham himself said he took many trips, and he was the kind of man who could forget what trips he had gone on when. But what reason could the Kasmer woman have for lying about the trips to Los Angeles?

"You don't appear to have made much progress," Janice Graham said. "Or are you just lying low?"

"I haven't made much progress."

"But you still feel that someone here murdered that poor girl?"

"I think something happened up here that got her killed."

"What do you think happened?"

"I think she found her mother."

"I see," she said, and looked at her watch. "Well, it doesn't appear that Judson is going to come back for me. He probably forgot all about it."

"Probably," I said, watched her walk away through the lounge.

This time the question wasn't whether or not to have another beer, I'd had enough. But Kay Michaels still hadn't returned, and outside the windows the sun was low across the immaculate lawn as the winter afternoon grew late. The bartender still wasn't bothering with me, but I don't like sitting at a bar without a drink any more than I like sitting in hotel lobbies. It looked like Hobson's choice, and I had just about decided on the lobby when Kay Michaels strode into the lounge.

"Come on," she said, "she wants to talk to you too."

31

The tall older model led me out of the lobby and around the hotel to the rear.

"It took a while to find her. She wasn't at the beach club where she usually is, and she hadn't gone back to her cottage over at the San Marino, so I had to ask some of the other girls before I found her right in the sauna back here!"

We passed around the small hotel pool where a few older guests wrapped in bathrobes were having drinks as the evening cold had begun to settle in the shadows behind the hotel. The sauna and health club rooms were beyond the pool in a new wing of El Mirador. Kate Lennon lay on a massage table in the massage room, a nice-looking young blonde covered with a towel. Covered but not hidden, a little heavier than most models from the contours under the towel, which meant still slim for an ordinary female.

"Hey," she said, raising her head to look at me, her voice light and young but very serious, "I didn't know you got hit and like that! I thought you'd just decided you didn't want to talk with me after all!"

I sat down on a straight chair, and Kay Michaels perched on the edge of another massage table. It was like a tropical swamp in the steamy room. A beefy masseuse in a white smock came in and began to squeeze the Lennon girl like dough.

"Why were you gone when I came out from under?" I asked.

"I got dressed, but you didn't come back, so when Miss Kasmer called and asked me to come in early I went."

"What have you been doing since? You weren't at your cottage this noon."

"Just working on the shows. I guess I was taking a swim after rehearsal at noon."

The masseuse stepped away from the girl. "I cannot work on a tense subject. You must be relaxed. I will return when your friends leave."

She stalked out leaving the Lennon girl under her towel on the table. I was old enough to be this one's father and then some, but I wouldn't have minded taking the masseuse's place. It's the middle-year girls who make me try to act noble. Kay Michaels half smiled and half frowned at me. She was reading my mind, or part of my mind. The other part was wondering why the girl was so tense the masseuse couldn't relax her.

"Was anyone around your cottage the morning I was attacked?" I asked. "Did you see anyone you knew?"

"No, I didn't see no one, Mr. Fortune."

"Dan," I said. "Why so tense then?"

She moved under the towel, "I guess 'cause Kay filled me in. I mean, about Dekker. I don't read the papers much, you know, so I didn't even know something had happened to her." Under the towel she shivered, the young flesh shrinking. "It's scary, you know? I mean, talking with her right here only a couple of weeks ago, and … and—"

She was too young for mortality to have become the great black pit dominating her life, but momentary flashes of inevitability catch even the young from time to time.

"I didn't know, you know?" she went on. "And maybe she was telling me something important that weekend and I didn't even know it. "She shivered again under the clinging towel. "I mean, if you really don't think she was killed by some crazy maniac."

"The police say she was, I don't think so. I could be wrong, but so could the police."

The girl turned to look at Kay Michaels. The older woman nodded to her.

"Tell him just what she said," Kay said.

I waited. The girl shifted her body under the towel. It was distracting even now. Kay frowned at me. Few women ever quite understand.

"Well," the Lennon girl said, "I'm not sure, you know? I mean, she liked to talk when we was in the room, but she was off on her own most of the time, so we didn't spend a lot of time together. When we did, me I wanted to talk about the shows and all, you know. Only she didn't. I mean, I didn't know her down in L.A., so I don't know what she was usually like, you know, but up here all she wanted to talk about was her family. I found out her mother'd run out on her when she was just a little kid, and her father got killed in some kind of brawl, and her brother and her'd been in and out of relatives and foster homes, and now she'd come up here to find her mother right at the fashion show!"

"She knew her mother was here?"

She shook her head. "Not exactly. I mean, she had this old photo, see, and that Alan Welker down at Regent told her someone at the shows here looked just like the picture only older. She said Welker was real sure, only he couldn't remember just who it was he'd seen or what she did up here, so he'd fixed it so she could come up and look herself. She was real determined, you know, only she didn't sound so happy. Almost mad, you know? And kind of sad, too."

"Mad?" I said. "Why?"

The Lennon girl squirmed under the draped towel, but this time my mind was on something else.

"Why sad?" I said.

Her voice was nervous, "She said she'd always known that her dad hadn't been killed in some accidental brawl. She'd always known the man who killed him had been paid to do it, and she knew who had paid him and why."

"Her mother?" I said.

Kate Lennon nodded. "That's how it sounded to me. She didn't tell me right out, but she said her dad had never given up trying to locate her mother, and right before he got killed he told her he thought he'd found her! He was excited because he was going to bring her mother home."

I watched her. "Did Suzy give any reason why her mother would have killed her father, or hired someone to kill him?"

"No," the girl said, "except maybe that he'd found her and she didn't want to be found."

She looked at us wide-eyed, but the implication was heavy enough to hang in the steamy room without any comment from Kay Michaels or me.

I said, "Did she find her mother, Kate?"

"I don't think so," the girl said. "She didn't act like it."

"How did she act?"

Under the towel the blonde girl was silent for a time. Then she looked up at me again. "Scared, Mr. Fortune. I can see her face that last day, you know? It makes me shake. It was like she wanted to get out of Santa Barbara fast. Like maybe someone was trying to kill her too."

"Did you see that photo of her mother?"

"Yes."

"Did you recognize it?"

"No. It didn't look like anyone I know up here."

I nodded to Kay Michaels. We thanked the Lennon girl, and left. Outside in the entrance room the masseuse was reading a magazine. I tapped her meaty shoulder and bowed. She gave me a vicious stare, snorted at my solitary arm, and stalked back into the massage room.

I had a feeling she wasn't going to find her customer any more relaxed than earlier. It looked like Kate Lennon was worried that she knew too much about Suzanne Dekker. Maybe she had reason to be.

32

It grew dark out over the lawn and the sea as I ate dinner with Kay Michaels in El Mirador's dining room. I had abalone. Kay ordered veal Oskar and ate slowly.

"A mother wouldn't murder her daughter," she said.

"If she'd killed her husband and the girl knew it?"

"No."

I shook my head. "I know at least three recent cases."

"Then the women had to be insane."

"Only under heavy pressures, Kay, intolerable conflicts."

"The husband, yes, but not a child."

"She abandoned them, both children. Something had to be very important to her. Her own life, probably."

Kay looked down at her food for a time. "We don't live in a very good time, do we? I wonder what they'll think of us in twenty centuries. Probably just about what we think of the Roman Empire of Caligula, Nero, and Messalina."

They probably would, but I had to work according to my time and its terms, and Kate Lennon's story could have changed the whole picture. Maybe Suzy Dekker hadn't found her mother after all, but maybe someone had found Suzy. Someone who didn't want her to locate her mother or rake up the past in any way. Not necessarily because her mother had killed her father, but maybe because someone else had—and not by "accident."

"On the other hand," I said to Kay Michaels, "it's possible the mother didn't kill the father or Suzy, but someone else who had wanted her father dead back then. Maybe what Suzy knew about her father that made her think her mother had been in on his murder would have pointed to someone else if she ever talked to her mother."

We ordered coffee but skipped dessert.

"What will you do?" Kay Michaels asked.

"Go down to Barstow and talk to the police. Then I'll try to locate the man who actually shot Dekker. If he's still alive, maybe he can tell me something."

"Will you return to Santa Barbara?"

"I don't know."

"Then you better have this."

It was her business card with her Los Angeles address and phone number. I left her to get ready for the first fashion show of the weekend, and drove to the De Anza to pack my bag. I decided not to check out. I didn't know if I'd come back to Santa Barbara, but in case I did I wanted the same room and Bill Dekker could afford the expense. I had my bag in the car, was checking the room to be sure I had forgotten nothing, when the phone rang.

"Hello?"

"Mr. Dan Fortune?"

It was a man's voice, and I came alert. A low voice, and nervous. Unfamiliar, yet there was something? ... A vague feeling that I *had* heard the voice somewhere before, and not so long ago, but not anyone I could place.

"This is Dan Fortune," I said. "Can I help you?"

"Maybe we can help each other."

"How?"

"I know why Suzy Dekker got killed."

"Why?"

"Meet me in two hours under the hotel boardwalk on San Marino beach."

"You have a name?"

"Maybe later."

"Maybe now, or maybe I don't come."

There was a silence.

"I thought you wanted help on the case."

"I think you want something too."

Another silence.

"Alan Welker."

The phone went dead.

33

I parked in the shadows where the dark road ended above a flight of concrete steps that led down to jumbled rocks and the beach. After nine on a Friday night the narrow road was deserted. I walked to the steps down to the beach. The surf was soft and silver in the night.

Had it been Alan Welker risen from the grave? Or was it some imposter who didn't know that Alan Welker was dead? Or someone just trying to make me come to the beach? And if it hadn't been Alan Welker on the phone, who had it been? If it was Alan Welker, who was dead?

At the foot of the concrete steps I studied San Marino beach in the night. Tall, thin beach houses lined the narrow strip of curving sand. Most were dark and shuttered in January, but here and there a window was lighted with the shadows of people inside passing across it. And some distance farther on I could see the massed light of the San Marino Hotel where it came down to the beach.

The beach itself appeared empty in the chill of the January night, but I moved ahead slowly toward the lights of the hotel. Meeting an unknown quantity in a remote rendezvous it had seemed sensible to bring my old cannon this time, and I put my hand on it in my pocket as I moved along the dark beach.

Twice shadowy shapes loomed up in the night, and I dropped to a crouch in the sand my hand tight on the heavy gun. But the first was a solitary old man who walked briskly between me and the ghostly line of surf with the manner of a man who did this every night of the year rain or shine, hot or cold, and the second turned out to be the advance guard of an adolescent beach party who set to work at once digging a deep fire pit in the winter sand.

When I reached the boardwalk I stopped. It was a short structure, maybe a hundred yards long, built by the San Marino in front of its two-story beachfront units. Most of the beach rooms were dark in January, most guests probably preferring warmer rooms farther back from the beach, but it was Friday and some rooms showed light and movement. There were two wide wooden stairways with railings down from the walk to the beach, and the blackness under the boardwalk was divided into cubicles of darkness at twenty-five-foot intervals by the supporting posts. I waited for some time in the open for some sign of my caller. No sign came. No one appeared.

I slipped my old pistol into my belt where I could get at it quickly with my lone hand, and moved into the darkness under the boardwalk.

I stood in pitch dark.

Alone now where the sun never reached, where the dark sand smelled wet and a cold chill rose like an unseen mist. The open beach and the hotel seemed miles away. Above on the heavy boards nothing moved. Even the silver line of the surf had vanished below the curve of the silent beach, and only the soft but steady pound of the waves reached into the darkness where I was.

Slowly the dim shapes of giant boulders and encrusted pilings emerged from the blackness. A litter of discarded papers and old beer cans. Broken bottles hazy in the dark. Bent low, I moved ahead under the heavy beams that supported the walk above between the pilings driven down into the sand. Now the odor of rotted garbage and urine mixed with the miasma of wet sand and cold chill. Until I saw the darker shadow directly ahead.

I moved closer. Slowly, my hand on the old pistol in my belt. To the cover of the last thick piling before which the shadow seemed to hunch motionless.

A man crouched down kneeling over another shadow that lay in the wet stink of the cold sand. I slipped the pistol from my belt and stepped behind the kneeling man. I put the muzzle to the back of his head. He stiffened.

"Fortune?"

I said, "Is he dead?"

"I think so. Who is he?"

"Don't you know who you kill, Dekker?"

"Kill?" William Dekker said, exclaimed. "I didn't—"

Dekker started to turn toward me, started to get up to his feet. I poked my pistol against his head. Hard.

"Stay down! Don't turn."

Out on the open beach the fire of the beach party leaped up the night in sudden sheets of flame that illuminated the dark under the boardwalk in sharp, flickering flashes. William Dekker twisted his head to protest, his dark hair and handsome young-looking face like some grotesque gargoyle in the light of the flames out on the beach.

"For God's sake, Fortune, I found him like this!"

"Shut up. Now listen to me carefully. Stand up, very slowly, but don't turn around. Put your hands behind your head. Now."

Dekker stood up with his hands behind his head. I patted his navy blue blazer and charcoal gray pants. He had no weapon.

"All right, now step away to the other side of the body. Hold it, that's far enough. Now turn, but keep your hands up."

He stood directly in front of me on the other side of the body on the ground, just far enough away so that he couldn't reach me in a single sudden lunge. I kept the pistol toward him, and looked down at the dead man. The voice on the telephone had been young, but the man on the wet sand was in his late forties or early fifties. His bullet head was bald, and he wore old denim work pants, sneakers, and a dark blue western style shirt. Not young and not a stranger. Welker, but not Alan. The working-man father of Alan Welker I'd run into in Alan's Los Angeles apartment: Clyde Welker.

Kneeling, and keeping one eye on William Dekker, I slipped my pistol into my belt and examined the dead man closer. He had been shot once in the head. A smallish gun, probably 7.65-mm again. Three times was too much coincidence. Same gun, same killer. I searched him quickly. He was unarmed, carrying a few dollars and not much else. I stood up. William Dekker had made no move, had watched me as if fascinated.

"You don't know him at all?" I said.

"No. Do you?"

"Then what are you doing here?"

"I followed you from your motel."

"And got here ahead of me. Sure."

Dekker shook his head. "No, I came after you, but I took a different way down to the beach. I didn't want to risk being spotted by following behind you on foot on an open beach, so I looked for a different access. I found one just before this boardwalk, came down, and hid under the walk. You took some time to get to the boardwalk, and when you did and came in under, I moved on ahead of you and stumbled right over him!"

"How did you find me? Why?" I asked as the firelight flickered brightly over his handsome face and dark eyes. "What were you doing in Santa Barbara at all?"

His eyes widened innocently, and he spread his hands to protest my suspicion. "The Santa Barbara sheriff's office called Marty about the Subaru. She told them you had it, but they said there had been no sign of you at the wreck. Marty was worried, so when I got home this morning she asked me to come up and find you. She told me about Elite Imports, so I went there, and sure enough there you were."

"Did Marty tell you to follow me?"

"That was my idea." His dark eyes flashed in the reflected firelight. "I told you I was going to find out the whole story, why Suzy died. I have to. She was family, and I failed her!"

I watched him for some time there under the dank boardwalk with the stink of stagnation and the dead Clyde Welker between us as the light of the flames played across both our faces.

"You still think the Canyon Slasher killed her?"

"That madman and her world. The world we gave her."

"And you have to get her whole story because she was family and you failed her?"

"I suppose we all failed her."

"Or do you have a more personal interest, Dekker? Maybe she was more to you than a niece?"

His face seemed to twist in the flickering light. "I don't think I'll even answer that."

Under the dim boardwalk we faced each other in silence. I hadn't expected an answer to the last question, not now and not in words, and the rest of his story was possible enough. The trouble was that even if it were all true it ruled out very little. He could easily have been here before me and either remained or returned. Clyde Welker had been dead at least a half an hour by my guess, and maybe longer.

"His name was Clyde Welker," I said. "Yeh, Alan Welker's father, and now he's dead too. You still think Suzy was killed by the blind chance of being picked out by an unknown madman?"

He said nothing, but his dark eyes flickered.

"Two dead in Los Angeles, one in Santa Barbara so far, and I don't think the Slasher had much to do with any of it."

His dark eyes were almost opaque in the firelight. "Perhaps not."

I didn't mention that one of the two dead in Los Angeles might have returned to life. Maybe he already knew, and there were still two dead no matter who the second one was.

"Let's go back down to Malibu," I said. "Where's the Subaru?"

"Out of impoundment but still in the shop."

"Okay, we'll have to leave it for now. You follow me."

He nodded down at the dead man. "Aren't we going to report to the police?"

I looked at Clyde Welker. "What can we tell them? We might be held here for days, and we can't help him now. Someone'll find him, I'd rather find who killed him."

Dekker's Lotus was parked in shadow up the road from my rented car. I didn't think it had been there when I arrived, but I knew that proved nothing much either as I led us back to the freeway and turned south. I drove through the night and thought about Clyde Welker, and a realization suddenly took shape in my mind.

There wasn't one unseen enemy, there were two! A cool, silent, almost impersonal force that had been trying to stop me but not necessarily kill me. And a force of violent fury that lashed out and killed. The only question was, were they two different menaces, or only two sides of the same menace?

34

William Dekker lost me before we reached Ventura. I swore out loud to the dark highway.

"Damn!"

He slipped past me on the last curve of the Rincon where the freeway ran tight under the shadows of the mountains and over the phosphorescent edge of the sea breaking on the rocks. I went after him, hit my horn long and loud, but it was no use. The rented car was no match for his Lotus, and with one arm I wouldn't try to match his speed. There's too little margin for error for a one-armed man in a speeding car that goes out of control. Wherever he went, I'd find him sooner or later if I had to.

Or maybe it wasn't a runout at all, only that restless need to push the gas violently to the floor and fly, and I'd find that he'd just gone on ahead to the big Malibu house and would be waiting for me.

It was past 11:00 P.M. when I drove up the twisting gravel road to the great Moorish hacienda with its sweeping view of the lights of Malibu far below, and I had been half right. Dekker had been to the house, but it was Marty who stood waiting in the courtyard under the olive trees. Her copper hair shined in my headlights against a dark green dress, and her eyes told me that she was expecting me.

"Where is he?" I said as I climbed out.

"He left again. Is something wrong?"

"Let's go inside."

She raised on her toes, put her arms around my neck, and kissed me. A hard kiss, deep and long. "I was so worried, Dan." Her face rested against my chest. "When the Santa Barbara police called and told me the Subaru had been wrecked on a mountainside, I thought something terrible had happened to you."

Her second kiss was softer, drawing me in.

"I was lucky," I said. I held her against me, the supple actress's body I knew so well, remembered so well. I wasn't sure that I wanted to hold her so close, but I knew that I didn't want to let her go either. Yet I had to, and to break the moment I told her of the two attacks on me in Santa Barbara and how the Subaru had ended up on the side of a mountain.

"Who could it be, Dan?" She raised her head to look up at me. "Why?"

"Let's go inside."

I went on into the large living room with its low beams and terra-cotta tile floor and made myself an Irish and soda at the well-stocked home bar in the corner before I turned back to Marty. She had stopped in the doorway to watch me. I didn't drink whisky very often anymore, and she knew that. She was small in the doorway, with her boyish face under the red hair but nothing boyish about her body in the dark green dress.

"Scotch?" I said.

"And water."

I made her drink, and sat down on the long couch. She remained in the doorway as if not sure where she wanted to go.

"What did Bill say when he got here?" I asked.

"That he'd found you and you'd be here in half an hour," she said, "and that he would probably write all night and had to be alone."

"Write?"

"He has a shack somewhere not too far away. In the mountains or on the beach, I'm not sure. He goes there to write when he wants to be alone. I don't even know where it is."

"Is that where he's been the last few days?" I said. "He said he wasn't home when the police called about the Subaru."

"It's where he said he was."

"Not even a telephone?"

"Not that I know. I don't have a number anyway." She came into the room and sat down facing me. "He writes there a lot, Dan. It began almost as soon as we were married, and lately he's gone more all the time."

"I hope it's to write," I said. I told her about Clyde Welker and how I'd found Bill Dekker. "His story could be true, or he could have been there before I was. When I just about proved the Canyon Slasher didn't kill Suzy, he acted a little odd and now he's gone."

She drank. "He'll be back tomorrow."

"Will he?" I said. "The Slasher has been a cover for the killer all along, and Bill was very insistent that the killer had to be the Slasher. Even when you and Diane Pasco were sure it had to be someone else."

She looked down at her drink. I got up and stood at the wide picture window that looked out over the clear winter night, the lights of Malibu below, and the glow of Los Angeles to the south. I heard her drink again behind me.

"Two different people in Santa Barbara," I said, "say Suzy was up there looking for her mother. But one says maybe not for the reason we think. She told a Kate Lennon she knew something about her father's shooting down in Barstow eight years ago. That it wasn't an accidental brawl, that there was more behind it. Miss Lennon is sure Suzy seemed to imply that her mother was somehow involved in Stan Dekker's death."

She shifted in her chair behind me. "Suzy did say once that no one had ever explained to her what the brawl was all about."

"It could be," I said, "that her mother was behind her father's shooting. Maybe he'd found her back then and was a threat to some new life, some important plan." I turned back to the room and Marty in her chair. "But it doesn't have to be only Peggy Hill Dekker. It could have been anyone who wanted Stan Dekker out of the way or just plain dead. A new husband of Peggy Dekker. A lover. Anyone she was involved with. Or someone who had a whole different reason for hating or removing Stan Dekker." I returned to the couch and my Irish.

"It opens a whole new bag, Marty. The killer could be anyone trying to cover a past no one knows exists. To hide what really happened to Stan Dekker, maybe even what really happened to Peggy Dekker."

"Peggy?" Marty said. "You mean Suzy's mother didn't just run away?"

"It's possible. Or maybe not alone."

"Not Bill," Marty said.

"How much do you really know about Bill? About back then? About his relationship to his brother, or to his brother's wife?"

She held her Scotch, but she didn't drink. She seemed to stare through me. "I don't want to be alone tonight."

"I can't stay here, Marty."

"Then I'll go with you. Some motel. Anywhere."

She finished her Scotch and stood. Almost rigid like a prisoner waiting to be taken away.

"All right," I said. "Get a coat, it's cold out."

The first motel with a vacancy had a noisy tavern out over the beach at the far end of Malibu. I had my bag, the clerk didn't even give us a fish eye. On the way to our unit, Marty stopped. Her hand was trembling lightly.

"Let's have a drink, Dan. All right?"

Her voice was shaky, strange, and I realized that she was suddenly shy. All at once hesitant. We were far from strangers, and yet we were strangers.

"All right," I said.

The tavern was crowded on Friday night, small tables packed around a miniature dance floor with a three-piece band blasting on an even smaller bandstand. We found a table as far from the noise as possible. She had another Scotch. I switched to beer. We drank and talked about nothing in particular and watched the dancers and the couples at the other tables going through the ritual of Friday night.

"It's not only what he might have done, Dan," she said.

"I know it isn't," I said. "Do you want to dance?"

The tiny dance floor was jammed like sheep in a pen, and a one-armed dancer can't get too fancy, so we danced tight together New York style.

"I don't think I'm right for him, Dan," she said.

"You mean you don't think he's right for you."

"I suppose so," she smiled. "You still know too damned much about people."

"I don't know anything about most people, only some. But I do know that six months isn't very long."

"Perhaps not," she said. "How long did we have?"

"A lot of years," I said.

We danced on in small circles in the dim light and noise of the crowded tavern. Somewhere out there in the night there was a murderer, and somewhere Bill Dekker worked or ran, but tonight I was dancing with Marty again.

"He's changed since we married," she said. "No, I know, you'll say he couldn't really have changed so fast. All right, I suppose I never really knew him that well. He was the dazzling writer, and I was ready. Now he seems to sell his work more than he writes it. Conferences and agents, movies and subsidiary rights, talk shows and magazine interviews, and when he writes it's alone away from me. I wonder why he got married at all?"

"Most men do," I said.

"Most men marry because it's easier than taking the trip to the Bronx or Burbank to visit Mom and get their buttons sewed on, and easier than chasing some girl all night when they want to get their ashes hauled. But Bill isn't a man who had to get married for those things. Girls chase him, and he's sewed on his own buttons for twenty years."

"Maybe he loves you," I said.

"I don't know, Dan," she said. "Lately I just don't know."

We danced and sat, drank and talked low, until the tavern closed at 1:00 A.M. Marty held my hand all the way to our unit.

"Don't put on the light."

She held me very close, her mouth moving on mine. Even with one arm I had always been able to carry her to the bed. A large bed where her tight body lay warm against me, where the neon lights outside the windows and the sound of traffic on the Coast Highway seemed to isolate us. I felt her hair against the pillow with my lone hand, her high breasts under me, the hollow of her belly even at thirty-five, her full thighs and the legs that rose and opened. We had always fitted. There are some things you don't forget.

The traffic on the highway was almost gone when we lay touching in the big motel bed.

"Could we, Dan?" she said. "Us again?"

"Maybe we never stopped."

"That's nice to think."

I said, "What do we want, Marty?"

"Whatever we can have. Go as far as we can."

"Do we have to go somewhere?"

"Everything moves, Dan. We can't let time pass us."

"I exist, Marty. All I want to be, maybe. In space not time."

In the dark room I couldn't really see her face. Only a pale blur under the hood of her hair. A blur and a pale body that moved close to me, her mouth finding mine in the big bed. Together. Again.

35

I left her sleeping in the dim early morning room, and drove the rented Chewy south through Los Angeles in the January dawn to Interstate 15 for Barstow. She would find her own way back to Dekker's mountain hacienda, or to wherever else she wanted to go. It was something Marty would handle herself. She always had.

I stopped for some breakfast in San Bernardino, and made a telephone call. To Ed Green, an old P.I. friend who'd moved out to Los Angeles from New York and hated it. I asked him to check on International Instrument Corporation, wherever it was located, and Joseph Murray, and to nose around the beach communities to see what he could dig up on Helga Kasmer twenty years ago. He was glad to hear from me, glad to get the work, didn't think he could do much about a twenty-year-old runaway girl, complained about southern California, and hung up. I had two eggs and toast, with coffee, and went back on the road.

The road climbed up and over the high precipices of Cajon Pass and on across the barren high desert to Barstow, the metropolis of the Mojave, where 15 goes on to Las Vegas and 40, or old 66, cuts straight across the desert to Needles and points east. It was lunchtime when I parked at Barstow Police Headquarters and told them what I wanted. A Lieutenant Campo agreed to talk to me.

It was a hot Saturday for January even in the high desert, and the lieutenant seemed half asleep as he waved me to a chair. He watched something very interesting through his windows as I told him my story. Or some of it. He nodded.

"I read about the girl. You remember the names in murder cases in a small city. I remember the girl pretty good. Nice looking, kind of touchy and eager at the same time 'cause her ma'd run out on her, and then her old man gets killed. She never had much chance."

"What can you tell me about her father's shooting?"

"Pretty ordinary killing," Lieutenant Campo said. "Guy named Buck Hayes, mean little bastard worked in the same garage with Stan Dekker. A local character, pretty well known and pretty well disliked. Dekker didn't go into that tavern too much, but Hayes was a regular. There was a waitress where they both ate lunch, and they were both after her. Standard, right?"

"They fought over the woman?"

Campo nodded. "She said at the trial that she liked Stan Dekker best but was afraid of Hayes so went out with both of them off and on. One night Dekker took her out when Hayes had thought he had a date. After Dekker took her home, he stopped in that tavern for a nightcap. Hayes was there and pretty drunk. They started yelling and shoving and Hayes pulled the gun and shot Dekker dead."

The lieutenant had a flare for the dramatic. He just let it hang there in the hot office.

"That's all?" I said.

"Yep. Hayes had been in trouble most of his life, Dekker had been unarmed, witnesses said Hayes just pulled the gun and shot, so the judge threw the book at him. Murder two, twenty to life. He's still in prison."

"No hint of anyone else being involved?" I said. "Maybe something more behind it than a simple brawl?"

"Like what, Fortune?" The lieutenant's voice had grown cool.

"Someone who wanted Stan Dekker dead."

"A conspiracy? Someone put Buck Hayes up to it, hired him?"

"Maybe you suspected back then but couldn't prove it?"

Campo laughed. "Fortune, when Buck Hayes sobered up back then he'd have involved his mother if he could. He'd have talked himself blue about anyone and anything. He'd have tried to make a deal to testify against anyone. As it was he tried to claim self-defense when ten witnesses said Stan Dekker never even hit him, and he tried to involve the waitress. Said she egged him on, told him she was tired of Dekker, got him drunk. Anything to weasel out, and you think he'd have kept quiet about some accomplice? Someone who hired him he could have made a deal to turn state's evidence against?"

"I don't know, Lieutenant," I said. "But I do know that I don't believe the Canyon Slasher killed Suzy Dekker, and that means that someone else did. For some reason."

"Lucky for me it's not my case then," Campo said.

"Did Stan Dekker's brother come to Barstow in those days?"

"I didn't know he had a brother."

"William Dekker," I said.

"A sister, yeh, but she never came to Barstow as far as I know until Dekker was dead. To pick up the girl. I never heard about a brother. The boy had to be sent to a foster home."

"Where is the boy now?"

"In Barstow. Doing pretty good, I hear."

"Could I have his name and address?"

"I'll find out." He left the office.

He seemed to have remained close to the case even after eight years, and I began to wonder if he could have missed anything important back then. Not William Dekker coming to Barstow regularly to visit his brother or his brother's wife, and not a hired murder. But you can never be sure of someone else.

Campo returned. "Sadie says you can go over. Sadie Carr, the foster mother." He gave me the address.

"You said Hayes was in prison? Can I talk to him?"

"He's up at the California Men's Colony at San Luis Obispo. I'll contact the warden, say you need him for a case."

"Thanks," I said.

"Fortune?" Campo said as I walked to the door. "Buck Hayes was a man out to kill someone all his life. He was born mean and stupid and mad at being born poor and mean and stupid. Mad at everyone who wasn't as low and dirty as he was. Mad at the whole world. Stan Dekker was just in the wrong place that night."

In my rented Chewy I found the address of the Dekker boy's foster parents on the eastern edge of town where the bare desert began again with its flat scorched hills and dry barrancas for a hundred miles to Needles. A nice little clapboard cottage with a small green lawn carefully watered and tended. A stout woman with gray hair met me on the front walk.

"You're Mr. Fortune?"

"Yes ma'am. Dan Fortune."

"I'm Sadie Carr. The boy is off in the desert with Carr. Rock huntin'. That's why I said come when Campo called. I'll talk to you, but I won't have the boy bothered. Not for anyone or anything. He's had enough. All he's going to."

"I hope so, Mrs. Carr," I said. "There are those who don't think Suzy was murdered by the Canyon Slasher."

She watched me a moment. "Who would they be?"

"Her roommate for one, her aunt for another."

"Jane Pearson says that?"

"Suzy's other aunt. Bill Dekker's wife."

"Him!"

"I'd like to ask some questions."

She watched me again. "Does he, the important brother, think the police are wrong about who killed her?"

"No," I said. "At least, he didn't."

"Ask me your questions."

"Was there any evidence that someone else could have been mixed up in Stan Dekker's shooting?"

"Not that I know. Buck Hayes was going to kill someone someday. Stan Dekker liked the wrong girl."

"Hayes couldn't have been paid by someone to do it?"

"I never heard anything like that."

"Was Bill Dekker around Barstow back then? Seeing a lot of his brother and Peggy Dekker?"

"I don't think he was ever in Barstow, then or later. We never knew Stan Dekker had a brother. The big writer wanted no part of his family then, and no part of the children later. He gave no help, sent no money, so when Jane Pearson could take only Suzy the boy was fostered out to us."

"And Bill Dekker never came near Barstow?"

"I don't think he even cared about Stan or his family. Not until Suzy grew up and went to L.A. Then it looked like he began to take a real interest in Stan's family. Suzy anyway."

There was a lot of anger in her voice, a lot of bitterness, but she was the kind of woman who would keep such weaknesses under control. They were an indulgence, like candy and ice cream, that gave her release from the demands of a hard world, but that would never be allowed to influence what she did or how she lived.

I thanked her, and returned to my car. It was getting late in the afternoon as I drove out of Barstow and back onto Interstate 15 toward Los Angeles. With luck, I would reach L.A. just in time to have some dinner, check into a motel, and get some sleep before flying north in the morning to San Luis Obispo.

36

A large, sprawling complex inside walls with towers at each corner, but a lot less grim looking than older penitentiaries, the California Men's Colony was set among high, lush mountains just north of San Luis Obispo, halfway between Los Angeles and San Francisco.

The warden was a polite man but busy. Thanks to Lieutenant Campo's call, he looked at my New York credentials, recorded them, and that was all.

"Hayes will usually meet with anyone, Mr. Fortune, but none of our inmates have to talk to anyone, is that clear? You're here because he okayed it, he can terminate it any time. You'll have up to an hour, we'll allow you to meet in private, and that means you'll have to be searched, I'm sorry."

He turned me over to a guard who searched me and took me to a private room. I sat down and waited. The same guard brought in a small, gnarled, terrier of a man with a thin, sneering mouth, a small broad nose, little pig eyes, and ears that stood straight out from a Marine-Corps style haircut. The guard left, and the small man looked after him with pure hatred, made an obscene gesture when the guard's back was turned. Then he looked quickly all around the room like someone hoping for something to steal, break, or use to escape. Finally he looked at me. He grinned. His teeth looked like he'd never cleaned them in his life.

"You a reporter? A lawyer, maybe?"

"Private detective," I said. "I'm interested in your case, Mr. Hayes, because—"

"Hey, listen, you got to help get me out of here!" He sat down with his face almost poked into mine. I could smell his heavy breath. "So I killed Dekker, he's a hell of a lot better off'n I am! I wish I was dead, he was in here! And that damned broad, she's walkin' around free! It was all her fault, the stinkin' little ass-teaser! Playin' me like some kid sucker, playin' both of us'n! Look, what's your name anyhow?"

"Dan Fortune. I'm only partly on your case. It ties in with another maybe. Stan Dekker's daughter was killed—"

"Shit, man, I don't ..." He almost jumped back in his seat, like a rodent at bay. "Hey, what the hell you tryin' to pull? You can't get me on that, I been in here! What do I know about no daughter? Jesus, what you people up to? Who gives a shit about no kid?"

"I didn't imply you had anything to do with Suzanne Dekker's murder," I said patiently, "but the two cases could tie—"

"Look, Fortune," he leaned back to me, his hand pulling at my pants. "I was out of my mind that night, you know? Drunk 'n crazy. I didn't know what I was doin'. That broad had me hyp'mtized, she drove me nutty. I wasn't responsible, see? I mean, I—"

I sat back now and let him rave on. He almost slobbered as he begged and fumed, whined and swore, defied and weaseled. Lieutenant Campo and the Carr woman had been right, there was no way he could have had an accomplice or been hired. He would have implicated anyone years ago. No amount of money would have protected a conspirator all these years, no degree of fear. He wasn't a man who remembered more than a week in either direction.

I stood up. "Thanks, Hayes."

"Hey!" he went slack-jawed. "We ain't talked yet. What'd you want to talk about?"

"We talked," I said. "I'll give the warden some money for cigarettes."

Hayes sat there angered and confused and hopeless. He couldn't understand what had gone wrong. He never would. For a moment I felt almost sorry for him, but not for too long.

On my way to the warden's office I knew that there had been no accomplice when Stan Dekker had died, no conspiracy. Only bad luck. A grubby, indifferent death without plan or reason.

I gave the warden some money for Buck Hayes. He let me use the telephone. In Santa Barbara the fashion shows had ended last night, and the San Marino Hotel reported that Kate Lennon had checked out. They didn't know where she had gone.

El Mirador said that Kay Michaels had returned to Los Angeles.

37

I called Kay Michaels from the airport as soon as I landed. Her voice had that same deep, quiet, perpetually half-amused quality. I had the feeling she would be easy to live with.

"This is a little sooner than I expected," she said, "or is it just business?"

"How do I get in touch with Kate Lennon?" I asked.

"Business, okay, but not that kind of business."

"I think she sold me a gaudy lie, Kay," I said from the airport phone booth. "A real snipe hunt. The question is did she do it for herself, or did someone put her up to it, maybe force her to hand me the cock-and-bull. Maybe the same one who hit me at her cottage."

The easy quality left her voice, "I'll get to her for you. Where can I call you?"

"Why don't I come to your place?"

"Why don't you?" she said. "I'll have Kate waiting."

The night was settling over Los Angeles as I drove out of the airport and headed for the Harbor Freeway north.

38

The address was on one of those small, curving side streets in the Hollywood Hills. A narrow three-story building of three apartments up a long flight of steps on the side of a hill and nestled deep in trumpet vine, plantain, bamboo, and oleander. Kay had apartment one on the ground floor. The street was silent as I climbed the steps. Two large shrubs completely hid her front door. As I reached the shrubs I saw someone standing in her open front doorway.

"Kay?"

"Come on in."

The tall, slender model led me inside to a comfortable little living room of furniture she had obviously picked out piece by piece herself. The picture window was a small one, but there was a long view of the city lights spreading wide to all horizons like a darkened ceiling of some planetarium. Kay had a beer ready. With one herself, she sat facing me.

"I can't find Kate," she said. "She's not at home with her mother, and her mother doesn't know where she is. None of her friends have seen her since Santa Barbara."

"Did she come home from Santa Barbara?"

"Not as far as anyone seems to know. Her mother isn't concerned though, Kate always goes her own way whenever she wants, it's not unusual." Kay took a good drink of her beer. "Has she run out because she doesn't want you to find her, or has she been taken away by someone?"

"One or the other," I said.

She thought about it. "You're sure her story was a lie?"

It was comfortable on her couch, and the beer was good. I nodded, "Unless Suzy Dekker herself was lying for some reason. That's possible, but I can't come up with a reason for her to lie that I can even half believe in."

"Perhaps she wasn't up there just to find her mother," Kay said. "But wanted to be sure everyone believed she was, so made her story deeper."

"You have any ideas about what else she might have been doing up there?" I asked.

"Me? Not a clue." She drank beer as if she really liked it. She shrugged. "Perhaps Regent can tell you tomorrow where Kate is. We're all supposed to leave word where we can be reached if we leave town."

I finished my beer. "You've got a nice place, Kay."

"I like it," she said. "Sometimes it can be lonely."

"Not all the time?"

"No, not all the time."

"How about tonight?"

"Tonight I was lonely, but now I'm not."

"Neither am I."

"Good," she said. "We can hold hands all night."

"Hands?"

"That's it for tonight." She smiled. "Sorry."

"At my age a hand can be enough."

"I wonder if you'd talk so much about being old if you didn't know you don't act old in any way?"

"Of course not."

She laughed, got up and got two more beers. This time she sat beside me on the couch after she opened them. "Who could have wanted to send you on a wild-goose chase, Dan?"

"Someone who wants me off his or her back, who wants any time he or she can get. Someone who tried to hide murder behind the Canyon Slasher, and who would very much like it to stay hidden. Someone grabbing at straws."

"Someone who very much wants you to stop what you're doing," Kay said, "who wants you out of the way."

"That's probably about it."

"And you have no notion who it is?"

"Not who, not why, not even exactly where."

"Then perhaps you should get out of the way."

"Can't," I said.

"Because you've been paid? Have a client?"

"That, and because no one likes to be beaten, especially not at his work," I said. "And because there are some things you don't let anyone get away with."

She took my hand and held it. We sat close and touching on the couch. So close her head rested under my chin and I couldn't see her face.

"I wonder if Kate Lennon is part of it, Dan? Of whatever got Suzy Dekker killed?"

"I wonder," I said.

"Or is she another victim? Lied to you because she was afraid of someone?"

I squeezed her hand, but said nothing.

39

I woke up in a double bed in a small, bright bedroom that didn't look much like my combination office/apartment in Chelsea. The bed seemed cramped and narrow—I'd spent a week in king sized beds, and we get used to new things awfully fast. The bed had been slept in on both sides. I was alone in it now.

The bedroom was light and pleasant but it wasn't fussy. Not a monk's cell, but not a boudoir either. I was getting to like Kay Michaels more each time. I wasn't sure I wanted to.

Showered and dressed, I found a note in the kitchen that told me that Kay had gone on an early modeling job, and anything in the refrigerator was mine. I had some cereal and milk, some toast and tea, and sat with my thoughts as I ate. Kay hadn't said anything about a job last night.

Over my last cup of tea I called Ed Green. He had choice words for the job of trying to check on Helga Kasmer.

"Best I came up with was an old landlord in Hermosa Beach who thinks he remembers a tenant named Kasmer. She wasn't married as far as he knows, and that's why he remembers her—she never had any men up to her room, and that was pretty damned unusual for a single broad in Hermosa in the early sixties. He gave me some other leads, said she seemed to move around a lot, but they all drew blanks. That's the whole report."

"How about Joseph Murray and International Instruments?"

"International Instruments Corporation has sales offices in L.A., New York, Washington, and lots of places overseas, and Joseph Murray sure works for them. They're high-pressure sales types, were very eager to have Murray get back to me. Had to hang up on them to stop their pitch."

"Where's their head office and their factories?"

"No factories," Green said at the other end of the line. "They're one of those jobbers, sell the products of a lot of manufacturers. In this case to the international market only. New York seems to be headquarters."

"Thanks, Ed," I said. "How much?"

"That Kasmer job was a bastard. Five hundred plus. The expenses weren't bad."

"Send me a bill for my records."

On the quiet cul-de-sac street with its cascading greenery and half-hidden buildings, I climbed into my rented Chewy and drove back to the Hollywood Freeway. I headed south to the Harbor and then took the Santa Monica all the way to the end and on along Route 1 to Pacific Palisades. This time I parked in front of the police station, and inside asked for Lieutenant Stepanic. I gave my name and business and Stepanic let me wait quite a time. Just long enough to indicate I was of no importance. The really long waits are reserved for those who *are* important and the police want to sweat.

He still swung in his rasping swivel chair when he finally had me ushered in. His hooked nose was a little red now as if he had a beginning cold, and his owl eyes were watery. Short and heavy, he seemed less frustrated and more resigned.

"Where you been, Fortune?"

"Santa Barbara."

"Why?"

"Suzanne Dekker was up there just before she was killed."

"Any luck?"

I told him about everything that had happened except the killing of Clyde Welker. He wasn't impressed.

"So she was looking for her mother, believed a crock of shit story about her father or you were sold, and someone tried to take you out a couple of times," Stepanic recited in scorn. "What the hell does that add up to? You've got nothing. None of it ties to her killing. You don't know if she found her old lady or not, and even if she did so what? You think her mother shot her, carved her up, and dumped her out in Collins Canyon? And if someone up there tried to stop you snooping, maybe you stuck your nose into something smelly and you better take it up with the Santa Barbara cops, it's not my jurisdiction."

"What if I said I'd run across another murder up there? Of someone connected to Suzanne Dekker?"

He studied me and toyed again with his switchblade letter opener. I sensed he knew that if he asked the next question he would be committed to a path he wasn't sure he wanted to be put on. The way I sensed that when I answered his next question I was risking jail, or even being tossed out of California.

"Who?" Stepanic said.

"Clyde Welker," I said.

"What's his connection?"

"His son worked with Suzy at a model agency. The same agency that sent her up to Santa Barbara. Alan Welker." And I explained the rest, that Alan Welker appeared to have told Suzy that someone around Elite Import's fashion shows looked like her lost mother, and arranged for her to be sent up there.

"Alan Welker?" the lieutenant said. "Did you talk to him about the Dekker girl?"

"Not yet," I said, a little evasively. "Haven't found him."

He reached for his telephone. "Wait outside."

I went out. In the glass-walled corridor I listened to the low voices, protests, typewriters, telephone bells, coming in a cacophony from all the police offices. Lieutenant Stepanic didn't let me listen long. "Fortune!"

Inside the office he pointed his switchblade at me. "I knew Alan Welker rang a bell. I just talked to Hollywood Division. Alan Welker was found dead in a parking lot on Vine Street last Tuesday night. The parking lot serves a building where Unicorn Productions operates. Suzanne Dekker once worked for Unicorn, and her roommate, Diane

Pasco, still does, and Tuesday was when we spotted you at their Venice apartment." He stabbed his desk with the knife. "You knew all about Welker, didn't you."

"Yes," I said.

"They didn't connect him to the Dekker girl because they didn't know his background or where he worked. You knew."

"Not then," I lied. In my work you have to lie sometimes, even to the cops. "You've got the connection now."

Stepanic swiveled in that rasping chair. "They contacted the Redwood City address on his registration, turned out to be a rooming house. They got his address here, but the landlord didn't know where Welker worked or where his family was if he had one, so they asked the landlord to identify the body. He did—but it wasn't Alan Welker. It was a buddy of Welker's named Frank Oglesby, about the same build but shorter, wearing Welker's jacket and driving his car but looking nothing like Welker."

Then the voice on the telephone Friday night at the De Anza motel *had* been Alan Welker. Unless it was someone else who knew Alan Welker was alive, or at least had been alive beyond last Tuesday. Stepanic was watching me as I speculated silently.

"So you knew about that too," he said.

"Not for sure," I said. Now I told him about the phone call and meeting where I found the dead Clyde Welker.

"William Dekker?" Stepanic said. He sat and thought about it. "You reported all that to the Santa Barbara police?"

"No," I said.

"You don't like to work with the police?"

There it was. Lying is sometimes necessary, but the truth is a lot better if you can use it. I leaned forward in my chair, tried it honest and earnest. And most of it was no act. I had to get him on my side or I wasn't going to go much farther.

"The police didn't seem to want to work with me, Lieutenant," I said. "I'm not in my own area, have no status, and am pushing an and-official position. I didn't think anyone was going to work much with me, and figured it was more important to keep moving ahead and not get tied up and held down. As long as I didn't hurt anything, and I don't think I did."

"You know how much trouble you're in?"

"I know."

He nodded, picked up his telephone receiver, did a lot of dialing. "Nils? Vinnie Stepanic in L.A. Fine, yourself? Good. Listen, Nils, we're looking for a guy could be up your way. Alan Welker. Young guy, we ... Clyde Welker? No, don't have a make on him. Last Friday night? What do you have on it? That's too bad. No leads at all? Look, this Alan Welker could be part of a homicide too. Right, we'll work close. I'll send you a report tomorrow, and you keep an eye open for Alan Welker. Roger."

He hung up and returned to watching me. "Some kids necking under the boardwalk found Clyde Welker soon after you left. Why was he shot, Fortune?"

"All I know is that when I ran into him last Wednesday in Alan's apartment he acted as if he knew Alan was dead, had met with the police about it, and wanted his son's killer caught."

"Hollywood never talked to any Welker," Stepanic said.

"I know. It's obvious Clyde knew that Alan was supposed to be dead but was alive, and I think the only person who could have told him was Alan himself. Clyde was probably in that apartment to get something for Alan who wanted to stay 'dead'."

Lieutenant Stepanic nodded as his telephone rang. He picked it up and listened. "Thanks," he said, hung up, and sat in silence. When he finally spoke his voice was quiet.

"You came to talk to me, you didn't have to. That was square. I don't like how you played most of it, but maybe you had good reason at that. Maybe I was wrong about Suzanne Dekker." He thought again. "That call was from ballistics down at the center. I called them when I called Hollywood. The bullets in the Dekker girl and the Oglesby kid came from the same 7.65-mm automatic, and from what you told me I'd bet on the slug in Clyde Welker being another match." He rocked slowly behind his desk. "It's possible the Slasher could have killed them all, but I'd have to say the chances are slim. Way out of his area, never happened in any other killing of his, and doesn't fit his M.O. That leaves us nowhere down here. This Alan Welker may be the only hope we've got, and he's probably spooked, hiding, and out of our jurisdiction. He contacted you once, he might do it again. One way or another I think you've got the best chance now of flushing out the killer, if there is one. So I'm going to let you go back up to Santa Barbara on your own."

"Thanks," I said. I stood to leave before he changed his mind, but his brooding face told me he wasn't finished.

"I'll delay sending a report to the Santa Barbara police as long as I can," he said. "You know, Fortune, most cops don't like their authority challenged or their conclusions questioned, but we don't like murderers much either."

I nodded.

40

Lieutenant Stepanic was a good cop, he knew what his work was. I hoped I knew mine.

There was a pay phone at the end of the glass-walled corridor outside Stepanic's office. I called Regent Model Management. They couldn't put me in touch with Kate Lennon. She wasn't at her home address, and she hadn't called in since leaving Santa Barbara. I left a message, and called Kay Michaels. There was no answer. I called William Dekker's hacienda in Malibu. Marty answered at once.

"You got home okay," I said.

"It looks like it," she said. I heard a nervous hesitation in her voice. "What happened in Barstow?"

"Dead end," I said. "There's no chance that anyone could have been part of Stan Dekker's shooting."

"No one?" I heard the slow release of tension in her voice, and yet a hint of disappointment. "What does that mean now, Dan?"

"It means that one motive is ruled out."

"That's all?"

"It means that Suzy had been told a big lie and led on by someone, or that I've been told a big lie to lead me away from Santa Barbara."

"What will you do?"

"Go back to Santa Barbara," I said. "Did Bill come home?"

"No," she said from the distant house. "I'm worried."

"For him, Mart, or about him?"

She was silent. "Perhaps both."

"I did get one hint in Barstow," I said. Somewhere along the police station corridor a woman was sobbing. "Suzy's kid brother's foster mother suggested that Bill's interest in the family took a big jump when Suzy appeared on the scene."

Silence again. "Perhaps he did change then."

"I'll get back to you, Marty," I said.

I called Diane Pasco's number in Venice. No answer there either. I could take Sunset Boulevard or the freeways to Unicorn Productions at Sunset and Vine in Hollywood. From Pacific Palisades it was a tossup—Sunset was direct and slow, but it would take three freeways in a big circle. I took Sunset.

It took over an hour, and it was after 11:00 A.M. when I parked in the lot behind Unicorn Productions and went through the alley to Vine Street. The ticket line was long but moving, and there was no crowd waiting to be interviewed. I told the man at the guard desk what I wanted. Diane Pasco came out.

"We're getting set to tape, come on inside."

The tall girl with the marvelous figure led me down a long corridor and through a door into the backstage area of a television sound studio. I watched her as we walked. She wore a tight pale blue sheath dress that showed off her figure and her long black hair to perfection. She knew her assets, and used them. We stood just inside the wings of the open stage.

"I mother the contestants," Diane said. "You passed all tests, you know? I could get you on today if you want. You could make a lot of money. The M.C.'d love a private eye."

"I could use a lot of money," I said. "I'll think about it."

We watched the eager audience filing in and almost clawing for the better seats while they stared around in search of the cameras that could beam their faces to millions. The stage set of the show revolved and bubbled like the gaudiest juke box.

"What have you found out?" Diane asked.

Out on the flashing, bubbling stage the M.C.'s assistants were warming up the audience with gossip and jokes.

"Suzy did go to Santa Barbara expecting to find her mother up there. She may have found her."

"Did you find her? The mother?"

"Not yet."

The audience still filed in, pushing and jostling in their eagerness, but those already in their seats paid no attention to anything except the bright stage where the assistants warmed them up for the event to come. They responded to every word, every gesture, every suggestion and command. An inflection in a voice from the stage could send them into great spasms of precise response exactly on cue.

"Why didn't she tell me if she'd found her mother?" Diane said. "She'd wanted to for so long, she should have shouted it to everyone instead of saying that nothing special had happened up there. She was excited, eager, talking about a new life, but she didn't say she'd found her mother."

"Maybe something else happened too," I said. "Or maybe her mother didn't want to be found. You said from the start you thought Suzy knew the man who called. I think you're right about her knowing the caller, but what makes you sure it was a man? Why couldn't it have been a woman? You said you didn't believe she'd have taken a call from some john that night."

Diane Pasco was watching the M.C. in the doorway of his star dressing room, ready to go on, surrounded by admirers he preened for. In the auditorium the ushers were closing the doors to the wailing of a few who had not gotten in. From the stage the warmup people were announcing all the money that had been won so far on "RISK!" and how much could be won. The eager audience applauded every dollar. I thought of some words of composer Charles Ives about the complexity of nature teaching freedom and the complexity of materialism teaching slavery.

"I never heard the caller that night, and Suzy just went out," Diane Pasco said. "Marilyn at the call service couldn't tell the police anything about the voice, says she gets so many calls she never even hears the voices. If a woman spoke low, Marilyn might not notice."

The audience continued to applaud the revolving neon sets of the glittering show, responding to the slightest cue to perform. Yet alone each one was probably a simple, responsible person with his own life, doing his own job.

"Alan Welker isn't dead," I said.

Diane looked at me.

"At least he wasn't last Tuesday," I said.

"But you told me that night he—!"

"It wasn't Welker. A friend of his named Frank Oglesby, in Welker's jacket and Welker's car."

A roar like a thousand lions greeted the arrival on stage of the M.C. for his own warmup. They leaped to their feet as the assistants urged them up, waved them up, up, up, commanded the cheers. And why were any of them here on a warm, bright, sunny day? The big prizes? Not for them, but for someone, and that was all right because at least they would know that someone won. The free show? Or just the need to DO something. Be part of an *event?* The need for recognition? Any recognition?

"I've never heard of Frank Oglesby," Diane Pasco said.

"My guess is it was Alan Welker who was supposed to be dead that night, the killer got the wrong man. Welker may even have been in the car and escaped. And I think the killer still wants Alan dead. I think he tried again in Santa Barbara and again killed the wrong man, Clyde Welker."

It was almost time for the show to begin now. The M.C. had the audience in his hands, hanging on his words and his smallest glance. They had all found what they were looking for.

"What is it all about, Mr. Fortune?" Diane Pasco said.

"You have no idea? Not even a vague hint?"

"No," she said.

"What if I said there seem to be two forces involved? A violent, desperate force, and a smooth, calculated force. Does it give you any thoughts about Suzy?"

"No," she said. "None. I'm sorry."

On stage they were going through one last mechanical check of the gaudy equipment. The M.C. was making sure of all his floor marks and camera positions.

"It's almost time," Diane Pasco said. "I have to work."

"Where could Alan Welker hide?" I asked. "Where would he go? Did Suzy ever mention anywhere they went or he went? Where his home was? Some relatives? Anywhere?"

"No, Mr. Fortune, nothing," she said. "It's time. Do you want to be on the show?"

I looked out at the stage with its flashing lights and ringing bells where three people would battle to show who knew more, faster, for more money. For an audience that would laugh or cry on command, and the vastly larger audience that would buy toilet paper and hair dye—the only real part of the show, the rest all surface fakery and revolving lights.

"No thanks," I said. "If I'm going to be a clown it'll be in real life, and what little I know I'd like to think has more use than selling soap. I'll call you."

She went off to round up her contestants, and I walked out to one last audience roar as the show announcer introduced the M.C. as if they had never seen him. The charade was on the air.

41

After I'd called Regent Model again and learned that they still hadn't located Kate Lennon, and there was still no answer from Kay Michaels, I drove north in the warm afternoon toward Santa Barbara once more. Inland this time, on Highway 101.

My theory said that Alan Welker was in Santa Barbara, and that he had to be there for a reason. That there was also a murderer in Santa Barbara, either a permanent resident or a temporary visitor, who had a reason to want Alan Welker dead. And that the two reasons had to be the same thing—that Alan Welker knew something danger-ous to the murderer. The sound of a man running scared, and maybe the sound of blackmail. And Alan Welker had contacted me once. I hoped he'd try again.

By the time I reached the sea at Ventura, I knew that the only place Alan Welker would know he could contact me again was the De Anza Motel, and the only way I could hope to let him know I was back in Santa Barbara was to show myself everywhere and with everyone and hope that he was watching. The prospect did not thrill me. I had a strong notion that someone else would be watching too. This time I would carry my old gun.

It was late afternoon when I got back to my room at the De Anza in Montecito. Nothing had changed except that the maid had cleaned and straightened. I unpacked only enough to get my shoulder harness and pistol. The harness fitted neatly under my empty sleeve, but I hated the weight. Back in the rented car I drove out into the hills to the massive concrete castle of the Grahams on its dusty mountainside.

The maid told me that the Grahams were out on business, but would be at El Mirador Beach Club at five o'clock.

I drove back into Santa Barbara itself to the big Victorian house of Eva Wayne on the upper east side. The testy neighbor wasn't in sight, but Henry Wayne's old yellow station wagon, and a small Toyota two-door, were parked in front of the turreted blue-gray house on its acre of trees and lawn. I parked up the street and walked back to 435. The street was empty as I climbed quickly over the low picket fence and slipped up to the side of the house. I heard nothing from the front windows, and worked my way back toward the high hedge that surrounded the back yard. The voices came from the last window, and the dog began to bark inside as a truck passed on the street.

"Can't you keep that animal quiet, damn it!"

It was Henry Wayne's voice in the room above where I crouched in the shadow of the hedge. The dog became silent.

"Dogs have saved my life more than once," Eva Wayne's clear, deliberate voice said. "They're more dependable than people, and sometimes a lot more intelligent and competent."

"I care about people, not dogs, damn it!" Henry Wayne said in a rage. "Why didn't you leave town the way I said!"

Helga Kasmer's voice came low, "What people, Henry?"

"My children! My wife! My family!"

"Only them?" Helga Kasmer said.

"Shut up!" Wayne shouted. There was something close to hysteria in his voice. "What did you ever do?"

"What I could," Helga Kasmer's voice said.

There was silence inside the room. I could hear the soft panting of the big, inscrutable dog. Then Eva Wayne's voice.

"I did not leave town because I did not want to, and because it was a stupid notion. There was no reason for me to go. Just more of your idiocy." I could almost see the contempt in the brown eyes of the tall, erect old woman. "You must learn to let those who know how to do things handle them, and let me take care of my own business."

"No!" Wayne's voice almost cracked. "No more. From now on I'm in charge, you hear? Helga, you hear that?"

"I hear it, Henry," Helga Kasmer said quietly.

"Someone has to take charge," Henry Wayne said.

The second silence in the room was broken by Eva Wayne's cool voice. A voice full of scorn.

"Not you, Henry. You don't have the brains or the nerves."

Something in the room hit a wall or a floor. Footsteps went away on a wooden floor. The dog growled. A door slammed. I slipped to the front of the house and watched Henry Wayne half run and half stumble out of the front door, his hair wild and his eyes angry. The small, wiry man climbed into his old yellow wagon and drove off without looking back.

When I returned to my crouch under the side window it was Helga Kasmer who was talking.

"… known it would happen someday, Eva."

"I suppose so," Eva Wayne's weary voice agreed.

"Your last triumph," her daughter said.

"Or my last failure. Things did not work out as we had expected, your father and I." There was an undertone of bitterness now in Eva Wayne's deliberate voice, and then a brief silence as a chair creaked. "This is a large house, Helga."

"I know it is," Helga Kasmer said. "It always was."

"You don't have to live alone."

"Yes I do."

This time I could picture them facing each other, the tall, tanned, angular-faced mother with her sharp nose and thin lips, and the overweight daughter with the ragged blonde hair and the shapeless clothes. Some deep gulf between them.

"I could have done better with my children," Eva Wayne said inside the room. "One a weakling and the other a nun."

"No, I think we're your logical children."

"Do you?"

Another chair creaked. Helga Kasmer's voice was flat.

"I better go back to work."

When Eva Wayne did not respond, I crawled to the front of the big house, brushed myself off, and hurried to ring the front door bell. A stocky Oriental in a white coat opened the door, and when I asked for Mrs. Wayne, nodded me into a narrow, spartan entry hall with polished wooden benches built in on either side. Before he could go to announce me, the two women came out of a rear room into the larger main hall of the old house.

"All right, Tasho," Eva Wayne said, and to me, "Is your mystery solved, Mr. Fortune?"

"Soon," I said.

"You must have learned something," Eva Wayne said.

"What have you learned?" Helga Kasmer asked.

"Come in and sit down," Eva Wayne invited.

I shook my head. "No time, thanks. The Canyon Slasher is definitely out now, even to the Los Angeles police, and whatever killed Suzanne Dekker wasn't her past. At least not anything that happened in her past. That friend of hers we talked about earlier, Alan Welker, looks like the key. Both the police and I thought he'd been shot and killed last Tuesday night in Los Angeles, but it's turned out that the wrong man was shot. I'm certain that Welker is here in Santa Barbara, and that he knows something very dangerous to the murderer of Suzy Dekker. Are you sure Welker was up here that weekend, Mrs. Wayne?"

"No," Eva Wayne said, "I'm not at all sure. I told you I had an impression from the girl, nothing more."

"If Welker was here New Year's," Helga Kasmer said, "it was unofficial as far as Elite or Regent were concerned, and no one ever mentioned meeting another man from Regent."

"Except Suzy Dekker," I said. "According to your mother."

"No, Mr. Fortune," Eva Wayne said. "My impression from the girl was that he could have been in Santa Barbara, not necessarily that she had met him."

It put a different angle on Alan Welker's being in Santa Barbara that weekend, very different. Did they know that?

"But neither of you knows anything about where Welker might be now, or what he wants in Santa Barbara?"

"Nothing," Eva Wayne said.

"No," Helga Kasmer said. "I've got to go, Eva."

I said, "If either of you hear anything from or about Alan Welker, let me know."

I went out with Helga Kasmer. She drove off in her small Toyota, but I didn't drive off. I sat in my rented car thinking about Alan Welker and another theory. Had he been spying on Suzy Dekker? Jealous? Obsessed? So killed her? Love, desire, need, possession, whatever you wanted to call it, men have killed for it since before history.

And other men, who wanted the same woman, have killed the killer.

The clock on the Moorish tower of the famous courthouse in downtown Santa Barbara showed almost five o'clock, so I drove back out
to Montecito and El Mirador Beach Club. After clearing me with a telephone call, the same guard sent me through the club and out to the
dazzling blue olympic-sized pool with its diving towers and rows of
cabanas. The cabanas on one side were small and on two stories like
a motel. But on the other side they were large and single-storied with
chairs and tables enclosed by low fences with a gate for each cabana
and waiters going in and out the gates.

Judson Graham sat alone at a table behind a cabana gate that
proclaimed "Mr. Judson Graham, Director." The big, barrel-chested
man had a drink in his massive hand and seemed to be watching
an elegant little party at one of the other large cabanas. He sat in
that chin-raised, head-tilted-back pose of his. All he needed was a
monocle. He wore a bathing suit under a short white beach robe that
enhanced his tan and his bull neck, but he wasn't wet. I guessed that
he wasn't a good enough swimmer to want to swim much in public.

"Fortune," he said as I walked up, "you're back. Come and take a
seat. Jan's in the pool. Drink?"

"I'll take a beer," I said.

A waiter materialized in a white jacket, and while Graham
instructed him on the drinks I looked out at the pool where Janice
Graham was swimming. She was swimming slow lengths of the hundred meter pool. She swam well, but I had the strong feeling that she
could swim a lot better and faster if she wanted to. Maybe if Graham
hadn't been there. He wouldn't be a man who enjoyed the athletic

prowess of his wife, unless it was in some activity he could do a good bit better. In the early winter evening she was the only one in the pool. She seemed to enjoy swimming all alone, totally absorbed in herself and what she was doing.

"So," Graham said as we waited for the drinks, "is your return good or bad?"

"If you mean have I found out who killed Suzanne Dekker," I said, "the answer is not yet but I'm getting close."

"Good for you," he said. "Can you name some candidates?"

"No," I said.

The waiter arrived, and Judson Graham went through the rigamarole of checking and signing the bill. All up and down the row of large cabanas behind their privileged fences other men looking a lot like Graham in their actions and manner sat around identical tables doing the same things. The women were all more or less slim in very well-fitting bathing suits over very well-tanned skin. The women seemed to enjoy both the suits and the skin. In the babble of talk the names of far-off resorts and international hotel chains were clear, as well as talk of stocks and brokers and real estate. They all seemed to feel good with themselves and each other. For some reason I thought about Suzanne Dekker.

"Hope Beck's is all right, Fortune," Graham said.

"Beck's is fine," I said. A good, imported premium beer that fitted well with the gossip of the far-off resort havens.

To feel good together was, of course, the reason they all gathered at the club. To reinforce their truths and ways and vital beliefs. It is important to not be alone in those things, to know others think the same as you, have the same truths, stand together. We all need some of that, even Suzy Dekker who'd never had much chance to feel good with herself or anyone else.

"You're still convinced the Canyon Slasher didn't kill that girl?" Graham said, watching the elegant little celebration at the nearby cabana.

"The L.A. police don't think so now. Or some of them don't," I said. "Can I ask you and your wife some more questions?"

"Jan'll come out soon," he said. He nodded toward the small private party. "There's a family in charge of its own space."

I looked toward the gathering. About ten people sat at, or stood around, the small tables of white tablecloths, silver, and heaped food and champagne. They ranged from the twenties to the seventies, with a short, rugged-looking middle-aged man in a blue blazer and yachting cap clearly the host. A small blonde wearing black velvet pants, a plunging black silk blouse, and a wide red sash around her narrow waist danced with some of the younger men to the music of a tape recorder. Alone at the center table an old woman, maybe seventy, neither ate nor drank but seemed to watch everyone in silence. In a pale blue dress and a small flowered hat she looked like the grandmother of the bride, but seemed to be the guest of honor.

"That's our club president, Baxter Pace, in the blue blazer," Judson Graham went on. "In the black pants and sash is his wife, and the old lady in blue is his mother. The others are some old friends and Bax's grown kids. The old lady's going into Casa Montecito Retirement Home. It's a swank place, Bax's business is a gold mine, and to top it off for the old woman he's thrown her this party. Pretty nice, eh?"

"She doesn't look as happy as your friend," I said.

"Well, who likes getting old and having to slow down?"

"Look at her. She's lonely, sad. She doesn't like the idea. It looks like a farewell party."

Graham became surly. "Bax's made sure she'll have the best, she's his mother. But old people have no right to lower the quality of being alive for their kids, for younger people in their prime years. Bax and Deborah and the kids have a right to their own self-realization. We have a responsibility to ourselves, Fortune."

"Maybe you're right," I said, "but in a way responsibility for each other is what life is. Even more so in a family."

"You sound like some tribal savage," Graham said. "This is the twentieth century, we've come a long way in understanding the individual human being, the need for self-realization. Old people and kids are a real block to self-fulfillment."

"Fulfillment or convenience, Graham?" I said. "Sometimes it seems to me that what people like you really mean is that kids and the old are inconvenient, annoying, nothing else."

Slender in a simple black tank suit, Janice Graham stood over the table toweling herself, her calm eyes considering me. Without a wig her hair was dirty blonde, a lot like Suzanne Dekker's from the picture but lighter. Her body had none of the cords and wrinkles of her neck. Slim and hard. The neck was the price of the slim body.

"News," she said to me, "or are you still working?"

"Both," I said.

"Wait, Jan," Jud Graham said. "You don't have a wife or kids, Fortune, how about a mother? Where is she now?"

"Dead," I said. "My father ran away from the world when I was a boy. My mother was young. I had 'uncles,' mostly cops because my father had been a cop and they were the men she knew, but she kept me with her until I went. She didn't live old."

"Then you don't know anything," Graham said.

"I'd have kept her with me," I said.

"It's easy to think so," Graham said.

Janice Graham sat down and sipped at his drink in the cooling evening sunlight. She didn't get a robe, sat with the towel around her shoulders. It made her very eye catching. That was probably why she did it instead of being warm in a robe. Graham seemed to notice and approve.

"What is the news?" she asked.

"That even the L.A. police now agree that it was someone who tried to use the Slasher as a cover, or maybe a copycat."

"I see," Janice Graham said. "You must have discovered something important to change their minds."

I told them both about Alan Welker and the wrong man being killed. "Welker looks like the key. I'm sure he's in Santa Barbara now, and he may have been New Year's weekend. Are you sure you never met or heard about an Alan Welker that weekend?"

"We never heard his name until you came," Graham said.

"And you had no contact with him since the murder?"

"Of course not!"

Janice Graham said, "We can't say that, Judson, we haven't the faintest idea what he looks like or sounds like, or anything about him. We wouldn't know him if he knocked on our door."

"Well," I said, and stood up to go, "if you do meet him, or hear anything about him, call me."

Janice Graham began to dry her hair vigorously. "What do you think he's in Santa Barbara for?"

"Either he knows something dangerous about the killer, the killer knows he does, so he's hiding. Or he killed Suzy Dekker himself, someone else is out to kill him, and he's hiding."

I left them in their enclosure, walked past the elegant party where the champagne and smoked salmon didn't seem to be making the old woman feel any better, and back out to my car. I drove up into the mountains along Sycamore Canyon, turned up Coyote Road, and into the dirt road to Henry Wayne's rundown ranch. I parked under the tall sycamores in front of the low stucco house in a deepening twilight.

This time I felt that sense of pleasant, benign living without any of the sensation of sudden silence and emptiness. The horses were out in the evening fields, the burros were quiet, and the cows chewed in front of the barn. Across the open corral, and beyond the barns and horse stalls, I could see a distant Henry Wayne out in a field. Through the haze of dusk children were gathered around him. He seemed to be telling them all a story, pointing to the fields and the mountains as he talked and the children listened with far off happy exclamations.

I started toward the field. Marian Wayne came out of the house and caught me at the corral. The sturdy red-haired woman wore the same sandals, and what looked like the same Mexican blouse and voluminous skirt but I knew wasn't because the colors were now green and orange. The blue eyes and weathered ranch-woman face looked toward her distant husband with the children in the field, and then up at me.

"We thought you'd left Santa Barbara, Mr. Fortune."

"I came back."

"For the same reason? That poor Dekker girl?"

"Same reason, only now I know it was the present not the past that killed her."

"You want to talk to Henry?"

"I've got some questions, a few facts to tell him."

She looked again toward where Wayne stood out in the fading dusk with the children. He was sitting on something now, maybe a boulder hidden in the grass, with the kids gathered around him listening raptly to some story. From time to time he touched one of the children.

"Could you talk to me?" Marian Wayne asked. "I mean, I'll try to answer any questions for him. We have no secrets."

"Everyone has secrets," I said. It sounded a little stupid even to me, a big cliché. But like most clichés it was true.

Marian Wayne was silent for a moment, maybe thinking about her own secrets.

"I suppose you're right, but Henry has fewer than most men, I think," the youthful woman said. "He's had a bad day with his mother, his job. A bad few weeks, I think. She's a hard woman, Eva."

"You don't like her very much?"

"I don't like her at all," Marian Wayne said. "Couldn't you just leave him alone with the children?"

"Tell him," I said, "that even the Los Angeles police now admit the Canyon Slasher didn't kill Suzanne Dekker, that it was someone using the Slasher's methods to cover up. Tell him a boy named Alan Welker from Regent Model Management is the key to the whole thing. I think this Alan Welker is in Santa Barbara hiding, and I'm going to try to locate him and talk to him. Ask him if he knows anything about Welker. Do you know anything about Alan Welker, Mrs. Wayne?"

"No, nothing at all," she said. "You ... you're implying that some-one in Santa Barbara killed that girl, aren't you? And that this Alan Welker knows who."

"That's one possibility," I said. "Another is that someone from out of Santa Barbara killed her, tried to kill Welker, and he ran up here to hide and contact me. Or he could have killed Suzy himself, and now someone who loved her wants to kill him."

She looked away from me. "You use that word so easily. I can't even think about it. *Kill.* Horrible."

"The word doesn't hurt anyone," I said. "Tell your husband to call me if he hears anything about Alan Welker."

"I will," Marian Wayne said. "Thank you, Mr. Fortune. His time with the children is important to him."

I nodded. She smiled and walked back to the battered old house. In time, she and Henry Wayne would make something of the rundown ranch. I looked across the corral to the field. Henry Wayne was standing and looking toward the corral. He had seen me. I nodded to him over the distance. He made no move. He only stood there in the far field, his children around him, staring toward me.

43

It was night when I drove out of Henry Wayne's ranch road, and everyone named on Alan Welker's list on the fashion show program I'd found in his room now knew I was looking to find Welker in Santa Barbara. I'd been to the beach club. That left Pietro's Shop out in its canyon, the San Marino Hotel, and El Mirador bar itself, as places where Alan Welker might have spotted me the first time and might be hoping to spot me again.

I was closest to Pietro's Shop, so I drove out and down into the dank canyon and had a beer. I was careful this time to keep my eyes on my glass. No one came close to me. I asked the bartender if he knew an Alan Welker. He didn't. I nursed the single beer for half an hour.

At the San Marino Hotel lounge the beer was better and the company better dressed. I sipped the beer and listened to the surf on the beach outside beyond the dark cottages and the boardwalk. Neither the surly desk clerk nor the bartender knew an Alan Welker.

El Mirador had the best beer and the most affluent patrons. It also had Marty and William Dekker seated on a couch in the big lobby room that served as a cocktail lounge. I took my beer and sat down facing them across a small table.

"How come?"

"To get the Subaru," Marty explained. "We've been calling your motel, but you've been out."

"Where have you been since Friday night, Dekker?"

"Working." The tall, dark-haired writer wore a denim suit with his western boots. "Writers do write sometimes."

"I hadn't noticed you doing much of that."

"That's why I had to this weekend."

"You ran off on me because you wanted to spend the last two days plus writing in your hideout?"

Dekker ate some of the oysters they sold in the lounge every evening at five. For the relaxed and affluent drinkers.

"I had to get to work," he said, "even if it meant neglecting Marty."

"I'll survive," Marty said.

"I expect you always will," Dekker said.

"Not like Suzy," I said.

Dekker ate a shrimp. "No, not like Suzy. Marty isn't going to meet the Canyon Slasher. She has so much more on her side than an eighteen-year-old prostitute with no parents, few brains, and little education."

"The Slasher didn't kill Suzy," I said, "and Alan Welker isn't dead. Or did you know that, Dekker?"

"No," Bill Dekker said, "I didn't know."

"You never told me," Marty said. "Who was killed?"

"A friend of Welker's named Oglesby. Probably by mistake. But Welker's alive, up here, and I'm going to find him."

"Find him?" Marty said. "Is he hiding, Dan? Why?"

"Because he knows something about the killer, and the killer is after him," I said, "or because he killed Suzy himself, and now someone close to her is trying to kill him."

Dekker drank his dark beer and ate the oysters and shrimp still on his plate. "If the Slasher didn't kill her, what did? Neglect, indifference, yes, but more than that. What we don't do, but also what we do. Family breakup, no discipline." His voice had taken on that deep tone I had first heard in Diane Pasco's Venice apartment.

"What killed her," I said bluntly, "was a 7.65-mm bullet from the same gun that killed the Oglesby boy and probably killed Alan Welker's father Clyde right here in Santa Barbara. A bullet, and a motive strong enough for murder in someone's mind. A motive maybe Alan Welker can tell me when I find him. Or a motive he had himself."

Dekker finished his beer. Marty waved to the waitress for another round of drinks.

"Not for me," I said. "You'll go back down tonight?"

"If the Subaru checks out," Bill Dekker said.

"I might wait until morning to drive it down," Marty said.

They were sitting silent over their fresh drinks when I left. I had shown myself where I wanted to. In the rented Chewy I drove back to the De Anza, locked my unit door, took off my jacket, turned on the TV, and got comfortable on the bed. There was no way of knowing when Welker would contact me, if he did.

The shows on the television were so much the same old one-dimensional dramas and canned-laughter comedies that I soon dozed and thought about Marty. Friday night there had been no sense of five years apart. Her face and body as they had always been in my mind and in all the dark store windows of cold New York winter streets. Could we be again what we had been? Why not? It was what I had hung onto all these years. The hope I had lived on day to day, a past more real than any present, the lost love.

Only as I lay there on the bed waiting for the light knock on the door, the cautious scratching on the window, the ring of the telephone, Marty's boyish smile faded into the almost sardonic smile, gaunt face, and angular body of Kay Michaels. I liked Kay Michaels. I wanted more of Kay Michaels. I wanted Kay Michaels in New York. I picked up the telephone receiver and dialed Los Angeles. But there was still no answer at the tall model's apartment.

I must have slept. I awakened with my hand on my old gun in its shoulder harness. The telephone was ringing.

"Yeh?" I said, my voice thick with the sleep.

"Dan? It's Kay Michaels. Asleep at this hour? What's her name?"

"Boring television," I said. "So I thought about you and dozed. I even called you."

"When?"

"Just a while ago. You must have just gotten home."

"I'm not at home. I'm in Santa Barbara."

"Why?"

"Maybe to give you another dream."

"Thought you were out of action."

"We could hold hands again," she said.

"Any time."

"But you're right. I really came up to see if I could get some lead on Kate Lennon for you. I thought she might have told someone up here where she was going, or left some address. But I haven't had any luck. No one seems to have seen her since last Friday, here or in Los Angeles."

"We'll find her sooner or later, Kay."

"Will we?"

"I hope so," I said.

I heard her breathe on the other end of the line. "You want to hold hands tonight? Maybe—"

"Yes," I said, "but we can't now. I'm waiting for a contact tonight."

"What contact? Who?"

"Maybe a witness, maybe a killer."

"Dan, don't! ..." I heard her breathe hard. "All right, I'll see you in Los Angeles."

"And later in New York?"

"And later in New York."

After she was gone, I hung up and thought about her. I didn't think for long. The telephone rang again.

"Fortune?" It was the same voice as on Friday. Male, low, and nervous. Unfamiliar, and yet not quite. I'd heard it somewhere before last Friday.

"Welker?" I said. "Where are you?"

"Not far. I still know about Suzy Dekker."

"I still want to know."

"What's in it for me?"

"Maybe your life," I said.

I could hear the sound of the surf in the background on the other end of the line where Welker was.

"I'm in the last house on Aurora Lane. One road past the San Marino Hotel. In exactly half an hour, and alone."

44

I checked my cannon and left the De Anza fifteen minutes after Alan Welker had called. It took five minutes to drive past the San Marino Hotel to Aurora Lane. I cut my lights, drove halfway along the lane toward the sea, parked in the shadows, and got out. Except for the steady breaking of the surf on the beach, there was no sound in the night, and no lights. A lane of small weekend houses, they were mostly empty on a January weekday night.

I walked along the dark road. There were no other cars. The last house stood above the beach with the line of surf behind it in the night. It showed a low light. I walked around to the back. Beside a closed garage, in the shadow of the palm trees, a red 1968 Mustang was parked. I knew where I had heard Alan Welker's voice before.

I knocked on the back door. A low voice spoke just on the other side of the door. "Fortune?"

"Yes."

The door opened a crack. Light from inside fell on my empty sleeve. The door swung open all the way. I went into a narrow kitchen and through into a living room where all the furniture had been covered for the winter.

"Whose house is it?" I asked.

He had followed me on into the living room.

"I busted in. Fifth empty house I holed up in."

He just stood there watching me.

"I should have known," I said.

He was the tall, blond youth I had met that first day in the alley below Diane Pasco and Suzy Dekker's apartment in Venice. The big, lean boy of twenty-three or so who had been polishing his red Mustang. So eager and helpful about Diane and Suzy that day, his round face and large blue eyes full of confusion when I asked too many questions. An ordinary and not too bright young man from Havre, Montana, who had been proud of being in "the talent line" but had lied about working for a TV or movie agency.

"You figured Frank was me," he said.

"Why did you lie about working at Regent Model Management?"

"You was askin' funny questions. I got to thinkin' I better clam up."

He hadn't been as confused as I'd thought that day. Now he was nervous, his big hands opening and closing spasmodically, independent of his mind or will. His clothes had been slept in for days, he needed a shave, and he seemed to be waiting for me to do something. As if he'd been running, hiding, and thinking for himself so long he desperately wanted someone else to tell him what to do.

"What happened to Oglesby?" I asked.

"I don' know," Welker said. That confusion in his blue eyes again. Thinking would always be hard for him, and he would never know that. "I mean, he got shot, on'y I don' know who it was, you know?"

"Why Oglesby?"

"I guess he wanted to shoot both of us, on'y I got away."

"Or maybe he only wanted to shoot you, Oglesby was a mistake," I said. "Maybe it was someone who liked Suzy Dekker too, maybe even loved her. Because you killed Suzy!"

The confusion left his big, round face, and his hands stopped their nervous twitching. A direct accusation was something to react to without thinking. Straight and simple.

"I didn't kill her! Why would I want to kill Suzy?"

"Because you loved her and she didn't love you," I said. "After she found her mother she had no more interest in you, dumped you, and you went crazy and killed her."

"*You're* crazy! She got killed 'cause of what she saw!"

His big, childish face was thrust toward me, the blue eyes wide and insistent. I let the loud echo of his voice fade into the silence of the dimly lit room and the low rumble of the surf out in the night.

"What did Suzy see?" I said.

"She said it looked like a fight, a beating, maybe a robbery. But after she got killed I figured it had to of been more, you know? I mean, she must of seen a killing!"

"Where?"

"Right here in Santa Barbara."

I sat down on one of the covered armchairs. "Start at the beginning. The whole thing."

Alan Welker nodded and sat down facing me. He leaned forward on the edge of the covered chair, his big hands clasped between his knees. "The way you said, Mr. Fortune, I liked Suzy a whole lot, but she never gave me much back. Then one day she showed me that picture she carried of her mother. I was sure right off I'd seen someone around the fashion shows up here that looked a lot like the picture. I mean, older sure, but not a hell of a lot different looking. Suzy always figured her mom could be around modeling and fashions, that's why she took up the modeling in the first place."

"Who up here looked like the photo?"

He shook his head. "I ain't sure, you know? I mean, I was only up here once before, for the shows more'n a whole year ago. I only saw that woman around a couple of times, she was too old for me so I didn't pay her much mind then."

"What about this year's shows? Didn't you spot her?"

"I didn't come up this year."

"You're sure about that, Welker?"

"Sure I'm sure. I didn't want anyone thinking about how Suzy got the assignment, you know? Especially old man Barton."

"And now? You've been up here some time now."

"My Dad 'n me come up last Thursday. We figured that list you swiped from my apartment, the one Suzy made on the show program, got to have the killer on it, you know? So we come up to snoop around while the killer thought I was dead. Only we didn't spot nothing about any killer, 'n we didn't see the woman."

"You've been snooping around Elite Imports, El Mirador Beach Club, and the hotels for five days and you haven't seen that woman?" I tried to see behind those empty blue eyes as he shook his head. It was hard to believe he hadn't seen the woman even once in five days. Unless she had changed her appearance, or hadn't been out in public since Suzy Dekker died.

"We just looked a day and a half," Alan Welker said, "then my Dad got killed, and I got so scared I been just hidin' out."

"How did your father get killed?"

He showed more reaction than usual on his dull face, rubbed at an eye. "Stupid! He didn't want me to talk to you, so he went to meet you first. I don' know how anyone knew we was meeting. He had to go 'stead of me!"

"We'll find the killer," I said. "Go on."

He sat there for a moment, a struggle on his still adolescent face. A transparent face that had trouble hiding things, and the confused battle of emotions was clear. Something was bothering Alan Welker. Maybe the conflict of talking on while remembering his father?

"We will get him, Alan," I said.

He nodded, looked up at me. "Yeh, sure. Anyway, Suzy come up here that weekend. I was in L.A. She got back the Monday, kind of real early, like she'd started down before dawn. She come to my pad, and she was all excited, but kind of nervous too, you know? I mean, almost scared. Happy, but … but—?"

"Worried?" I said. "Uneasy?"

"Yeh!" He nodded. "That's it, uneasy. Not real scared, just sort of uneasy. Like enough to take the shine off finding her mom after all them years."

"She really found her mother up here? You're sure?"

"That's what she told me," Welker insisted. "Found her, was gonna quit modeling, get out of L.A., start a whole new life. Her and her mom. Start over, only not right away, and it wasn't gonna be all simple. They had to get to know each other, and her mom had stuff to work out, so they wasn't going to tell anyone for a while. But she had to tell me 'cause in a couple of days or maybe a week she was leavin' for good to join her mom up north somewhere."

"Why not tell?" I said. "Why not stay with her mother?"

"I sort of wondered too," Welker agreed, licked at his lips as if they were bone dry. "She said she didn't stay because her mom got worried about what she'd seen. Her mom told her it could mean a lot of trouble for Elite Imports and for Suzy too, so she should go back to L.A. fast and they'd meet later in Frisco."

It had the sound of a stall, as if the long lost and still unknown mother had been playing for time. On the other hand, I had suspected some kind of trouble at Elite Imports all along. Or maybe it had been a combination of both.

"Exactly what did Suzy see up here?"

The big blond youth chewed at his dry lips and literally wrung his hands clasped between his knees. "She said she went to this house and got a real lead to the woman who looked like her photo, but she stayed too long, so had to run off to rehearsal and forgot her sweater. After rehearsal she went back. It was night and the house was dark. She looked around at the side and heard these violent voices. They came toward her, so she hid behind some bushes or a hedge, and saw it was two men. She said they was really arguing wildlike, and one of them hit the other with something. The one who got hit went down, and Suzy thought he took out a pistol when he was down but the other man hit him again, and again, and Suzy ran." Alan Welker twisted his hands between his knees. "She never did get her sweater back."

"That's all?" I said. "Who were the two men?"

"Suzy said it'd been too dark to see them, she wasn't even really sure they were both men. Maybe only one was."

"What house was it? Whose house?"

"I don' know, she never told me. Or maybe she did but I don' remember."

"Go on," I said.

He looked up at me. "Then she got killed! They said it was that crazy Slasher, but right off I didn't believe it, you know?" The big youth brushed at the air of the dim room. "I mean, I knew what Suzy did sometimes for a fast buck, what she was really sayin' when she said she was gonna quit 'modeling.' She didn't go out with no john that night. If she met a guy it was for somethin' else, you know? So I thought about her seein' what she did up here, went over to her pad to look, and found that program with the list of names."

"And took the list with you?"

His round face looked as foxy as it could. "I figured them names had to be the people she'd talked to up here about her mom, you know? I mean, one of 'em was probably in that brawl she'd seen, maybe two of 'em, and maybe what she'd seen was what got her killed."

He let it hang there in the small room. So did I. We both looked at it for a time.

I said, "You didn't tell the police what you thought? In fact, you didn't go to the police at all."

His blue eyes shined. "Not me, 'cause that's when I got the idea."

He watched me as if he was sure I could never guess what a great idea he'd had back then.

"A little blackmail." I said.

He went sullen and defensive. Sullen, I suppose, because I'd guessed his clever idea too easily, and defensive because my voice didn't sound too approving.

"Suzy was dead, it wasn't gonna hurt her, and it was maybe a gold mine, you know? A real chance to beat the action, get a big start! I mean, if one of those richies up in Santa Barbara killed her it'd be easy."

"Without even a name or a motive?"

"I didn't need to know all that! I mean, all it had to be was one of them names on the list and we was in!"

"We?" I said. "Oglesby?"

"Frank come in with me, yeh. I needed a guy could write real good, and it'd take maybe two guys to pull it off the way I had it figured out."

"Tell me," I said.

He was almost eager, even now. "Frank wrote up a letter and we sent it to everyone on the list, 'n even some that wasn't, like Graham's wife 'n Henry Wayne's wife: *Suzy Dekker brought something interesting down with her from Santa Barbara. For the right person it's a great buy. Come to her apartment in Venice. Come alone. Suzy and I talked, and I know how she died.* We figured that'd bring someone runnin' for sure!"

"It did," I said. "With a gun."

Some of his eagerness evaporated. "We sent the letters 'n took turns watchin' that apartment. That's what I was doin' the day you saw me. Just a guy out washin' his car, right? Frank used a cover, too, when he watched the apartment. I never did figure yet how we got spotted."

"Why was Oglesby in Unicorn Production's parking lot?"

"When I told Frank about you comin' to the apartment in Venice, he said maybe you was a scout sent by the killer! You'd asked all about Diane Pasco, so we figured if you was on the level you'd go to her studio to talk to her. If you didn't go, that'd mean you was playin' some kind of game, right? So we drove over to Unicorn—"

"You had the red Mustang when I saw you. Where'd you get the Datsun?"

"At my place. I never drive the Mustang at night if I can help it. That's when you get scratched, you know?"

"You don't want a classic scratched," I said.

"No sir! I mean, when you got—"

"Go on," I said. "You drove to Unicorn that night."

I brought him back to his story, to reality and the present. Reluctantly. He didn't want to come back, preferred to talk about his cars, any cars, not violence and murder.

"Yeh," he said. "So we got to the lot and saw your Subaru. That made you look on the up and up, but Frank thought maybe we better watch a while, since we was there, and see what you was up to. We hung around until the lot was pretty near empty, but you didn't show. Then there was just us, your Subaru, and some cars way across the lot behind the buildin', when Frank suddenly yelled and I saw this shadow and a gun shoved in the window on Frank's side."

As he sat there leaning toward me in the small room he began to sweat. A heavy sweat, beading and trickling. In memory of the past danger in that parking lot? Or did thinking about the parking lot remind him of present danger? Or maybe both.

"I ain't sure about anything after I seen the shadow and that gun," he went on, his wide blue eyes seeing that shadow and that gun. "I guess I took a dive out my side door. I heard Frank kickin' and grabbin', and then I heard a shot. God, I never knew a shot sounded so loud up close. I was out by then, and runnin'. I remember I slammed my door back and heard another yell, and then another shot, but nothin' hit me so I just kept on runnin'. I ran a hell of a way before I knew there was no one chasin' me." He was seeing the dark, silent streets of Hollywood now.

"I sat down right on the curb. I was shakin' bad 'n didn't even know for sure where I was. So I just sat there a while in the dark. Then I started to calm down 'n stop shakin' and I figured I had to go back and see what happened to Frank. It took a while to figure out where I was, and when I got back to the lot the cops was there. I heard 'em using my name! Then I saw Frank, 'n he was wearin' one of my jackets with the name tag my Ma sews in. The cops thought Frank was me! I didn't want to have to explain the whole thing to the cops, so I got out of there, and I still haven't figured out what went wrong."

The defeat on his face was too real to be a put on. He really didn't understand how his brilliant plan had gone wrong. I swore.

"Damn! What the hell do you think went wrong? The whole stupid plan was wrong from the start! Anyone could guess what you planned to do. The killer turned it around on you, found where you lived, and tailed you and Oglesby to the parking lot!"

"The plan was okay," he said. Sullen and stubborn, and yet I had the feeling that he didn't really mean it. Once, but not now. Everything had changed and his heart wasn't in it.

"Oglesby was dead, you were running scared, but you still didn't go to the police," I said.

"Because my Dad said we had it better than ever," Welker said. "I called him that night, told him the whole story, so he flew down from Montana. He said the killer thinkin' he'd shot me was great. If the killer was after anyone now it was Frank. I mean, maybe the killer knew what I looked like, but he'd think I was Frank, so if I kept out of sight any diggin' he did would lead to the wrong guy! Dad figured it'd keep the killer mixed up long enough for us to spot him and maybe make some big money. My Dad thought it was a real opportunity, you know?"

"A gilt-edged investment," I said. If he heard the edge in my voice he didn't respond. His mind was on other things. "So you and your Dad came up here after the killer, but he found you two first and killed again. Why did you want to meet me that night under the boardwalk?"

"Because I wanted for us to work together," he said. "You and me could clean up. I mean, you know how to handle this kind of thing, you know? You're smarter at it than me or Frank or even my Dad was. I mean, three murders, you know? We can really squeeze him now."

He'd seen too many bad movies and TV shows, read too many bad novels, listened to too many people with no more idea of right and wrong than a rabid jackal. He'd heard too much about the main chance, the big score, and all the other clichés of an amoral time in a material world. The new American dream.

"No police even when he killed your father?" I said.

"I … I still figured maybe we could team up," Welker said. "It's a real big chance."

"It's no chance at all," I said.

His head moved back as if he'd been slapped. Then he sat there with his head down and his big hands clasped together between his knees, the knuckles showing white.

"I guess you're right," he said. "We better go to the cops."

I felt my feet press against the floor of the dim room, the fingers of my solitary hand dig into the shrouded arm of my chair. Welker had stayed as far away from the police as a man could. No police—not for Suzy Dekker, not after Frank Oglesby, not for his father. Why now? His dreams of blackmail had cost him a lot so far, why give up so easily, so suddenly? He hadn't really tried to sell me. Not really.

"The police?" I said.

He stood up. He stumbled, caught himself. "Why not? You parked your car up the lane a ways? Out front?"

"The Mustang's closer."

"Like I told you, not at night, you know?"

Something was wrong. He was too nervous. In five days he hadn't found the woman who looked like Suzanne Dekker's snapshot. He didn't know who Suzy had seen in the violent fight, or what house it had been. He had told me everything and nothing. Now the police. Something wasn't right at all.

"Okay," I said. "My car and the police."

I stood up. He turned toward the front door. I hit him on the back of the head with my heavy old gun. He let out a cry, but he was a big, strong boy and only went down on one knee. I hit him again. He fell on his face, bleeding but still moving. I ran to the back door. If I was wrong I'd apologize, but I didn't think I was wrong, and out in the cool, dark night my face poured sweat. He'd given the one cry. If I was right, I didn't have much time.

The red Mustang stood ghostly in the moonless night. Beyond it the garage was dark, and the beach was wide and open to the right. There were trees and a high wall to the left, and behind me the house and the dark, deserted rural lane. Alan Welker had wanted me to go out front, and there was no cover on the beach. There was no safety in the Mustang or the garage, and no way to climb the wall with one hand. That left the trees. One with low enough branches hung over the flat roof of the house.

On the roof I lay flat over the back door.

I heard the footsteps inside the house. The quick steps of two people, sharp and echoing. A silence. Then the footsteps moving swiftly toward front and back, and a man came out the back door and stood in the light from inside. A man with a gun. The gun had a silencer.

The man was the tall man who had danced with the models that night in El Mirador bar. A man who, I knew now, had to have been in Pietro's Shop the day I was drugged, who drove a blue Chrysler, and who had to be the man Henry Wayne had met in the fog—the salesman for International Instruments Corporation, Joseph Murray.

A man who didn't hold his gun like a salesman.

Who waited in the night until a shadow came around the outside of the house from the front. A shadow with another gun.

They met at the back door below me.

I shot them both in the back.

Emptied my gun from four feet away.

When my hand and knees stopped shaking enough to reload, I climbed down. The tall man was dead. I bent over the other one. It was Henry Wayne. He was dead too.

I went into the house. Alan Welker lay on the floor where I had left him, but he wasn't on his face now, and he wasn't moving. He lay on his back with a single bullet hole in his forehead. I stood looking down at him. Then I sat down.

After a time I went out to my car and drove to the San Marino Hotel to call the police.

45

They read me my rights, gave me my phone call (to Marty at El Mirador, she and Dekker had stayed over after all), then put me in a private cell. I told Marty not to bother with a lawyer, the police and I had work to do.

"Henry Wayne and Murray must have killed them all," I said. "Suzanne Dekker because she witnessed something, Oglesby and the Welkers because they tried blackmail."

"What did the girl witness?"

"I don't know for sure. Some kind of fight or killing."

"Who is Joseph Murray?"

"I don't know that either."

"You don't know much."

"I know Alan Welker had me set up for them. Somehow they got to him, scared him or promised him a deal to finger me."

"Then they shot him?"

"He knew who they were."

"Pretty dumb kid."

"Pretty dumb," I said.

"But you're not dumb, are you, Fortune?"

"They were waiting to kill me."

"They were shot in the back! All six slugs!"

"I knew they were killers, I've got one arm. Warn them, try to take them, and I was a dead man."

After the first night they stopped questioning. They would check everywhere, talk to everyone. I began to fall into the power of the jail. Began to get the prisoner's sense of peace, of separation from an outside world, of detachment. Timeless, in a timeless world without responsibility, without pressure to perform. No sense of duty, no demands, nothing that must be done except the mindless and automatic routines. A microworld unrelated to a forgotten "reality." No more need to do the job, produce, perform. Floating beyond other people's reality, other people's truth so important on the other side of the walls.

A day. A night. The morning and noon of another day. And the one who came on the afternoon of whatever day it was had my old gun with him and a file folder. He opened the folder.

"The gun Henry Wayne was carrying was a 7.65-mm Mauser that shot Suzanne Dekker, Frank Oglesby, and Clyde Welker."

"Alan Welker?" I said.

"One shot from the gun on the man you call Joseph Murray."

"He'd only tried to put me out of action before," I said. "But if they had to kill me they had to kill Alan Welker too." I stopped. "The man I *call* Joseph Murray?"

"You're licensed in New York, it's legal to carry here, so we'll forget the gun. Lieutenant Stepanic in L.A. told us about you and Clyde Welker. You should have come in then, but we can forget that too."

"Tell me about Joseph Murray."

He looked out the high cell window as if he wanted to forget about Murray but couldn't. "International Instruments Corporation never heard of Joseph Murray. We checked their records. No Joseph Murray."

"No," I said. "I had a man call them last Saturday. They had a Joseph Murray then. A salesman."

The detective nodded. "Mr. Ed Green. They agree he called. They say either he gave the wrong name or their people heard it wrong. They have a George Murray. In their London office. Very much alive." He turned away from the window. "They say that either the man lied to Henry Wayne or Wayne lied to you. They flew in a top man, he couldn't identify the body."

"What identification did Murray have?"

"Driver's license, credit cards, health insurance, all with an address in Los Angeles. The L.A.P.D. checked the apartment. It was empty, stripped, and the landlord had no idea when Mr. Murray moved out. The landlord didn't know where Mr. Murray had come from or gone. He was staying up here in a motel on upper State. Nothing in the whole room older than yesterday."

"Rental papers on the L.A. apartment?"

"International Instruments given as place of work, two previous addresses in Tucson, Arizona. The Tucson cops found that no Joseph Murray ever lived at either place, no one there could identify pics of the body, and they had no Joseph Murray in their records."

"F.B.I.?"

"We sent his prints and a photo to the F.B.I., Internal Revenue, Treasury, Social Security, Pentagon, Veterans Administration, and the police of New York, San Francisco, Washington, and L.A. He fits no missing persons tracer, no one's come to claim the body." He turned back to the window. "We've got a body, a name, and an empty L.A. apartment. After that, Joseph Murray doesn't exist, and no one can identify the body."

"Or will identify the body," I said.

He took out a cigarette, gave me one, lit them both, and leaned against the cell wall. "The name's Trenka, Fortune. Captain Nils Trenka. They've held the inquest, verdict was self-defense, you can go any time you want."

"You've got the killers."

"We've got Henry Wayne and a body no one can, or will, identify. Wayne wasn't a man I'd have expected to kill anyone, and we don't know why he did. I don't like having a dead man someone doesn't want me to know anything about. It gives me a feeling that I'm being used, and I don't like that feeling. I want to know what it was all about."

"Do you have any John Does in your morgue?"

"Three." He moved from the wall. "Come on."

We collected my things in his office three floors below in the court-house and went out to his car. Santa Barbara County has no morgue so it uses Cottage Hospital on the west side. A modern hospital with a modern morgue. The first body was a bloated man in his late fifties with thick dirt under his nails and in the folds of his skin.

"Found knifed near the railroad tracks off lower Santa Barbara Street. Our hobo jungle."

The second was a woman. "Fell or jumped from the roof of the Californian Hotel on lower State. Found the Saturday of New Year's weekend. Not registered in the hotel."

Third and last a small, skinny man. "Found in the harbor a few days after New Year's. Fractured skull, other bruises. Lab says he'd been carrying a gun in his jacket pocket."

"Have you traced the gun Henry Wayne used?"

"No. It's not registered to Wayne."

I looked down at the third dead man. His thin face was scarred. There were more scars on his body, one a small welt like a burn inside his forearm. His sparse hair was gray-white. He didn't look like a man who would carry a gun or be found dead in a California harbor.

"What do they all say?" I said. "Wayne's wife, his mother, his sister, the Grahams?"

"We're wrong, he couldn't have killed anyone. No motive, no reason. He never had a gun. They don't believe any of it. Some mistake."

"Can I talk to them?"

"Any time."

Marty was waiting in the corridor when I walked out. She jumped up. Her eyes were wide with a kind of surprise as if she was startled to see me walk out without a striped suit and chains.

"I've been waiting since you called! Who was this Henry Wayne? That other man? Why did they kill Suzy?"

"I think because she witnessed an earlier murder. That weekend here in Santa Barbara."

"Witnessed?" Marty blinked. "That's all?"

"It happens," I said.

"Yes," she said. "So it's all over, Dan?"

"Not yet," I said. "Where's Dekker?"

"He went down to Malibu the night you were arrested," she said. "What else is there?"

"There's why," I said.

46

My rented car was in the police lot. I drove out to Coyote Road in Montecito and raised a solitary cloud of dust in the late afternoon on the dirt road into Henry Wayne's rundown old ranch. Under the two sycamores Marian Wayne stood in the open doorway. When I parked she had vanished. The children were playing in the field beyond the corral just where I had last seen Henry Wayne playing with them. I walked slowly to the house.

Marian reappeared with a knife in her hand. A kitchen knife. She came at me. I took the knife away from her. She turned and leaned her head against the wall of the low stucco house.

"I'm sorry," I said. What do you say to a woman whose husband you've killed? "There was nothing else I could do."

"You killed him!"

"I didn't want to."

I hadn't made her trouble, but I'd helped it along. You change things when you mix in them. I've said that before. Just by being part of something you affect it, change it, make it something it might not have been. If I hadn't been here Henry Wayne might or might not be dead. Maybe someone else would have killed him, or maybe he would have survived and gotten away with it. But I'd been called from New York, and Wayne was dead.

"Can I help?" I said. "I mean, are you fixed okay for—?"

"Blood money?" She looked at me and turned back to the wall. "We'll be fine. Eva will see to that. I'll have money, and I'll keep the house, and even go on fixing it up, and the children will go to college, and everything will be the same, except they won't have a father and I won't have a husband."

"I'm sorry," I said. I'd go on saying it.

"He never harmed anyone in his life." I heard the tears there behind her eyes, and maybe that helped her. She came away from the wall, looked toward the corral. "He was gentle, a builder not a destroyer. He loved life, children, animals. He lived for his children, for me, for the ranch."

"He murdered three people and tried to murder me."

"He couldn't have!"

"To hide another murder that Suzy Dekker saw."

"No!"

"Think about New Year's weekend, about the days since."

She sat down in the dirt under the old sycamores, her long red hair hanging down from her bent head, her peasant skirt spread around her as if she were a flower growing out of the ground.

"He's dead, can't you let him rest?"

Her voice came from beneath her hair, on an edge of tears.

"When a man makes me kill him I have to know why. I don't know why."

"So you'll feel better?"

"What would make him kill, Mrs. Wayne? Trouble at Elite Imports? In the family? With Judson Graham or his wife?"

"Nothing would make Henry kill."

"Money? His past?"

"No!"

"Your past?"

"No!"

"His mother? Eva Wayne? You don't like her, do you?"

She only shook her bent head.

"For his children?" I said. "To protect his family?"

Across the fields I heard the childish voices, high and happy without the artificial cares of growing up. These children were going to have to grow up faster and harder than most. After she told them. Maybe she'd lie. I hoped she would. Let them be happy another few years. Truth and life hit soon enough.

"He would have killed to protect his family," I said. I didn't need an answer, her silence now was enough. "That New Year's weekend, did he act strange any time?"

She raised her head. "Why should I help you?"

"To know why he did what it was impossible for him to do."

She brushed her long hair out of her eyes, traced a pattern in the dirt. "The Saturday night of New Year's. He came home almost violent, paced the fields in the dark. In the morning I found him asleep on the couch still in his clothes. When I asked he said he'd had a fight with Eva. He was strange all the time after that, except with the children. Brooding, working very hard downtown, going on trips, always preoccupied."

She looked around at the ladders against the house wall, at the tools rusting on the ground, at the whole ranch that was hers alone from now on. An expression of hope and loss on her weathered face. Like a refugee from an invasion returning to her empty village after many years.

"The man Henry called Joseph Murray," I said, "what did you really know about him?"

"Not much. He'd been around for years. At Elite, at Eva's, even here once or twice. He seemed close to Eva. No, not close, but familiar, as if they'd known each other a long time but didn't really like each other. He was a taciturn man, I can't recall him ever speaking to me. He never seemed to have anything in particular to do. He did come looking for Henry the Monday after New Year's. He seemed anxious to find Henry, but never said why."

That had been the day of the night Suzy Dekker was killed somewhere in Los Angeles.

"Thanks, Mrs. Wayne," I said. "And I'm very sorry."

"It doesn't help, Mr. Fortune. Even if he killed a hundred people I'd want him back and he won't come back. Not to me, not to the children." She was silent. "Someday I'll have to tell them the truth." Looked at me. "I don't envy you your work."

Later she would come to really hate me. She would forget what Wayne had done, forget that she had in the clarity of the tragedy understood what I had had to do, and I would become the man who had killed her life, killed her good man, and she would no longer believe there had been any reason. She would remember me as a killer, cruel and merciless, a destroyer.

But she had told me what I had needed to hear.

47

I made my calls from a pay phone in Montecito Village. Then I drove into Santa Barbara to the courthouse and Captain Trenka's office.

"I think I know what made Henry Wayne kill, and what Joseph Murray had to do with it all. Come on."

He came without asking questions, got into his car, and followed me back to my room in the De Anza In n. I went to the room phone. I dialed "9" for an outside line, then dialed the time. The recorded time kept repeating as I talked into the phone.

"I know about Joseph Murray and why Wayne killed that man in the morgue. Gerald Forbes is coming up from Los Angeles now. You've got a top man up by now, I'll give him an hour to contact me."

I hung up. Trenka looked at the silent telephone.

"The killers beat me to Alan Welker twice," I said. "Once could be chance, twice had to be something else."

"A bug on your phone here?"

"Probably at the motel switchboard."

I poured three glasses of Irish, gave one to Trenka, kept one, and let the third stand untouched. I took soda, so did Trenka. We drank slowly, talked about California weather, New York weather, and the way the country was becoming so homogeneous neither looking out the window nor talking to people told you where you were. We both regretted the passing of regions. The knock came half an hour later. I opened the room door.

"Mr. Fortune?"

He was a large man. Graying, well dressed in a conservative brown pin stripe with vest and Ivy League tie. A one-time football player from a good college, now vice president of a large company or president of a small one. Only he was none of those, except maybe the one-time football player, and he had a gun under the pin stripe. Behind him a long black car was parked parallel to my unit. A driver sat in the front seat. He would have a gun too, but it wouldn't be under his coat now. It would be aimed, unseen, at me.

"Right," I said. "Come in. Drink? I've got Irish."

He took the drink, nodded in appreciation as he tasted it, and sat down. He looked at me, and waited.

"About halfway along," I said, "I realized that there were two forces working. One violent, murderous. The other silent and efficient. That was Murray, right, Mr.—?"

"Jones." He smiled. "Murray was our man, yes."

"Yes," I said. "The Central Intelligence Agency. C.I.A."

"Jones" sipped his Irish. "Murray had no orders to kill. He used bad judgment, was carried away by the need to do his job. Understandable in a way, we train our men to do the job."

"No orders," I said, "but if he'd managed to hide everything you'd have given him a medal."

He shrugged. "Probably."

"Henry Wayne killed Suzy Dekker, but it was Murray who covered by imitating the Canyon Slasher. Right?"

"Yes," Jones said.

"Who's the dead man in the morgue?" I said. "The little man they fished out of the harbor. The man with the scar on his arm where the tattooed number was burned off."

"Ludwig Scharf," Jones said. "He came to break our operation. Photographs, documents, the works. Wayne killed him. Murray had no part in that, but he stripped identification and dumped the body in the harbor. Wayne learned that the Dekker girl had seen him kill Scharf, located her, and shot her with Scharf's gun. Murray was too late to stop him, but conceived the plan of making it look like another Canyon Slasher victim." Jones nodded approvingly. "That was excellent field improvisation, but later that young fool sent his blackmail letters, Wayne slipped Murray and shot the Oglesby boy." He shook his head. "Not a very well-handled operation by then."

"Sloppy," I said. "Regrettable."

He looked at me over his whisky, but went on. "Murray's immediate job was to prevent exposure of an on-going operation. He enlisted aid from L.A. to watch the Dekker and Pasco women who were causing trouble. They spotted you, tried to discourage you at Welker's apartment. When you came up here Murray attempted to neutralize you with a car accident. When that failed, he must have decided it was necessary to kill you and Alan Welker. He did not clear that decision with us."

"You would have stopped him?" Captain Trenka said.

Jones put down his glass. "Captain, any decent agent knows that you must finish a job. You can't leave any loose ends, trust to chance, promises, or even bribes. People don't stay bought. When you do a job you must clean out all possible problems. A final solution. But no more than that, nothing unnecessary."

He picked up his glass, drained it. "This entire affair was botched. Ludwig Scharf should never have reached Henry Wayne. When Murray let Scharf get to Wayne he opened the floodgate. Wayne went crazy, panicked, and Murray overreacted."

"Counterproductive," I said. "What happens with Murray now? How do you explain his death? Whoever he really was."

"He was killed in the line of duty in enemy territory, was buried there. Medal, pension, and memorial."

"Enemy territory? California?"

"Everywhere we work is enemy territory, Mr. Fortune."

"Yes," I said. "Of course."

I stood up to pour fresh drinks when we all heard the car stop outside. I waited until the door opened and a short, muscular man with steel-rimmed glasses and a brusque manner came in. Mr. Jones nodded to him.

"Hello Forbes," the C.I.A. man said. "You got here fast."

"Fortune called Washington. I happened to be in L.A., they put him onto me, and I came running for this one.

"Yes," Jones said.

I introduced the muscular man to Captain Trenka. "Gerald Forbes from the Office of Special Investigations, Justice Department. Some Irish, Forbes?"

He shook his head, "Let's get at it."

Jones got into his chauffeured car, Forbes went back to his, and Captain Trenka brought up the rear as I led the way into the city. Trenka stopped at the courthouse for two deputies in a squad car.

48

Gerald Forbes stared for a full minute at the woman working in the garden in the low early evening sunlight.

"Eva Beck. Reported killed fighting beside her husband in Berlin in 1945. Her body wasn't found so the books were kept open. We knew that if she was alive she was being protected."

Helga Kasmer had opened the door of the big Victorian house. She had stood there all in black, heavy and silent, and looked at each of us in turn. Then she had led us through the dim house and out into the garden where I had first seen Eva Wayne. In the incredible but precise profusion of rigorously tended plants the tall, erect old woman was pruning her roses this time. In her smock, on her canvas stool, cutting away dead wood. When Forbes spoke she turned to look at him. Then at me, at Captain Trenka and the one deputy, and finally at the C.I.A. man, Jones. She looked at Jones for some time.

"Eva Beck," Gerald Forbes said. "Born in an ethnic German area of Croatia on December 12, 1904. That was the Austro-Hungarian Empire then, and her father fought in the Austrian Army in World War I. Later he fought for the Poles against the Red Army of Budenny, and then turned up in one of the Free Corps of Germans like so many of the future senior SS officers. Bitter freebooters looking for success and a leader. But Rudolf Beck died in a street brawl in Danzig, and Eva bounced around among German relatives and fascist groups. In 1936 she showed up in the SS at Sachsenhausen, by 1939 in Buchenwald, 1941 in Treblinka, and in 1944 Auschwitz under Mengele himself."

On her stool Eva Wayne continued to trim and prune, methodical and silent.

"She was married in 1939 to Bjorn Kasmer, an early Norwegian Fascist volunteer who served first in the regular SS, then in the Fifth SS Panzer Division 'Wiking,' and later in the Eleventh SS Volunteer Division 'Nordland.' She had a daughter in 1940. At Auschwitz she used to stand behind Mengele as the men, women, and children were marched in and separated into those who could still work or be used for his horrible experiments and those who would be exterminated immediately. She often stood with her small daughter beside her dressed in an identical little black SS uniform. That was how she got her name from the inmates—Mother Death."

The sun was all but gone now, the last rays slanting through the palms and olive trees in the back garden, giving the thick vegetation the aura of a savage jungle half in shadow. In the half-light, Eva Wayne spoke with her back to us.

"My maiden name was Eva Bauer. I was born in Dresden, not Croatia. I have never been in those places, I did not do those things. I was in the SS with Kasmer, we served our country, the rest is lies. They always make up lies about the SS. In the SS we were only soldiers like any other."

In the fading light of the city the only sound in the back garden under the palms and the flowering hibiscus was the low growl of the dog under its hedge. It did not like so many people in a small space. The deputy watched the dog with his hand on his pistol. The rest of us watched the rigid back of Eva Wayne as she went on pruning her roses. Helga Kasmer seemed to watch no one and nothing in particular. She had not spoken since we arrived, and now her voice was a strange monotone.

"Sometimes I think I can still see their faces as they come in through the gates, the barbed wire. Pale faces, hopeless and afraid yet trying to somehow comfort the children. I was only five in 1944, but I think that sometimes I really do remember. So many faces, like dark visions in a fog, all passing me to meet death as I held her hand all black above me."

The C.I.A. man, Jones, said, "Miss Kasmer suffers from hallucinations. The war years were hard at the end. She was too young to remember anything."

"I remember a girl," Helga Kasmer said in her monotone. "She was no more than ten or eleven. She broke some rule, and my mother took her out in front of the camp and hanged her. There were no children in that camp, only Jews and Slavs and communists and criminals. I remember that girl."

Eva Wayne paused in her pruning, the shears suspended in the fading light. Was she remembering that hanged girl?

"Eva Beck's fingerprints are known," Forbes said. "There are identifying marks, witnesses from the camps, and surviving SS men who will point to her."

Eva Wayne returned to her gardening. Jones sat down on the back steps in the dusk, closed his eyes.

"Why hide her?" I said. "Protect her all these years?"

Jones sat with folded arms, silent.

"It's not hard to construct the scenario, Fortune," Forbes said. "Captured by the O.S.S. at the end of the war, and became a valuable anti-communist tool. Probably had Gestapo information on the Soviet secret police, the German communist underground, other radicals and socialists, and contacts with the anti-communists in her native Yugoslavia and other countries. A contact with the opposition behind the Iron Curtain ever since. In return the C.I.A. brought her to the U.S., hid her, helped her to prosper, and protected her. I've seen it many times."

The twilight seemed to hold us all in a great hand of darkness with a glow of light all around. There was no wind, the plants of the garden standing motionless. Only Eva Wayne moved, pruning her roses. I turned to Helga Kasmer.

"What happened to Henry?"

"The little man came here that Saturday afternoon," the tall, heavy woman in black said. "With his scarred face and his worn old suit.

Mother assumed he had come to blackmail, she understands that kind of thing. She told Scharf to return that night, and called our C.I.A. friends. Two things went wrong. Mr. Murray did not respond in time, and Ludwig Scharf did not want money. He wanted the world to know that Mother Death was alive and enjoying a tranquil old age in the paradise of southern California. He wanted the voices from the grave to rise and destroy her. He wanted justice."

Helga Kasmer watched her mother. I suppose that no matter how old we get, or what we think of our mother, we still have to talk to her and hear a response. Helga Kasmer got no response.

"Then," she said, "Henry arrived at the house."

Captain Trenka filled his pipe. Jones seemed to be asleep on the back steps. The last glow of day hung like a pale shroud over the mountains to the west, and Helga Kasmer's voice came now out of the night itself.

"I had always known about Mother Death, most of it, despite the biography the C.I.A. invented for her. She was always good at languages, and English was her best; but at first she still had an accent so they built a half-true biography for her, complete with fake fingerprints and forged SS papers, as the loyal wife of honest right-wing Norwegian Bjorn Kasmer who had the courage to act on his beliefs and join the Nazi armies and die fighting bravely. Eva Bauer who had fought honorably for the Fuhrer but had seen the truth and had come to America to start a new life as a good anticommunist democrat."

If Eva Wayne heard her daughter she gave no sign. From time to time she paused in her work and glanced around her darkening garden with an expression of satisfaction. There was a detachment about her, as if the Eva Beck we all talked about didn't exist, or was of no interest to her. Left behind in some far away time and place. Unconnected to today.

"I tried to run away from what I knew twenty years ago," Helga Kasmer said, "but I found I couldn't. I could never escape what she had done, what she was. The horror was too large. I knew, and that made me an outsider no matter where I went. I couldn't run away, and

I couldn't denounce her. All I could do was live alone, never pass the horror on to anyone else, to innocent children. AH I could do was live alone but near her, a living accusation to her."

Let herself become too heavy, wear shapeless clothes, never groom herself, the rejection of anyone's interest or desire. Her life determined by her mother's life. Horrified and haunted, carrying her mother's guilt as her whole existence. Unable to live in today, unable to escape those past years and her mother. An outsider everywhere. Inhuman. Hating her mother, and yet only with her mother could she feel human.

"But Henry didn't know the truth," Helga Kasmer said. "He didn't know about Mother Death. He only knew the story they had invented of the misguided fellow-traveler Eva Bauer and her SS husband, and even that had made him feel guilty as a boy. But his father, Wayne, had forgiven this bland past, so Henry got over it finally. But it hadn't been easy for him."

She looked at Trenka and me. "Can you imagine that Saturday night of New Year's when he saw the past as it had really been? Pictures, statements, documents, statistics. All those terrible, endless numbers. The faces. The hanged children. The voices from beyond the grave. There was no way Henry could accept it. No way he could ever live with it."

I saw Henry Wayne in my mind. Not the Henry Wayne with his gun at the beach house or slipping through the fog, the Henry Wayne who played in his fields with his children and rebuilt his house with his own hands. Mother Death within those barbed wire gates condemning the stream of victims to slow death or quick death but always and without exception to pitiless death. He had to reject it and hide it, both at the same time. Something had to break, and it broke inside his head. It could not be true—and no one could be allowed to know about it.

"I don't think he meant to kill Scharf," Helga Kasmer said, "and Eva was furious. The C.I.A. would have handled Scharf, that was their job. Somewhere else, quietly." She looked at Jones, but the big C.I.A. man sat on the steps in his elegant pin stripe with his eyes closed as if he had to sleep where he could. "But Henry killed Scharf. After he had denounced him, cursed him, begged Eva to deny it all, to explain that Scharf was all wrong. Eva said nothing. She just sat in the living room that night with the dog at her feet, denying nothing and explaining nothing."

Eva Wayne paused now in her work to examine a particularly old bud union in the last light of day. Then she firmly cut a thick cane back to the union itself.

"So Henry killed the little man," Helga Kasmer said. "In the side yard in a violent argument, a sudden rage. He hit him and hit him. Scharf had no chance to use his gun."

A sudden insane rage striking out to kill not Ludwig Scharf but the past, the truth, Mother Death. Insanity, accident, even self-defense—Scharf had a gun. Perhaps he could even have gotten away with it, acquitted, and at worst manslaughter. But then the truth, the past, would come out, and that could never happen. To admit that he had killed Scharf, to let anyone know what he had done, meant letting the world know why he had done it, and that the world must never know. His wife must never know. His children could never know they were the grandchildren of Mother Death! He had to protect his wife and children at any cost.

"Murray, Eva's watchdog, came too late, but he took charge and somehow covered all traces of Ludwig Scharf—his car, where he'd been staying, everything. Wiped him off the face of Santa Barbara and any connection to us. Eva and Henry were safe, and then Henry found out that Suzanne Dekker had seen him kill Scharf. She could connect him to Ludwig Scharf, and if she did the whole story would come out."

I said, "And we know the rest. He killed Suzanne Dekker, Murray tried to hide that behind the Canyon Slasher, Alan Welker blackmailed, Henry killed twice more and Murray went on covering it all up to the point of killing Alan Welker and trying to kill me. You all knew what had happened, yet you covered it up. You all knew when Alan Welker sent his blackmail letters, and still you hid it, lied, made up stories about trips to L.A."

"He was my brother," Helga Kasmer said.

"And Eva's your mother," I said. "Maybe you really want it all forgotten too."

"I've spent my life atoning for her guilt! Alone. I've been her conscience. Isn't that enough?"

"I don't think so," I said. "She has no conscience."

And suddenly it was night, the house and garden in complete darkness. Then strong spotlights came on at each corner of the big house, bathing the garden in a bright glare like a flare above a battlefield or the lights of a concentration camp. I saw a flicker in the eyes of Eva Wayne, as if for one instant she was remembering the lights and the barbed wire of so many years ago. In the glare, Jones opened his eyes, stood up.

"So you know," he said. "What do you plan to do?"

"She'll be deported to either Germany or Poland," Gerald Forbes said, "depending on which indictment takes precedence."

"You know what would happen to her in Poland," Jones said.

"She'll get a trial," Forbes said. "Probably a fairer trial than she and her Nazis ever gave their victims."

"We'll fight you," Jones said. "We made a commitment to her, we'll keep it."

"Fair play and morality, Jones?" I said.

"Your absolutism doesn't interest me," Jones said. "We protect the nation, we don't ask those who help us who they are or what they've done at other times, we keep our word to them."

"They'll hide her again," I said to Forbes, "if they can."

"I'll handle that," Captain Trenka said. "Withholding evidence, accessory both before and after, even conspiracy. That should hold her until Forbes gets his papers ready."

"Let Miss Kasmer stay free." I said. "Someone has to feed the dog."

Jones's manner changed. I had the feeling that he was suddenly fighting for himself. Someday it could end this way for him. The understanding of one elite guard for another.

"Eva's nearly eighty," he said. "She's lived a different life for thirty-five years. A straight, normal, hardworking life. She won't have a lot longer. She hardly remembers those days."

With full darkness Eva Wayne had put down her pruning tools. In the glare of the floodlights she opened a box and began to clean and oil her tools. She had a small, thin smile, but there was no way of knowing if the smile had anything to do with what was happening, no way to know if she had heard anything or not.

"We want her to remember," Gerald Forbes said, "and I wonder about her normal, hard working life. I have a feeling that her import business owes more than a little to her old Nazi and SS contacts. They're all over South America, they had the capital they managed to get out of Germany, and they know how to exploit cheap native labor, eh? I expect her business is based on those old contacts."

Jones looked up at the spotlights on the corners of the old house, watched them. "She's lost her son, her daughter hates her. Isn't that enough? What did she do that thousands didn't do in those days? What thousands are still doing all over the world. What we'll always do. In thirty-five years she's hurt no one. Contacts, profits, exploitation? That's how business operates. She has a business like any other. She was no Heydrich, no Eichmann. She did her job."

Eva Wayne on her canvas stool paid no more attention to Jones defending her than she had to Forbes accusing her or her daughter condemning her. She wiped her garden tools one by one with the oily rag and put them carefully away in the box.

"She's not Heydrich, or even Mengele," I said. "She may not even be a monster, but she served monsters, and that's why I'd have to blow the whistle if she were a hundred, on her death bed, and couldn't remember even last year. She's got children, a business, neighbors just like everyone else, and that's why I have to turn her in. She's a murderer, and we don't just live in time, we live in space, and in space her crime is constant. They died today, those murdered men, women, and children."

Forbes said, "We have to bear witness, Jones. We have to remember. As long as one Nazi lives we have to expose him so that those millions who died aren't forgotten. As long as we remember her we remember them. They were really here among us. When we forget the first SS killer then we forget the victims, they never passed this way with us, there was no horror. To stand up and point the finger is to remember that hanged child, the grandfather beaten to death, the gassed mother. They lived among us."

Eva Wayne oiled her last set of shears, wiped them, and put them into the box. She closed the box and sat looking at it.

Jones said, "The past is past. It's no danger. My job is to protect us from today's horrors not yesterday's. You had some murders to solve, you've solved them. The rest is just revenge."

"You'll never understand what we're talking about any more than Eva Beck," Forbes said. "You'll always be 'Mr. Jones,' nameless, doing your job no matter who tells you to do it or what it is you're told to do."

We stood there under the glare of the spotlights that cast a cold, eerie light over the lush garden with its profuse, orderly plantings. All I could think of was the barbed wire, the towers, the desolate landscape that was the final world of so many. The machine guns and the floodlights.

Eva Wayne removed her gardening gloves and stood up. She took off her smock, folded it, and folded the canvas stool.

"You'll have to shoot the dog," she said. "He won't be fed by Helga or by anyone."

"We'll send the Humane Society," Captain Trenka said.

"Only they don't shoot them," I said, "they gas them."

It was a mean shot, but I'm human, and all at once I had seen Eva Wayne clear. What she had done thirty-five and more years ago destroyed her son and determined her daughter's life, but for her it had never been more than an episode, an incident, in her whole life. She wasn't haunted, she wasn't horrified, she felt no guilt. Something that happened, no more. A time and a circumstance, she had done what she was supposed to at that time and in those circumstances, and when it ended she went on with her life as most people do. An ordinary human being, doing what she had to.

She didn't even glance toward me as she went into the big house with Captain Trenka. Helga Kasmer turned on the lights, got her mother's coat. Eva Wayne followed Trenka out to the police car. A group of neighbors had gathered around our cars. The old man who had been across the street the first day I came to the house was with them, and now I knew why he had been belligerent when he saw me nosing around Eva Wayne's house and asking questions. He knew about Eva Wayne, they all did. The bland official "confession" of her Nazi past the C.I.A. had cooked up to whitewash her by admitting small guilt, and now they saw our array of official cars and were rallying around to defend her against persecution.

"Why don't you just leave her alone!"

"She's a damned good neighbor. You should be so good!"

"I don't believe she did half of what you people say!"

"Those commies are always telling lies!"

When they had Eva Wayne in the police car, I got back into my rented car and we all drove off into the Santa Barbara night.

49

At the courthouse Mr. Jones did not come in with us. His long black car with its silent driver went on past and vanished in the night in the direction of the freeway. He had a lot to do if he was going to save Eva Wayne from being deported.

I dictated my statement. Captain Trenka said I could return to sign it later. He and Forbes had Eva Wayne now, my job was over, and I had a client to report to.

At El Mirador Hotel I found them in the lounge again. I sat down, ordered a cold beer, and told them.

"She saw this Wayne kill some man who wanted to expose his mother as a Nazi?" Marty said. "Poor Suzy."

"His mother, himself, his children," I said. "I think that's what drove him over the edge, his children growing up with Mother Death hanging over them, always part of them. A horror like that, knowing it, knowing *they* were part of it. The world knowing."

"Just another victim of the Nazis," Marty said. "Maybe the last victim."

"No, Henry Wayne himself is the last," I said.

"Mother Death," Bill Dekker said. He seemed to roll the name on his tongue as if listening to the sound, the impact. He sighed and shook his head. "Witness to a mundane murder, and a cover-up by a stupid C.I.A. man. Hell."

"Can't use any of it, can you?" I said. "Not for the big book. Maybe for another one, a thriller, but not for the big one."

"Book?" Marty said. "What are you talking about, Dan?"

"The book he's writing," I said. "That's what he's been doing, working on his next novel. Suzy's death must have given him the idea. All that talk about where are our children."

Marty looked at Dekker.

"He's been running around," I said, "following me, watching. To get material for the book, ideas, colorful incidents, scenes."

Dekker said, "A writer has to gather his material, Fortune, move around in the world. Find what's worth writing about, what people will want to read about."

"And you found a book in Suzy's death," I said. "Our wandering children, the decay of the family, the abandoned, the fakery of self-realization. Guilt, love, violence, sex, and gore."

"A hell of a book!" Dekker said. "A big book. I know what I have to do to be a writer in this country. I'll write a book they'll all drool to read."

"Before you even write it," I said. "You go the Hollywood huckster one better, don't you? Those letterheads you had printed with that slogan on top: *Where are your children?—Watch for the BIG one!*" I took a long drink of my cold beer. "I can see all those promotion blurbs now: SOON TO BE A MAJOR MOTION PICTURE. But you top that, right? SOON TO BE A MAJOR NOVEL! One hundred thousand dazzling words. Count 'em. One hundred thousand gorgeous words! All yours when you read THE BIG BOOK! A major event soon to burst on the country. Watch this space for more exciting details."

Dekker watched me in the quiet lounge with its hum of low conversation and soft tinkle of ice in glasses. Marty had begun to tear a paper napkin into small pieces. Dekker drank.

"I want my share of the cream," he said. "I want the gold. Why should only the doctors and lawyers get rich from their work? If an artist's work is true and honest and beautiful it will be recognized eventually? Shit, you hear? In this country now the market is too big. If you're not known early you'll never be known because you'll never be published! If by luck you are published you'll wait forever for the lightning to hit. You've got to be the lightning, shout yourself from the rooftops. The big public takes a man at his own estimation. Tell them you're a great writer and you are a great writer. Keep quiet, do your work, and no one'll know you're alive today."

"Sell before you write," I said, "and you'll never know what you can write."

Our voices had risen in the hushed lounge, and people were looking at us. Marty slowly stirred her whisky and soda. I finished my beer. Dekker drained his glass.

"You thought I could have killed her, didn't you?" he said to Marty.

"Yes," she said.

"And all I was doing was writing a book."

"You could have told me."

"No," Dekker said, "I couldn't."

"It's too bad you can't use what happened then."

"I can use what might have happened. Another round?"

As he walked to the bar he smiled at everyone he passed. A tall, slim, handsome man with dark eyes, an expensive vested suit, western boots, and a manner that knew all eyes were on him.

"It's not going to work," Marty said.

"I'm sorry," I said.

"So am I," she said. "Us?"

"Always us," I said.

"Always how, Dan?"

"How do we want it?"

"Does it matter? How?"

"I'm not sure," I said. "I think so."

She looked away toward where Dekker was standing at the bar talking to three men. Holding forth, his fine *hidalgo* hands describing sweeping vistas in the air, his dark eyes brilliant, his words flowing in a confident stream. He was smooth and dazzling and all surface. I wondered if his writing was all surface too?

Marty read my mind, or I had read hers. "The odd part is he's a hell of a good writer. He may be great, if he doesn't destroy himself with hype and promotion first." She looked back to me. "Turn in your rental and use the Subaru. I'll go back to Malibu with Bill. Drive the Subaru down and I'll pay you. Then we can talk."

Dekker brought the drinks. He was keyed up, all about his new novel, the abandoned children, our guilt. It was sure to be a block-buster. Marty and I drank and listened. Suzy Dekker seemed long ago, far away. Forgotten, if he'd ever really remembered her. I finished my beer and left them together.

I drove to the De Anza to pack before I made one more stop and then signed my statement at the Courthouse. Kay Michaels was sitting on my bed.

"Look what I found," she said.

Kate Lennon sat in a chair.

"Where?" I said.

"Right here at Elite Imports."

Kate Lennon grinned. "I forgot my check when I left. I must have been in a hurry."

"Which check?" I said.

"The company one, I'm not an idiot." She laughed. "I got the other check before I ever told you that dumb story."

"Lucky," I said, and told them about Henry Wayne, and Joseph Murray, whoever he had been, and Alan Welker.

"Good God," Kay Michaels said, whispered.

"Hey," Kate Lennon said, stood up, "I didn't know anything about all that!"

"No," I said. "You just helped them do it."

Kay Michaels said, "He *was* acting oddly for him, Henry Wayne, not himself at all. I never thought about it, Dan."

"Why would you?" I said. "You didn't know him that well."

"I suppose not," Kay said. "Why—?"

Kate Lennon said, "He sure acted funny when he came to me that morning after taking you out. I was going to throw him out until he started talking extra money for a little job of acting. That's what I'm really going to be, you know? An actress." She grinned again. "Hey,

I was pretty good, you know?" She went wide-eyed and innocent in imitation of herself telling me the phony story." 'No, except maybe that she didn't want to be found.' I thought that line up myself." She laughed again.

"They told you what story to tell me, but not why?"

She nodded. "Wayne took me to the C.I.A. guy, and he, the C.I.A. guy, gave me a lot of jive about spies and national security. I didn't believe it much, but I believed the money. So I did their little job for them, and then got lost the way they wanted it. That's the whole story."

"You could have told it sooner, Kate," Kay Michaels said.

"Staying out of sight was part of the deal."

"So I'd go off in the wrong direction looking for her," I said. "Another trick to get me out of the way while they found and killed Alan Welker."

"Hey, it didn't work, right?" Kate Lennon said. "Everything turned out okay. I got paid, and the good guys won anyway."

With a wink to Kay Michaels, she walked to the motel room door and out. She'd go far in this world. With a little luck.

"Sweet kid," Kay Michaels said.

"Sweet kids don't go far out here, or anywhere."

"How far do you think I'll go?"

"You're not a kid. As far as you want to go."

"That's the first time I've been told I'm not so young and it's been meant as a compliment," Kay said. She smiled at me. Then she stopped smiling. "Why did Wayne do it, Dan? There's something missing. I know why he killed Suzanne Dekker and the others, but why did he kill that man in the first place?"

I told her about Eva Wayne, or Eva Beck. All of it. She was silent for some time. She got up from the bed and walked to the one window and looked out as if she had to reassure herself that the world was still there.

"How can people do such things to other people?"

"Easily, it seems," I said. "They don't think of them as people. Not human beings like themselves, like *us*. It didn't begin with Hider and the SS, it hasn't ended with Hider and the SS, but that doesn't mean that one single SS man or woman can be forgiven or forgotten."

"The children, Dan! How? ... No, I suppose if I could understand it at all I'd understand about the children. I don't understand, I hope I can never even begin to understand." She turned from the window. "I want to just walk a long way all alone, Dan. Not have to talk to any people. No people at all. Just the sky and the mountains and the sea and the trees and even the concrete." She crossed to the door. "Will I see you in L.A.?"

"I think so," I said. "In New York too?"

"I think so," she said.

After she had gone I smoked a cigarette. I thought about her, and about Marty. Then I took a long, hot shower, dressed again, and went back out to my car. Later, after I'd signed my statement for Captain Trenka, I'd pick up the Subaru and have the motel clerk return the rental car in the morning.

But now I had one more stop.

50

The unique and bizarre concrete-and-glass castle stood high on its mountain slope above the winding road. A giant shadow in the night showing light through its wide picture windows like a dragon in the dark. Its gray squares and circles and angles were shadowy as I drove up the twisting driveway, and it looked like some prehistoric beast, an ancient demon. Far below a sweeping crescent of light stretched from the oil platforms in the channel across the snake of the freeway and the mass of the town to distant lights in the mountains to the west. The view and the house of a man who could have everything.

Judson Graham himself opened the door. He stood in that head-tilted-back manner of his. Big and burly, his voice curt.

"What do you want, Fortune?"

"So you heard about Eva Wayne?"

"Helga called us. Wasn't Henry Wayne enough blood for you?"

"Can I come in?"

He would have said no, it was all over his face, but he had some anger he wanted to vent and I was an audience. He walked ahead of me into the mammoth living room with its daring paintings. Janice Graham sat near the dark picture window that spanned the whole width of the room. Tall and slim, she wore a dark wig now, and a soft purple houserobe. She did not turn, but sat looking out at the world beneath her. Graham glowered at me.

"You solved your damned murders. A two-bit prostitute and three blackmailers!"

"With no help from any of you," I said. "You could have saved time and maybe some lives. Alan Welker, Wayne, and that CIA man could still be alive. You all knew who Suzy Dekker was, you knew someone up here had killed her if not who or why, and you knew about Alan Welker's blackmail. I know why Eva Wayne and Helga had to lie, they had Wayne to protect. But why did you two have to lie? What did you have to protect?"

"I never lied! I said I barely remembered the girl and I didn't. I knew nothing about her murder or about blackmail."

"No," I said. "You got one of Welker's blackmail letters the same as everyone else up here."

"Letters? I got no letter," Graham fumed. "Damn it, Fortune, Henry Wayne is dead, isn't that enough? Why Eva too?"

At the window Janice Graham turned to look at us. She didn't speak, but sat there in her long purple robe framed by the vast black of the window and the distant lights far below.

"You know it's the end of Elite Imports?" Graham said. "Without Eva there isn't any company. Her knowledge, taste, contacts were the key. Especially her South American contacts. Helga can't keep it going. We'll have to bail out fast with what we can get, cut our losses before it all goes under."

"You'll survive," I said.

Chin raised, he looked at me. In the end I had been bad news for him, and I guessed that another reason he'd been willing to talk to me now was the hope that I could, somehow, still get Eva Wayne off the hook and save his investment.

"Couldn't you have left Eva alone?" he said. "What did she do except try to save her son? What else would anyone have done? Whatever the hell made him do it all, and I still don't know, all she did was try to cover for him."

I looked toward Janice Graham. She was still watching us from where she sat at the giant window. Straight and rigid, the cords in her thin neck stood out like ropes, and her eyes seemed to have the same question. They really didn't know what had made Henry Wayne do what he did. Helga Kasmer had not told, maybe to protect Marian Wayne and her children. But Forbes and his office had it now, and the world would know soon enough.

"It's not what she did for Wayne," I said. "Wayne killed to hide Eva's past, and her past is why she's been taken away."

"Her past?" Graham said. "Because she was a Nazi once? Our enemy once? How long does she have to pay for that mistake?"

"You knew about her past?"

"We knew she was a Nazi, married to an SS man. We knew he was killed, she fought hard. What else is there to know?"

It was the C.I.A. cover story. I told them what else there was to know. All of it. Judson Graham took a cigarette from a box on a coffee table, lit it. The first I'd seen him smoke. Janice Graham remained unmoving in her chair in front of the wide black window.

"Mother Death?" Graham said.

"With Helga beside her at the gates. Thousands and thousands, old and young, strong and weak."

"Eva Beck?" Graham said.

He smoked and looked down at the floor. Yet I saw a quick light in his eyes. Excitement. He had heard of Eva Beck, and realized he was in the center of an event, something important.

"I never knew," he said, almost eager. "Eva Beck! I had no idea, you know? But, it's been a long time. She's made a new life, Fortune. Everyone deserves a second chance."

"For her, Graham, or for you?"

His eagerness vanished. "She was young, what did she know? A lot of people believed Hider."

"Because she's a good investment? Good business?"

"Thirty-five years," Graham said. "Isn't it time?"

"You must have guessed there was more to her past, guessed who those vital South American 'contacts' were. You had to suspect they were Nazis, SS men. But she was a good investment."

"A businessman can't worry about the morality and politics of everyone he does business with."

At the wide black picture window Janice Graham shifted in her chair. She was looking out again at the far-off crescent of lights across the night sky.

"The worst danger," I said, "isn't the Hiders and the Himmlers, the Eichmanns and the Mengeles. We'll always have monsters. We can live with monsters. The danger is the ordinary man with his wife and children, his pleasant house, his friendly community. Those perfectly ordinary neighbors who serve the monsters, who do the work of the monsters, who cheer the monsters. The perfectly normal people who use the monsters for their own profit, their own privilege, their own advantage. We know we have monsters among us, but they can't go far without those who serve them and those who join them. The plain people who do their bidding and their business. Who say yes to monsters."

"You would have said no to Hider, Fortune?" Graham said.

"I don't know," I said. "I'm not sure I would have said no, but I know I should have said no."

At the dark picture window Janice Graham turned again. She didn't look toward me. Her gaze was fixed on the back of her husband's head where he stood smoking and watching me.

"We'll always have monsters," I said, "but without the Becks to serve them and the Grahams to work with them they'll remain nothing but bitter, violent misfits with their delusions, end in solitary rooms, or prisons, or insane asylums. Canyon Slashers, not Hiders. Canyon Slashers and Hillside Stranglers and Son of Sam murderers preying on a few unlucky victims instead of the whole world."

Graham stubbed out his cigarette. "You want a world that never existed and never will. I live in a real world."

"Maybe you do at that," I said. "But I didn't come to talk about Eva Wayne anyway. That's the job of a lot of governments now. I came to talk to your wife."

Janice Graham stood up. She walked toward me in her long purple robe.

"No," she said. "You don't have the right."

Graham looked at her. "Jan?"

"No," she said. She walked closer, held the long skirt of her soft robe in her left hand, her slim ankle showing above her purple slippers. "It's my life."

"Suzy had her life," I said. "Stan Dekker had his."

"No," she said.

Judson Graham watched both of us. His chin was up again, his leonine head tilted back and looking down in a scowl. At both of us. "What's going on? Jan? Fortune?"

"She's Suzanne Dekker's mother," I said. "I wasn't sure, both Helga Kasmer and Marian Wayne could have been. But I believe Helga Kasmer didn't marry and never will, and Marian Wayne couldn't abandon a child for any reason. Tonight at Eva Wayne's I became sure it was your wife, and you just made it certain."

"Me?" Graham said.

"You really didn't know about Alan Welker's blackmail letter. You haven't been lying, you never saw the letter sent to you—because Janice intercepted it. She couldn't risk your knowing anything about Suzy Dekker. Not if she was to go on hiding her first marriage, her dead husband, her children abandoned in Barstow sixteen years ago."

The tall woman in her black wig had stopped halfway between the window and me. The elegant features of her long, cool face were composed, without expression. She stood with the wide black window behind her like the dark tube of some gigantic television set of the future.

"Eva Wayne knows," I said, "and probably Helga Kasmer too. It had to be Eva Wayne who sent Suzy to her, recognized the photo. They both kept quiet because they didn't want to admit any real involvement with Suzy to protect Henry Wayne, but they have no reason to keep quiet now. Then, there'll be records in Flagstaff and Barstow. Scars, teeth, maybe even fingerprints. It's hard to vanish in this country once someone suspects who you really are. I expect you can dig it all out if you want to Graham. I'd check New York for the phony maiden name she gave you, but you won't find any records. You will in Flagstaff and Barstow."

Janice Graham stood between me and the window without a sound. She watched me. She had never taken her eyes from my face since I'd begun to talk, never looked toward Graham.

"Suzy came to you that Sunday," I said. "Somehow you'd gotten rid of Graham. He'll remember. You pretended to accept Suzy, pretended you and she would make a new life together. You played for time to think, to plan some way out. She told you about seeing Henry Wayne hit a man, and you used that to scare her into going back to L.A. early. Then you told Henry Wayne that she'd seen him hit Ludwig Scharf."

Self-contained, erect, even haughty, Janice Graham neither moved nor looked at Graham, or the room, or the rich furniture, but only at me.

"You fingered her," I said. "Wayne didn't know Suzy had seen him. He found out. No one else could have told him. No one knew she'd seen anything except Alan Welker and you. Not her roommate, not Bill Dekker, only Alan Welker and her mother. You told Henry Wayne, and he went down to L.A. and killed her."

She stood in the purple robe with that calm, well-born manner that was so much a part of her now, that she must have dreamed about having in the grubbiness of Barstow, wanted, and later worked hard to develop in herself. In New York or San Francisco.

"You didn't tell Wayne who she was, or let him know that you knew what she'd actually seen. He might have come after you too. Just a hint, an innocent remark about this model who had turned out to be, say, the daughter of an old friend, and who'd looked you up and told you she'd seen something at his mother's house that scared her, a fight or something. Suzy wouldn't have met a john that night, or Henry Wayne, but she would have met someone using your name, and that's what Wayne did. He used your name to lure her to him, and killed her."

Our breathing was loud in the room. Graham turned to the long, dark picture window now, looked out at the night. Janice Graham still looked only at me. Then she walked to the long, rich, glove-leather couch trimmed in dark wood. She sat down.

"I didn't mean to hurt her," she said. "I only wanted her to go away, to leave me alone. I wanted to scare her, make her run away, run anywhere away from me. I never thought he'd really hurt her. I never thought he'd kill her."

"You didn't think about her at all," I said. "Only about yourself."

I walked to the steps up out of the enormous living room. Graham had not turned at the window.

"There's another child," I said. "I'm not sure he would want a mother now, but you never know about kids."

I left her looking at Graham's burly back where he still stood at the long window surveying the sweeping night view of his world. He wasn't a man who liked complications, who would want to share "his space" with abandoned children and the shadow of a dead first husband. Not a man who wanted to be cheated.

I drove back down the curving mountain road and through the dark trees and silvery chapparal on the steep slopes. Was it inevitable in our world, the mad search for "self"? The ultimate corruption? The total break with "others" until you can abandon children and work with monsters as long as it is an advantage to you? Send a killer after your own child?

51

I got a few hours sleep at the De Anza, showered, dressed, and walked through a clear, crisp morning to El Mirador and the Subaru. I left the rented Chewy and a check with the clerk of the De Anza, drove to the courthouse and Trenka's office. I signed my statement and told him about Janice Graham. There was nothing we could do about her, and Trenka had heard that she'd already been seen at the airport leaving town. Not south, north. Not Barstow, but San Francisco again. Where there might be a new Graham for her.

As I left the courthouse I saw a battered old camper stop in a red no-parking zone. A woman and a girl got out and came toward the courthouse entrance. The woman wore a faded print dress and carried a shabby plastic handbag in front of her in both hands. Her face was flat and empty. The girl was no more than twelve, carried a ragged bouquet of wilted flowers and wore a small hat perched on her long brown hair. The woman stopped me.

"Cap'n Trenka?"

"First floor," I said. "Third office down the corridor, on the right."

The woman looked around uncertainly.

"They told us to see this cap'n," she said, squinted in the morning sunlight as if unable to understand what the sun was doing in the sky. What she was doing standing in the sun. "My son and my husband, they've got 'em both in the morgue."

"Mrs. Welker?" I said.

She brightened. "You knew my husband? My boy?"

"A little," I said.

She nodded. "We had eight kids, Clyde and me. People they don't have kids no more like we did, the way God meant we should."

"Momma?" the girl said, nervous.

"I'm sorry," I said. "I'll show you Trenka's office."

They followed me into the courthouse. The woman talked as we went.

"Clyde was in printing. He was going to get his own shop when Alan got all that money. Clyde had the shop all picked out. Alan had this girl, was going to make a lot of money. He wrote us, you know?"

I left them at Trenka's office. For some monsters there is no last victim, always another.

Outside again I got into the Subaru and drove through the rich old city to the freeway and turned south. The ocean was on my right, bright and blue in the morning sun with the Channel Islands towering clear in the winter morning. I would stop to see Diane Pasco, report to Lieutenant Stepanic, and then go to Malibu and Marty. And we could not go back.

I had kept the dream of Marty alive, but it was only a dream. I had forgotten the reality, no matter how good it had been in bed again. The pleasure of memory not of discovery, and a dream is only a shadow. A dream is for one, not two. I had forgotten the person, the real Marty who had her own needs.

I had forgotten, and in Germany they were marching again in their minds. Thirty-five years is a long time, and the young need a heroic past. They were publishing books about the glory of the SS, the heroes of Hider's war. The memoirs and the medals, the flags and the uniforms, the fine faces of German courage. Soon the horrors would be history, and history is important to no one.

Our strength and our weakness.

We forget our lost loves, move on. And we forget the monsters with bloody hands, the victims of yesterday.

THE END

Read the first chapter of the next exciting Dan Fortune mystery

Freak

by Dennis Lynds
#11 in the Edgar Award-winning Dan Fortune mystery series

From New York City to Chatham, New Jersey, the Erie Lackawanna commuter railway crosses the Passaic River twice within fifteen miles, but no one who didn't know would ever guess that the river at Newark and the river at Chatham were the same river.

At Newark, it's a sluggish body of black water under slimy pilings and looks as if it'd catch fire if you dropped a match near it. At Chatham, it's a swift little stream running clear over gravel between banks of leafy trees and bushes. At Chatham, there are canoes, not scows; houses, not junkyards; ranch-style tracts and two-story Colonials, not tenements or urban-renewal cellblocks.

Yet only fifteen miles separates them.

I thought about the human-made time bomb ticking in the vast gulf of those fifteen short miles, the ecological time bomb, the political time bomb, as my train crossed the part of the river that ran clean over shallow rocks. What had brought me out to Chatham today was a more private time bomb. A taxi took me through the old town with its tall oaks and elms, frame houses, antique shops, and discreet real estate offices. At last we turned into a long side street, where the cab stopped at a collection of low buildings fronting the Passaic River. There were no windows in the main building, just skylights. It was a large two-story affair with a sign announcing Computer Methods Corporation.

In the lobby, they sent me to the second floor and a secretarial office between two executive offices. The secretary was a redhead who stared at my missing arm as if it were an insult.

"Dan Fortune to see Ian Campbell," I said.

"You're to go to his home. Five River Lane."

"Do I walk?"

"You don't have a car?"

"Sorry about that."

"Well, wait over there. I'll have to call a taxi."

There was no apology for the change of meeting place. The main drawback to the detective business, aside from a little violence now and then, is that you make your living from people's trouble, and people in trouble tend to forget their manners. Then, maybe it's better to make your living from other people's trouble than from other people.

The same taxi driver returned and took me back through the town and down another long road that ended at a stone bridge over the Passaic. A steel chain blocked the bridge, and a bright red Lincoln limousine was parked in front of the chain. Beyond the Lincoln, and the chain, the road continued in a loop up through branching trees and past a rolled green lawn to an impressive manor house straight out of eighteenth-century England – as befitted the home of a squire in a village named for William Pitt the Elder, Earl of Chatham.

Besides the taxi driver and me, there was a third man. He was on the stone bridge, leaning over the parapet, looking at the water. He didn't move as I paid the taxi driver again and walked out onto the bridge toward him.

He spoke straight down to the river. "Campbell's already got a visitor."

He was small, short and slender, with soft hands, a narrow head, and a pale face under a broad-brimmed pearl-gray fedora that didn't suit his wan coloring. His fitted black topcoat was nipped in at the waist, his gray trousers narrowed at the ankle, his shoes were black patent-leather oxfords, and he wore gray spats above the shoes. His hair had been slicked with brilliantine. The Roaring Twenties.

"You're waiting to talk to Campbell?" I asked.

"No."

"Then you must be waiting for Campbell's visitor," I said.

He turned. Despite the narrow head, his face was almost round, the cheekbones wider than his forehead, and as soft as his hands. Thick eyebrows and pale eyes without any particular expression. Youngish, maybe in his late twenties, but seemed older. Whatever he'd been going to say, he didn't.

He looked at my empty sleeve and missing arm. "How'd you lose it?"

There was something about the way he asked, simple and direct, that made me hold back on the gaudy yarns I tell the thrill seekers enjoying the event of a crippled man.

"Fell into the hold of a ship when I was a kid," I said.

"How old a kid?"

"Seventeen."

He turned back to the river. I had the feeling that I had somehow failed him.

"Not young enough?" I said.

He didn't answer, or even move. I didn't interest him anymore, and if something didn't interest him it was as good as not there. But the big black man in the pale blue leisure suit who was walking down the circular drive from Campbell's manor house toward us did interest him. Enough to make him watch, if not to say anything. Tall, broad, and muscular, this new arrival had the rolling, flat-footed walk of a trained boxer who had been no butterfly in the ring. The kind of fighter who could hit and be hit, with the bent knuckles, thickened ears, and broken nose to prove it, and his interest in me was even less than the small man's. He gave me a single glance that weighed me, measured me, judged me, chewed me, and spit me out as neither threat nor profit to him.

"Left town," the big man told the small man as he reached the bridge. "Sold out and faded."

The small man's expression didn't change, but somehow there was a wave of menace from him, a predator irritated enough to momentarily show his fangs and claws. He climbed in the rear seat. The big man closed the door and got behind the steering wheel. There was no doubt who was boss. Neither of them looked at me as they drove away.

●　●　●

I rang the doorbell to Campbell's manor house. The door opened.

"Fortune?" He was as tall as the black in the powder blue leisure suit and almost as thin as the small man, but with a dark tan from somewhere other than New Jersey in November. Ivy League handsome, he had an aquiline nose, firm jaw, cool blue eyes, a boyish smile, and slightly rumpled black hair without a trace of gray. He was Ian Campbell.

"Who were they?" I asked.

"Who?"

"The men who were just here."

"There was only one. A Negro. I don't know who he was."

"What did he want?"

"He was asking for my son's wife."

"Your missing son?"

"Yes."

"Just the wife? Not your son, too?"

"He never mentioned Alan. Fortune, I – "

"Did he say why he wanted Alan's wife?"

"No. Damn it, Fortune, I don't give a damn about that man or why he wanted Helen Kay! I didn't like Alan's marriage. I like it less now. I'm hiring you to find Alan, nothing else!"

Meet the Author:
Dennis Lynds

A raconteur and Renaissance man, Dennis Lynds changed the mystery form and along the way created colorful private detectives who consistently won awards as well as the hearts of readers. He was a tall, lanky man with a nose the size of Gibraltar and a generous nature that made him a soft touch for friends, panhandlers, and his children. He published some 40 novels under various pseudonyms, won awards such as the Edgar, the mystery world's highest honor, and received accolades from legendary authors like Ross Macdonald. "A novelist of power and quality, ... one of the major imaginative creators in the crime field," Macdonald wrote of him.

The New York Times named several of Lynds's novels to its Best Mysteries of the Year lists. Remarkably, two of them written under different pseudonyms appeared on the same list – *Silent Scream* by Michael Collins and *Circle of Fire* by Mark Sadler.

Amused, Lynds said that none of the *Times* editors realized he was both Collins and Sadler. "I don't think they ever figured it out," he explained. And he never bothered to tell them.

Seldom does an author change the course of a genre once; rarely twice. Lynds is credited with being the writer who, in the late 1960s and early 1970s, propelled the detective novel into the Modern Age. His most famous pen name was Michael Collins. With that name, he created the opinionated Dan Fortune, the star of one of America's longest-running private detective series. The first book, *Act of Fear*, won the Edgar Allan Poe Award for Best First Novel. "Many critics believe Dan Fortune to be the culmination of a maturing process that transformed the private eye from the naturalistic Spade (Dashiell

Hammett) through the romantic Marlowe (Raymond Chandler) and the psychological Archer (Ross Macdonald) to the sociological Fortune," according to *Private Eyes: 101 Knights* by Robert Baker and Michael Nietzel.

At heart, Lynds was a rebel. Two decades later, he rattled mystery critics and changed the field again, this time by introducing literary techniques into the genre, beginning in the late 1980s with *Red Rosa, Castrato*, and *Chasing Eights*, and continuing well into the 1990s with The *Irishman's Horse, Cassandra in Red*, and *The Cadillac Cowboy*. Other authors followed, proving the flexibility and durability of the suspense world. "No one could accuse [Lynds] of reworking the same turf in his novels... . His last several books have pushed the private-eye form into some fascinating new shapes," according to *The Wall Street Journal* in 2000. *The Los Angeles Times* commented, "It takes style to bring that off. Bravery, too, of course."

Lynds also published mainstream novels, short stories, and poetry. Five of his literary short stories were honored in *Best American Short Stories*.

During World War II, he was a rifleman and carried books of poetry in his knapsack as he fought across France. He was a strong swimmer, so when he and fellow infantrymen were surrounded by Nazis, he plunged into an icy river, leading them to escape. He earned two Purple Hearts and a Bronze Star. Later he graduated with a degree in chemistry from Hofstra and a masters degree in journalism from Syracuse. A lifelong New Yorker, in the mid 1960s he finally left the East Coast's bitter winters to settle in the warm sunshine of Southern California. He was married three times, to Doris Flood, then Sheila McErlean, and finally to Gayle Hallenbeck Stone Lynds. He had two daughters, Katie and Deirdre Lynds, and two step children, Paul and Julia Stone.

Dennis Lynds died at age 81 in 2005. Jack Adrian wrote in *The Financial Times*, "Unusually for a mystery writer – as a breed, they tend to favor things as they are, rather than as they might be – the American author Dennis Lynds, politically, came from left of center.

This did not mean he preached bloody revolution. He wrote to entertain." Entertainment was something Lynds never forgot, that and to be generous to his friends.

Obituaries celebrating his work appeared around the globe. In a typical understatement, he commented near the end of his life, "I had a good run." His career had lasted more than fifty years.

The Slasher
#10 in the Edgar Award–winning Dan Fortune mystery series
by Dennis Lynds
Originally published under the pseudonym Michael Collins

Dan Fortune doesn't forget. Particularly, Fortune has never forgotten actress Martine Adair – Marty, the woman he loved, and maybe still does. Five years ago, she abruptly stopped seeing him. The next thing he knew, she'd married her Broadway director. Fortune read in the trades about the two plays she did with her new husband. That's when he accepted there was no way a private detective could ever give her what she wanted, the money, the prestige, the theater roles. Next he heard she'd moved to Hollywood, divorced the director, and married again, this time to some kind of movie magnate.

Yesterday she called from the West Coast and asked for his help, and all of it came back to him, the years together, the intensity, the sex – he still missed her. Marty was the woman he thought about late at night alone, the way he thought about his missing left arm.

And now she needed his help. *His* help. Her new husband's niece is dead, the victim of a vicious serial killer the newspapers were calling the Canyon Slasher. According to the police, the niece's murder fit the psychopath's *modus operandi* in every detail. But Marty tells Fortune the police have it wrong, and then she says she's not the only one who thinks so.

Can it be, Fortune wonders as he rides the train from New York to Los Angeles, that Marty has doubts about her new husband, about his real relationship with his niece? And is she counting on Dan's loyalty no matter what?

First published in 1980, *The Slasher* kicked off Dan Fortune's second decade as the iconic private detective from the rapidly changing Chelsea district of New York. Hailed with rave reviews, *The Slasher* is also a transitional book, introducing Fortune to Southern California and to Kay Michaels, who might eventually become Fortune's greatest romantic love. Still, when the case is finished, Fortune returns home to New York and the next job.

"*The Slasher* is smashing, [with a] plot that leaves the reader breathless." – *Publishers Weekly*

"A compelling novel of people with dark secrets." – *The Raleigh News and Observer*

"[Lynds] carries on the Hammett-Chandler-Macdonald tradition with skill and finesse." – *Washington Post Book World*

###